Praise for the Demon Underground series:

"Love, betrayal, vampires, and a mystery. How much better can it get than that?"
—*That Teen Can Blog*

". . . fast paced, exciting storylines...The ending took me by surprise; I can't wait for the fourth book to come out!"
—*C.J. Harris, Vampire Librarian*

". . . big, shocking and intense."
—*Lara Taylor, Fresh Fiction*

Val Shapiro has a secret she's desperate to keep—she's lost her slayer powers.

As the new guardian of the *Encyclopedia Magicka*, Val expected the books to give her powers to replace those that disappeared after she lost her "V card" to Shade. But the encyclopedia exacts a price for every spell, making the job of guardian a tricky proposition.

When a rogue demon kidnaps Val's roommate Gwen and Micah, leader of the San Antonio Demon Underground, Val is plunged into the middle of a Solomon's Choice. The rogue wants the dangerously potent *Encyclopedia Magicka* in exchange for her friends' lives; the succubus leader of the Demon Underground in Austin is demanding the books be destroyed rather than let them fall into the wrong hands and wants Shade for herself, swearing to do everything she can to prevent Val's turning over the books.

The kidnapping isn't the only crisis Val faces. She's been betrayed by Fang. Demons and vampires are disappearing. The vamps of the New Blood Movement are forcing Val to keep the terms of her agreement to work for them to combat this new threat. The Demon Underground is challenging Micah's leadership, and everyone is depending on a now-powerless Val to set things right.

Val needs all the help she can get. Even if it means forgiving Fang and spending time with a dangerously sexy cowboy-vampire.

Other books by Parker Blue

DEMON UNDERGROUND SERIES

Bite Me

Try Me

Fang Me

Make Me

Donnell—

Make Me

Demon Underground Series, Book Four

by

Parker Blue

Bell Bridge Books

Thanks for all your help on this— really appreciate it!

Parker
(Pam)

Bell Bridge Books
PO BOX 300921
Memphis, TN 38130
Print ISBN: 978-1-61194-120-3

Bell Bridge Books is an Imprint of BelleBooks, Inc.

Printed and bound in the United States of America.

We at BelleBooks enjoy hearing from readers.
Visit our websites – www.BelleBooks.com and www.BellBridgeBooks.com.

10 9 8 7 6 5 4 3 2 1

Cover design: Debra Dixon
Interior design: Hank Smith
Photo credits:
Cover Art © Christine Griffin
Spine and back cover art- C Unholyvault | Dreamstime.com

:Lmm:01:

What Has Gone Before

My name is Val Shapiro, but they call me the Slayer since I've made a hobby—and a living—hunting vampires. Up until now, that's been easy, seeing as how I'm one-eighth succubus lust demon. I call that part of me Lola, and she gives me the power to make men fall instantly in lust with me. While I was still a virgin, I had incredible power, speed and healing ability—all the better for pounding vamps into dust. My mom thought I was a bad influence on my little sister, so my parents kicked me out of the house and the family business a few weeks ago when I turned eighteen.

It worked out okay, though. I found a new friend in a part hellhound, part terrier mix named Fang. He's telepathic with demons and keeps the snark level pretty high, but I'm okay with that. I also discovered there was a Demon Underground in San Antonio to help people like me pass in human society. They're pretty awesome, so it's almost like having a family again. Almost.

I worked for a while with the San Antonio Special Crimes Unit hunting vampires and had a thing going on with my human cop partner, Dan Sullivan, until he discovered what I was. He couldn't deal with it, or the fact that I beheaded his ex-fiancée, even though she'd become an evil bloodsucker herself. And when I reluctantly helped the New Blood Movement, a vein of "good" vampires to identify and eliminate the bad bloodsuckers, that was it for him.

Luckily, I found a new boyfriend, a totally hot shadow demon named Shade. All you can see when you look at him are the interdimensional energies swirling through his body, unless he's touching someone. Then he looks like a normal human. So, I touch him a lot. Purely to keep his demon identity a secret, y'know.

As long as I still had my V-card, I had all my slayer capabilities, but when I gave in to lust and lost it to Shade, I also lost my powers. Now I have this rep as the invincible Slayer with nothing to back it up but Lola. Doing the deed with Shade was kinda awesome, but losing my mojo sucks.

Anyway, before he committed suicide when I was five, my father gifted me with a set of magickal books, *The Encyclopedia Magicka*. Someone stole them, but with Shade's help, I found them again and kicked the thieves—an evil rogue mage demon and his father—into a pocket universe where they can't do any harm.

Now the books have adopted me as their keeper, and their old keeper agreed to teach me how to use them and their powers. It's a good thing, 'cause I lost a bet and promised the New Blood Movement I'd work for them until we could find the books *and* the Movement revealed their existence to the world.

One down. One to go.

Chapter One

I crouched in the darkness of an ancient live oak, armed with only my wits, listening for any sign of the vampire. Nothing but the rattling of branches and the soughing of the wind through the leaves here on the longest night of the year.

Creepy.

I wasn't hiding out of fear. I just wanted to get a bead on him before he found me first. Now that I'd lost my strength, speed, and healing ability, and I hadn't seen hide nor hair of any of my new powers as keeper of the *Encyclopedia Magicka*, I needed any advantage I could get. The live oak, with its leaves and gnarled branches as big around as my waist, shaded me from the revealing flood of moonlight.

"Val Shapiiiro," he crooned, the eerie mocking sound seeming one with the breeze. "Come out, come out wherever you are . . ."

Too close! He'd found me.

Lust for the hunt sizzled through my blood and I whirled toward the sound. "Make me," I growled.

He rushed me, inhumanly fast.

I leapt up to one of the low branches hugging the ground and lashed out with a *savate* kick, hoping to score a field goal with his head. He ducked.

Too slow, damn it. I stumbled for a nanosecond on the uneven surface, then regained my balance as he appeared on the bough beside me. His infuriating grin flashed in a sliver of moonlight. I struck out with my fist, hoping to smash the fangs off his face. Blocked.

I couldn't let him take the offensive. And though I might have lost my speed and strength, I still had my martial arts training. I battered him with a series of blows, but he was so fast, none of them connected where I wanted. I tried a low blow—a kick to the 'nads, but he stopped that, too.

Frustrated, I leapt up to grab the branch above me, planning to swing up and over it and use the momentum to knock him off his perch. Instead, he tackled me. I lost my grip and we both hit the hard-packed earth, knocking the wind out of me.

Taking advantage of my momentary pause and gasp for air, he straddled my waist and hooked his legs over mine so I couldn't move, then grabbed my wrists and pinned them above my head.

Crap. He was too strong—I couldn't get free, no matter how hard I struggled.

He grinned, looking way too happy with the situation. "Yield, darlin'?"

Never. I still had one weapon left. I hated to use it, but I hated to lose even more. I called on the succubus inside me and she leapt to the fore, eager for action. The purple eye flash that came with the use of my demonic powers reflected in his eyes as my succubus Lola surged forth and slammed into his chakras, instantly making him my slave.

His lust for Lola made it impossible to disobey me. I paused for a moment, trying to catch my breath enough to tell him to shove off.

His smile turned wicked as he released my wrists and his hands started to wander where only one man's hands had gone before.

This was *so* wrong. "Get off me," I yelled, shoving against his shoulders.

He took his time rolling off, his lascivious gaze and knowing smile never leaving my face as he hooked his thumbs in the belt loops of his jeans.

I scrambled to my feet, releasing him from Lola's clutches so fast it made us both stagger. *"Seriously,* Austin?"

He looked different without his Stetson . . . edgier, more dangerous. Alejandro's cowboy lieutenant ran a hand over his face and chuckled softly. "Hey, you were the one who played your ace in the hole . . . darlin'."

My face heated. Crap. He always made me feel young and foolish. No matter that at eighteen, I'd been slaying vampires for years. No matter that I could make any man alive do whatever I wanted. No matter that brave cops, vampires, and demons feared me as the Slayer. None of it mattered when Austin gave me his knowing look, reminding me he had at least a hundred years more experience than I did. It was as if he gazed deep into the insecurities of my soul and laid them bare.

I averted my gaze and pretended I was absorbed in brushing twigs and leaves from my shirt and jeans. "I had to," I muttered. "It was the only way I could win." He'd already beaten me once. I couldn't let him win two out of three.

"I know," he said softly. "Took you long enough."

I shrugged. "I don't like to use my powers unless it's absolutely necessary."

"And that's why you lost the first time. If I'd really been out to get you . . ." He shrugged.

"I know, I know." I'd be dead. Thank goodness this was only practice. I didn't want the word to get out to the general vamp population that the Slayer had lost her powers, or I'd be challenged by every one of them not affiliated with the New Blood Movement. And maybe even some *in* the Movement.

"Best two out of three?" I asked. This time, I'd be faster on the draw with my secret weapon.

"I'll pass," he drawled. "Now that you've figured out when to play your trump card . . . well, let's just say I don't think either of us would be comfortable doing that again."

Boy, make me squirm, willya?

Someone slammed into me from the side, taking me down again. Another vamp—Luis. I shoved Lola into him so fast, he didn't get a chance to try anything.

"Stop. Don't move." I scrambled to my feet and, just in case Austin tried anything more, I hooked him with one of Lola's energy tendrils as well. "You, too."

I'd learned my lesson and wasn't about to—

Wham. I was down on the ground again. A third vamp? *You're kidding me.*

I shook my head. No problem. I could handle three without even breaking a sweat. I lunged out with Lola to take care of *numero tres,* and got nothing but a hard slap across the face.

Crap. It was Rosa. Lola wouldn't work on her. "Stop her," I gritted out, sending a surge of power along Lola's energy strands.

My two marionettes obeyed instantly, grabbing Rosa and pulling her off me. They looked murderous, so I added, "Hold her—don't hurt her." Alejandro wouldn't be pleased if he found out I'd let two of his lieutenants tear the third limb from limb.

Rosa—smart girl—didn't fight them. She just smirked at me.

"Lucky hit," I said, rising up on one elbow to feel my jaw. She packed quite a wallop.

"Not lucky," she spat. "You, you call yourself the Slayer? If I used my knife, you'd be dead right now. *Muerta.*"

I could have pointed out that she'd be one dead undead

bloodsucker with a single word from me, but kept my trap shut. After all, they were helping me regain some skill and confidence by sparring with me in private. It was my own damned fault that I'd assumed they'd come at me one at a time. The least I could do was act grateful.

And I was, I really was. I hadn't known until tonight that the Movement used the clearing in the center of the woods around the mansion as their private training grounds. But I'd ignored their suggestion to stick to the open space. Instead, I'd taken to the trees, hoping it would give me some advantage. Not so much.

I cast around with my senses but didn't detect any more bloodsuckers. "Any others waiting in the wings to take a swing at the Slayer?" I asked before I got up again. I didn't want to meet the ground up close and personal for a fourth time.

"No," Austin and Luis answered in unison.

Good. I got slowly to my feet. The adrenaline was gone, so I was starting to experience the pain of tonight's punishment. Dang, it sucked to feel human. It was times like these that I regretted giving up my powers. "Why do you care anyway?" I asked Rosa. She'd sounded so pissed.

Still held captive by the other two vamps, she rolled her eyes. "Because you need to protect Alejandro."

"Why? I'm not his bodyguard. Doesn't he have, like, a whole *vein* of bloodsuckers to do that for him?" I knew he thought of me as his personal talisman, but sheesh, that was taking it too far.

"For when he goes to Austin," she clarified.

I glanced at the cowboy vamp, confused. "Goes to Austin for what?" And, realizing the two guys were both still in Lola's thrall, I let them go, despite Lola's protest.

Rosa rubbed her arms and sulked. "Stupid *chica*. Not him, the city. Maybe you've heard of it? The capital of Texas?"

Oh. But . . . "Since when are we going to Austin, where I'll apparently have to watch his back?" I asked.

Luis folded his arms. "Alejandro hasn't told her yet."

He and the cowboy vamp exchanged an unreadable glance. "Better take her to him," Austin said.

I heaved a sigh. Secrets. I hated secrets.

Luis nodded briefly, and the three of them headed back to the house. They didn't even look back, just assumed I'd follow them like a good little girl. Hell with that. They could keep their secrets.

Fang finally trotted up from his place on the sidelines. Part scruffy terrier, part telepathic hellhound, part smart-aleck-bane-of-my-existence, he sat on his haunches and grinned up at me. POUT MUCH?

We'd decided to have him sit this one out to see what I could do without him. I thought he'd be upset that he couldn't mix it up with me, but with that snarky comment, I wondered . . . "Did you enjoy watching them beat the crap out of me?" I asked.

He snorted. NOT SO MUCH. BUT IT WAS NECESSARY.

"Maybe," I muttered. "But is this meeting necessary? Not so much."

YOU DID AGREE TO WORK FOR HIM UNTIL THE BOOKS WERE FOUND AND HE COMES OUT OF THE CLOSET.

I know. I'd found the books, but he hadn't done the second part yet.

SO, THIS IS PART OF YOUR JOB. WHAT'S THE MATTER? YOU'VE ALWAYS WANTED TO TRAVEL MORE.

Yeah, but not as a bodyguard. Okay, yes, I was pouting. So sue me.

Fang didn't say a word, just looked at me with reproachful brown eyes framed in his adorably fuzzy face. Dang. He'd pulled out the big guns. I gave up. "Okay, okay. I'm coming."

I hobbled toward the house, feeling every ache and pain the vamps had hammered into me. More like eighty than eighteen.

NEXT TIME, WEAR SILVER, my unfeeling hellhound advised me.

I'd thought of that, but it seemed like cheating when the vamps were supposed to be helping me. Then again, being a vampire was kind of cheating, too, wasn't it?

Fang just snorted, which I took to mean he agreed with me.

Alejandro's people had been careful not to create any paths into the woods that would reveal the location of their training ground, but it was easy to follow the lights to the house. I trudged up to their back door where Austin waited for me, holding open the door. He'd put his hat back on, too, so he looked more like himself.

"I'm coming," I muttered.

"I know." He grinned again, but didn't move when I passed him.

Our energy fields intersected in the close confines of the doorway and Lola licked into him. I didn't pull back—he deserved a good licking.

The tall, lean cowboy didn't react, though. He just raised an eyebrow as if to say, "You really want to go there?"

POINT TO AUSTIN, Fang said with a laugh.

Shut up. I shoved past Austin into the kitchen, disappointing Lola once more. "In his study?" I asked without looking back.

"Yes, ma'am." Austin didn't bother to hide the amusement in his voice.

I tried not to stomp out my frustration as we headed to find Alejandro. Luis gestured me into the room I'd visited far too often. Very masculine, very Mediterranean, very dark . . . except for the sun-drenched mural of a beach scene covering the wall across from Alejandro's desk. Then again, if I'd been unable to see the sun as long as he had, I'd probably want a view like that, too.

I flopped into a chair across from Alejandro and his massive wooden desk and said, "So, boss, what's this I hear about you going to Austin?"

Luis scowled. He hated it when I treated Alejandro so informally. That's why I did it, of course, and Alejandro didn't mind. Luis and Austin took up positions behind their boss and I wondered where Rosa was.

MAYBE SHE WAS PUT IN A CORNER FOR SPILLING THE BEANS, Fang suggested.

"I am afraid *our* trip to Austin is necessary," Alejandro said.

"Why?"

The vamp leader absently rubbed the bust of Cortes he kept on his desk. "The situation in the state capital has changed. The legislation we were counting on to protect us when we come out and keep the unaffiliated ones in their place is stalled."

I grimaced. I hated politics as much as I hated secrets.

MAYBE BECAUSE THEY GO HAND IN HAND.

Probably. "What does that mean, stalled?"

Alejandro shook his head, a puzzled expression on his face. "I wish I knew. My calls are not being returned, and there has been no communication from my supporters. We shall have to go there to see what is happening."

I was all for getting those laws in place so the Movement could come out and I could satisfy my contract with Alejandro, but . . . "Why do you need me?"

"Because you can go where I cannot," Alejandro said with a smile.

Who was going to keep a vampire out of anywhere he wanted to go? "Like where?"

Austin's mouth quirked up. "Like daylight."

Oh.

"Indeed," Alejandro agreed. "You are the only one I can trust to protect my interests while I'm there, to live in my world and not reveal what you discover, to act for me during the daytime."

Fang huffed with amusement. HE WANTS YOU TO BE HIS RENFIELD.

I didn't find that at all funny. It was a pretty tall order. But, unfortunately, I couldn't argue with the vamp leader's logic. "Rosa seemed to think you wanted me to be some kind of bodyguard."

Alejandro waved away my objection. "Rosa is overly protective. We cannot invade another vampire's territory without permission. Without it, we risk much. I have gained that permission, but have agreed to bring only four with me. I shall take Austin and Vincent, and leave Luis and Rosa in charge here."

No wonder Rosa was peeved, with only two vamps to guard her boss's back. "If I'm the third, who's the fourth? Fang? Does Fang count?"

FANG ALWAYS COUNTS.

"No, Fang does not count as the fourth," Alejandro said with a smile, "though I see no reason why he cannot come. The fourth will be Jack Grady."

Grady? The former keeper of the *Encyclopedia Magicka* was an odd choice. "Why him?"

"The encyclopedia can be a powerful weapon in our favor. He knows how to wield it, and you do not. We need him to get you up to speed as fast as possible."

Good luck with that. I'd tried with no luck. He was supposed to be training me on how to tap the magick potential in the books, but the only thing he'd done the past few days was pig out on Gwen's food and hog Shade's bed.

"I have already spoken with Mr. Blackburn and the Demon Underground has agreed to let me take both of you," Alejandro said. "I have made arrangements for a place to stay so we can leave tomorrow night when the sun goes down."

Why not? I'd only been to Austin a few times, and it would be something different than the same old, same old. "Do you have any idea how long we'll be gone? Mom will kill me if I miss Christmas." And since Mom and I had kind of a truce going on, I didn't want to screw that up.

"It's little more than an hour away," Austin drawled. "I think you'll be able to come home to Mommy when you need to."

Parker Blue

I clamped my lips on an unwise comeback and resolved not to let him get to me. "Okay. Should I pack?"

"Yes," Alejandro said. "Pack for a couple of weeks. It'll make it easier than returning here for a change of clothing or necessities. You may go now if you wish."

I definitely wished, though I didn't care for his master to servant phrasing. Glancing down at Fang, I asked, *You ready?*

In answer, he got up and trotted away, pausing in front of the study door to glance expectantly over his shoulder at Austin.

The cowboy rolled his eyes, but followed Fang's unspoken bidding and opened the door for him.

How do you do that?

CHARISMA, BABE, SHEER CHARISMA.

Shaking my head, I followed him down the hallway and out the front door. I straddled my Valkyrie motorcycle and waited for him to jump up into his own leather and sheepskin seat, then helped him on with his goggles.

I sped home on the dark, silent streets of San Antonio. There weren't many people out in the early hours of the morning, so I was able to drive on autopilot and make plans for the unexpected free time. I could take a hot bath to soak out my aches and pains, maybe even get some extra sleep before I had to show up at Alejandro's tomorrow. After all, who knew what awaited us in the state's capital?

When we arrived home, I took off Fang's goggles and he jumped down.

"Hungry?" I asked. Usually, he'd be pestering me for food right about now.

SORRY, BABE.

"For what?"

A dark cloth fell over my head and someone grabbed me, trying to pin my arms. What the . . . ? I struck out with my foot, connecting with someone who let out an *oof.*

YOU'LL HAVE TO SEDATE HER, Fang said, and I felt the sudden prick of a needle in my arm.

My mind grew fuzzy. *Fang? What's happening?*

No response.

"Thanks, Fang," a man said. "We owe you one."

I had only one thought as I lost consciousness. *Traitor.*

Chapter Two

I woke feeling groggy, as if someone had stuffed cotton candy in my head. As I fought to clear strands of sticky pink cobwebs from my brain, I realized I was lying on my side on some yielding surface—a bed?—with something covering me. I didn't seem to be bound at all, which surprised me. Without opening my eyes to alert my captors that I was awake, I tried to get some idea of where I was. It smelled dank and musty, with a strange hint of vanilla, but I couldn't hear any sounds of life.

Tentatively, I opened my eyes a slit. No help. The room was dark, with only a small bit of flickering light—a candle somewhere nearby, which must be the source of the vanilla. I lay facing a wall, and there was nothing I could see to help me figure out where I was or who had done this to me.

The beginnings of panic threatened to consume me, followed by a gut-wrenching feeling of betrayal. Why had Fang helped them? He was the best friend I'd ever had, the one I could always count on. Or at least, he used to be. Loss and pain swamped me, made me unable to think for a moment.

But I gritted past that and wondered what to do. Heck, I knew what I *should* have done. I hadn't even thought to use Lola on my kidnappers. Austin was right. I'd let down my guard and look what had happened. I couldn't continue to ignore what I was. That was going to get me killed.

Embracing Lola could help me find out if there were any men nearby I could coerce into helping me. I reached for her, but couldn't find her. It was as if she were imprisoned behind that sticky web.

A male voice suddenly appeared from somewhere beyond me. "Fang says you're awake."

That pissed me off. I leapt up, or rather, tried to. The blanket covering me tangled my arms and legs and I ended up falling on the floor. I fought my way free, struggled to stand and discovered it didn't do me any good. Silver bars had me penned in like an animal. I was in a prison cell, fergawdsake.

I swayed dizzily on my feet. The drug in my system, coupled with the dim candlelight, made it difficult to focus, but I could see there were two people standing on the other side of the bars and a smaller, fuzzy blob that had to be my ex-friend, Fang.

What the hell is going on? I asked Fang.

No answer. It was as if the web caught my thoughts and bounced them back at me. Nothing penetrated except a dull, throbbing headache.

I stumbled forward and grabbed the bars, trying desperately to clear my brain. Now I could see that one of my jailers was a guy, maybe in his midtwenties, with dark curly hair and a concerned expression. He looked a lot like Micah, except for the burn scars that puckered the left half of his face. The other person was a girl, maybe fourteen years old. She was petite, with long dark hair, half of which she'd piled sloppily on top of her head with hairsticks stuck in haphazardly. The other half fell partially over her face. The hair and the determined look on her face made me revise her age upward. Okay, maybe seventeen.

"Who are you?" I demanded. "Why did you do this to me?"

"I'm David and this is Pia," he said, nodding at the girl. "It's all right, we don't want to hurt you. We just want to talk."

"That's why you drugged and imprisoned me?"

"Your reputation precedes you." He glanced down at the hellhound. "Fang said it wasn't necessary, but we couldn't take the chance he was wrong."

"Fang said?" For the first time since I'd opened my eyes, the weight crushing my heart lifted the tiniest bit. I looked at Fang. "He knew you wanted just to talk to me?"

"Yes, but Pia didn't feel safe until your powers were tamed and you were kept at a distance."

"And it's all-important that Pia feels safe?" I asked incredulously.

"Yes, it is," he said, gazing earnestly into my eyes. "Have a seat and I'll explain."

"Let me out first."

He shook his head. "After we talk, I'll let you out. I promise."

Yeah, as soon as I was able to use Lola, he'd do anything I wanted. "At least turn the lights up," I said. I wanted to see more of the area, figure out where I was, locate potential weapons.

David shook his head. "The low lighting is for your benefit. The drug makes you hypersensitive to light. If I turn them up, you'll get a migraine."

It pained me, but I looked at Fang for confirmation. He nodded to indicate David was telling the truth. The hellhound's big brown eyes pleaded with me to understand, to forgive him. I closed my eyes, desperately wanting to believe my best friend really did have good reason, a reason I didn't yet know, but I couldn't *hear* him to get that reason. And I couldn't *hear* him because he'd let someone drug me. *I hate this.*

"Please," David said. "Have a seat."

Why not? I was still feeling wobbly. I glanced around and noticed that there was a soft-looking armchair sitting next to the bars, with a sink and toilet on the other side in the small cell. The chair looked really out of place, so I guessed they must have put it there to make me comfortable.

I sat in it, and the guy seemed to relax. He and the girl pulled wooden chairs from along the wall opposite my cage and set them on the other side of the bars. David stared at me solemnly for a moment, turning the ruined part of his face away from me. "This is what it used to be like, you know," he said softly.

"What?"

"During the Inquisition and the Salem witch trials. Humans didn't understand us, were afraid of us, so they labeled us *witch* and imprisoned us, drowned us, burned us."

"Us?"

"Part-demons," he explained. "Like you and me. And Pia and Fang."

Part-demons? I wondered what their powers were, why they felt it necessary to take mine away. Why Pia didn't feel safe until I was behind bars. Or so David said. *She* hadn't said anything so far. I wasn't willing to give them the benefit of the doubt yet. "Well, you've got the imprisonment part down pat. What's next? Drowning or burning?"

He looked taken aback, offended even. "Neither. What kind of people do you think we are?"

I didn't really believe it, but wanted to throw him off guard. "I think you're the kind who would drug and kidnap someone just to talk to her. Are drowning and burning really that much of a stretch?"

He shook his head, and the soft light created shadows on his scars, making the side of his face look like a pockmarked, desolate moon. "We're not monsters. And we did this partially to show you what it's like to feel helpless, under someone else's control. How . . . awful it is."

I glanced at Pia whose eyes hardened as she gave me a challenging stare. No help from that quarter. And I revised her age upward again. "Okay, so why was it necessary?"

"Do you know why the Demon Underground was formed?"

I felt my brain start to clear. I wasn't sure where he was going with this, but I played along. "Sure. To help us find our place in the human world, find us jobs, help us blend—that sort of thing."

He shook his head. "That is what it has become, but that isn't why it was originally formed. It was created to *help* people like us, to protect us, keep us safe from human witch hunts, and to ensure no one learned of our existence who could harm us."

"Is that really necessary anymore? I haven't heard of any modern-day Inquisitions."

"Haven't you?" David asked with a raised eyebrow. "And why is that?"

"Uh, because there aren't any?"

"Oh, but there are. You just don't hear about them."

"Like what?" I poked at the limits of the sticky strands encasing Lola. They seemed to be giving way a little.

"Like a small town afraid of a family who were a little different. So afraid that they torched their house and burned them alive—a part-demon father and daughter, and a human mother lost their lives, killed horribly. Only the eleven-year-old son survived."

Pia ran her fingers lightly over the ruined half of David's face, looking sad.

Horror rippled through me. "You?"

He nodded. "And the father who was so afraid of his daughter's voice that he made sure she could never, ever sing."

He made some kind of strange gesture to Pia who pulled her hair aside so I could see the ragged scar where her larynx used to be. "Her *father* did that to her?" I asked, horrified. No wonder she hadn't said anything. "Why?"

"Because she's a siren."

"Siren . . . like in *The Odyssey*?" If I remembered my reading, sirens were women who bewitched sailors with the sound of their voices.

He nodded. "That should have been enough, but he went even further." He glanced at the girl. "Show her, Pia."

Pia hesitated, then opened her mouth. I didn't know what I was supposed to see, so I leaned forward to get a better look. Unfortunately, I did. Where her tongue should have been, there was nothing but a stump.

Nausea churned through me and I threw myself back in the chair, covering my eyes with my hands to shut out the sight. "I'm so, so sorry." It made me want to find the people who had done these horrible things and rend them in two.

David added softly, "How about the parents who treat their daughter like a freak, encourage her to fight deadly vampires, then kick her out of the house when she turns eighteen?"

"M—me?"

Pia nodded solemnly. And I finally heard Fang's voice in my head. YOU, he confirmed.

Startled, I glanced at him. *What's this all about?*

PLEASE, JUST HEAR HIM OUT, Fang said. HE'LL EXPLAIN.

If I could hear Fang, maybe I could reach Lola. Yes, I could. Maybe I could reach David, force him to let me out. I'd still listen to him, but on my terms.

I WOULDN'T DO THAT IF I WERE YOU, Fang warned.

Why should I listen to you? I sent a few tendrils toward David.

"What are you doing?" David asked suspiciously before I even reached him. Apparently, I couldn't hide the purple eye flash.

Pia's eyes narrowed as she whipped up her hand to yank out one of those hairsticks and threw it at me. It thumped into the chair arm and pinned my sleeve. Startled, I let Lola go.

TOLD YA, Fang said. BUT WOULD YOU LISTEN? NOOOO, NOT THE SLAYER. SHE ALWAYS THINKS SHE KNOWS BEST.

I glared at him, and David said, "That was just a warning. She's very, very good with her knives."

That was a knife? I pulled it out of the arm and checked it out. Sure enough, it was a small thin blade, the handle made to look like a hairstick. Very sharp, very deadly. "Who's going to protect *me* from *her*?" I asked.

Pia's fear turned to a smile and she laughed silently. Never to be able to talk, to sing, or even laugh . . . I couldn't imagine. I put the small stiletto down on the floor and slid it back to her, hilt first, as a sort of peace offering.

Okay, I got it. She had reason to be frightened. I fingered the hole in my sleeve. And if she was still afraid of me, even with those lethal weapons of hers, then she must really need the reassurance of me behind bars and out of David's chakras.

SHE DOES, Fang confirmed. PLEASE, HUMOR US IN THIS? HE'LL MAKE EVERYTHING CLEAR.

Okay.

As Pia retrieved her knife and inserted it very carefully back into her hair, David said, "So long as you don't harm us, we won't harm you."

"All right." I glanced at Pia. What were we talking about, again? I mentally rewound the conversation. Oh, yeah. "My parents didn't abuse me," I said.

David cocked his head. "There are other kinds of abuse than the physical."

Pia nodded solemnly, and I imagine she had experienced both. Despite myself, I hurt for both of them.

David said, "Be honest. Did you grow up in a loving family? Did they care about you, nurture your gift, help you to find others like yourself, encourage you to be all you could be?" When I remained silent, he continued, "Or were they ashamed of you, did they hide you away from the world, did they try to turn you into something you were not . . . stunt your powers?"

"It was for my own good." But I didn't believe it, not really.

He was only voicing the thoughts I'd had for so long. Wonder where he'd learned that?

I glanced at Fang.

I DIDN'T TELL HIM, Fang said defensively. I DIDN'T HAVE TO. THEY KNOW WHAT IT'S LIKE.

I sighed. "Okay, I get your point. It sucks being part demon in a human world. So?"

"So that's why the Demon Underground was really formed," David said, sounding intense. "Tonight is the winter solstice. In times past, all of the part-demons who turned eighteen during the year would be brought in on this night to participate in a ritual to make them full-fledged members of the Underground. They would be kidnapped and bound to experience the horror of the past, learn about the history of our persecution, then set free to make a choice. Join the Underground and be protected . . . or leave and have their memories of the Underground removed, as well as the memories of everyone they've ever told about us."

"So that's why you kidnapped me? To initiate me?"

"One reason," David confirmed.

"So let's do this ritual and get it over with."

David grimaced. "I can't. I don't know what it is. Micah does, but he's not sharing."

"What do you mean?"

"Micah and the other Underground leaders throughout the US want to pretend we're past the hatred. They won't do what needs to be done." David's voice rose. "So what happens? My family is killed, Pia is maimed, and you're left without training, bound to a family who doesn't love you. And who eventually shunned you."

I wasn't sure I'd go that far, but he had a point. "I'm sure if Micah knew—"

"What makes you think he didn't?" David spat. "His father knew we were in danger, but chose to leave us where we were. He knew what might happen, but decided to give the humans the benefit of the doubt." He leaned forward. "See what happens when you do that? You get Pia, me, you. Damaged goods."

WHOA, DUDE, Fang said. INTENSE MUCH?

Just what I was thinking.

David relaxed a little. "It was preventable. If only he'd held to the old ways. The rituals and traditions were there for a purpose. They were put in place to keep us *safe*."

Standing up for Micah was getting me nowhere. "Okay. Why am I here? What do you want me to do about it?"

"*Think*. You're a victim of the new ways, just like us. We want you to stop helping the damned vampires. We want you to convince Micah to reinstate the old practices, convince him to be the leader he should be and help his people, not hurt them."

Pissed off now, I said, "And how are the old ways any better? You can't make people accept you. You can't force them to change their ways. People will still get hurt."

"Not demons. The only people who would get hurt are those who try to hurt part-demons who can't help the way they were born. Do *you* want to see someone else maimed like Pia was?"

I stared at the poor siren, her abilities cruelly ripped out of her by her own father. I didn't want that to happen to anyone. I shook my head mutely.

"Then, please, help us."

"Why me? Why not ask Ludwig or Tessa or someone else?" They'd been in the Underground a lot longer than I had.

"Because you were one of those who should have been helped.

And because, with the *Encyclopedia Magicka,* you're a catalyst for change in both the vampire and demon communities." He shrugged. "Or you can be, if you choose. So, will you cut all ties with the vampires and convince Micah to reinstate the old ways?"

I watched him for a moment. He obviously believed what he was saying, and was certainly passionate about it. But I couldn't promise anything without hearing both sides of the story. "Okay, I'll talk to Micah before I do anything else, I swear."

David glanced at Fang, who told him, VAL IS TELLING THE TRUTH. SHE WON'T HARM YOU AND WON'T GO BACK ON HER WORD.

How could I, when they'd been through so much pain already? "Okay, now let me out and I'll talk to Micah."

David smiled crookedly. "Not necessary. We'll go get him for you."

I rolled my eyes. "Kidnapping again? Seriously?"

"Again, not necessary. He's just upstairs." He nodded at Pia who opened a door at the far end of the room and let Fang out.

"Huh?"

"Don't you know where you are?" David asked.

"No. Where?"

"You're in the basement of Micah's club."

I knew it was the Underground's headquarters in this city, but . . . "Club Purgatory?" I asked incredulously. "I-I had no idea this was here."

David snorted. "So ask yourself, what other secrets has he kept from you?"

A very good question—one I was suddenly determined to learn the answer to.

Chapter Three

Micah finished totaling up the Club Purgatory receipts for the evening and leaned back in his desk chair, running a hand over his face. God, he was tired. And without much to show for it, either. The economy might be picking back up, but he hadn't seen it yet in the club's income this holiday season.

The club had flourished under his father's management and Micah had continued his policies after he died, but Micah doubted even his father would have been able to do any better during the recession. He'd tried everything—what else could he do? He'd stepped up the number of sets each night, hoping to entice more women to the club, and it had helped, but not enough. He couldn't lay anyone off—the demons needed the jobs he provided. He'd been supplementing the club's income and the Underground with his own savings, but he couldn't continue doing that forever. Maybe—

A scratching noise came at the door and Fang's voice came through loud and clear. MICAH, I NEED YOUR HELP.

Surprised, Micah rose to let the hellhound in. "What are you doing here?" He glanced down the hallway. Fang couldn't have gotten in without someone's assistance. And everyone else was gone for the night. "Is Val with you?"

SORT OF. THAT'S WHY I NEED YOU. SHE'S . . . IN THE BASEMENT.

The basement? Alarm gripped him. The basement and its contents were a closely-guarded secret—one of his father's less pleasant legacies. How did the hellhound know about it?

Fang rolled his eyes. PLEASE, DUDE. YOU DO KNOW I CAN READ YOUR MIND?

"Yes, but how does Val know about it? Did you tell her?"

NOT EXACTLY. BUT SHE'S LOCKED IN ONE OF THE CELLS AND NEEDS YOU TO LET HER OUT.

What? Adrenaline spiked through him. "What the hell is going on here?"

GO DOWNSTAIRS AND YOU'LL FIND OUT.

Micah rushed down the stairs. Part of the basement was used to hold wine at the proper temperature, but there was a hidden door to another section that others rarely saw . . . and Micah knew all too well. One of the wine racks was hinged, and he swung it out from the wall, then opened the hidden door. Beyond the door, several cells stood side by side, each kept private from the others by solid walls. Val was in the closest one, clutching the bars from the inside. What the—?

The only light came from a fat, stubby candle. He reached for the light switch, but Fang said, NO, DON'T. SHE'S BEEN DRUGGED WITH PERDO.

Perdo? Who would want to remove her powers and lock her up . . . in *his* club's secret basement? Alarmed, Micah grabbed the key ring on the wall and hurried to unlock her cell door. That's when he saw David and Pia standing in the shadows.

"You," he said in annoyance. The Underground's two biggest troublemakers. And Pia was one of the few women he couldn't control. Incubus abilities were too similar to a siren's for his power to work on her. "Did *you* do this to her?"

"They did," Val confirmed. "But they think they had good reason."

He unlocked the cell door to free her. "Oh, yeah? Like what?" And why couldn't they have let her out instead of sending Fang after him?

Val slipped out of the cage. "They wanted to tell me a few things, have me ask you some questions."

"So they locked you up?"

Val shrugged. "There were safety concerns."

He glanced from Val to the two troublemakers who had yet to speak. Yeah, well, he understood how cornering Val might be a tricky proposition, but locking her in a cage . . . "I'll deal with you two later. Come on, Val." He nodded toward the stairs, not knowing how much she knew or had seen. "Let's talk upstairs, where it's more comfortable."

Val leaned back against the bars. "No, thanks, cuz. I think I'd rather do this here."

Hell. What did that mean? Micah's mind whirled as he debated how he could keep her in the dark about everything that was down here.

Fang snorted. SORRY, DUDE. AIN'T GONNA HAPPEN.

"So, how about a few questions?" Val asked.

Annoyed, he said, "Okay, ask."

"Why do you have jail cells in your basement?"

He told her a partial truth. "My father put them in, in case we needed to restrain vampires or violent demons. It's where we held Josh and Andrew for a while after they stole the encyclopedia, until we figured out what to do with them."

"In a *jail* cell?" Val asked. Her expression was both thoughtful and uncertain.

"Yes," he said, hating how defensive he sounded. "Would you rather we'd turned them over to the police?" He headed toward the door. "Come on. Don't you want to get out of here?" He knew he did.

Stubbornly, she sat in one of the chairs outside the cell, locking her arms over her chest. "Not yet. How many people know about your dungeon?"

He winced at her word choice. "Not many." Too many, now that Fang and Val knew . . . not to mention David and Pia. He wondered how much more they'd told her.

SHE KNOWS A LOT. BUT NOT EVERYTHING. YET.

Was that a threat? Suddenly, Micah felt as though everything he'd tried to hide was about to become public. He turned on David. "What's this all about?"

The scarred demon stepped forward into the candlelight, then sat in the other chair and leaned back, giving Micah a challenging look. Pia came to stand behind him. "You know," he said.

Micah sighed. "That again? You think imprisoning Val would make me agree to go back to the old ways?" What was this, a play for his position? He wouldn't put it past David.

"No," Val said. "He wanted me to hear both sides of the argument."

"Okay, fine." Micah crossed his arms. "What do you want to know?"

Val shrugged. "Tell me why you don't want to go back to the old ways."

At least she could usually be reasoned with. He wasn't so sure about David and Pia. Micah grabbed a chair from against the wall and dragged it over to them. Turning it backward, he straddled the ladderback and leaned forward to address Val earnestly. "My father did away with those traditions a long time ago. I agree with him. They're archaic, no longer pertinent in today's modern times."

Val shook her head. "That's not an answer. That's a sound bite."

"Outdated policies and meaningless rituals, with guys in robes standing around talking a bunch of mumbo jumbo? Come on, Val. It's straight out of a B movie."

"They're not meaningless," David said.

"How would you know?" Micah asked. "Have you ever seen one?"

"No, have you?" David challenged.

Micah shook his head. "My father did away with most of them when I was young."

"So you don't really know the purpose or what they're all about?" Val asked.

"Yes, I do. I've read the Book of Rituals. Trust me, Val, the rituals are antiquated, obsolete. We need to progress with the times."

THEY WORKED FOR CENTURIES, Fang said.

"Maybe. But if I tried it now, they'd laugh me out of the Underground."

"I doubt it," David said. "I think they'd be glad you were reviving traditions that once protected us."

"Well, I don't, and one of those rituals you love so much chose *me* as leader of the San Antonio Demon Underground. I make the decisions here. We're done." Pulling rank wouldn't solve anything, but neither would this conversation. He stood. "Come on, it's late. Let's go home."

"Not yet," Val said. "Sit down."

She looked stubborn as only Val could. And he didn't want to leave her down here alone to explore, nor did he want to bodily carry her away. Sighing, Micah sat back down and spoke directly to Val. "David and Pia have had a hard time of it, but don't let their bitterness and prejudice affect you. The part-demons they champion are a very small minority."

NOT AS SMALL AS YOU THINK, Fang said, obviously broadcasting to everyone.

That was news to Micah. "What?"

COME ON, DUDE, CAN'T YOU SENSE IT? DEMONS ARE GETTING RESTLESS, WORRIED ABOUT YOU AND YOUR LET'S-ALL-JUST-GET-ALONG POLICIES. SOME HAVE EVEN MOVED AWAY, TO OTHER PLACES WHERE THE UNDERGROUND IS MORE IN TUNE WITH THE OLD WAYS.

Moved away? Seriously? He hadn't known. Hadn't noticed. That bothered him, but it wasn't his fault. Progress was hard for some people. "It's just because the vampires are all stirred up. Val has helped

Alejandro get that under control, so things should calm down again."

NOT IF THEY COME OUT TO THE WORLD. THAT'LL STIR UP A WHOOOOLE CAULDRON FULL OF TROUBLE. AND THE WITCH HUNTS WILL BEGIN AGAIN.

"Yeah," David said. "It's a holocaust waiting to happen."

"So that's what this is all about?" Val asked. "You want me to stop working with Alejandro?"

"Hell, yes," David exclaimed. "Misery loves company. How much you wanna bet that as soon as the humans turn on them—and they will—that every vampire out there starts pointing fingers at the demons in their midst?"

"Maybe," Val said doubtfully. "But I have a contract with Alejandro. I promised to work with him until the vamps come out."

Micah kept quiet, letting Val convince herself.

David let loose with a bitter laugh. "Some things are more important than contracts . . . like species survival."

Val looked as though a lightbulb came on. "So that's why there are suddenly fewer vamps harassing the city. Some of them were killed by demons like you, weren't they?"

He shrugged. "Only the bad ones, none in the Movement. What did you expect us to do? Stand back and watch as they terrorize San Antonio? Their bloodlust threatens to reveal their existence, and by extension, ours. Humans way outnumber us. Revealing ourselves would be suicide."

The effect of David's words on Val, clearly obvious from the dumbstruck look on her face, worried Micah. Could David be right? Micah knew there was a strong faction inside the Underground that didn't want to help the vamps, but he figured it was the normal fear of change. He didn't realize they feared for their lives. That thought was a knife in his gut, but he wasn't ready to concede changing their ways would protect them. "You think turning vigilante is safer?"

"Safer than doing nothing," David retorted.

Val held up her hands for them to stop, then turned to Micah. "Okay, you say you're the leader, but what do you do, really? Besides throw parties and help people find jobs?"

Is that how she saw what he did? For some reason, her defection hurt. Micah said, "I keep a watch on the city. You know that—Shade is one of my agents."

"And what do you do with that information?"

"I pass it on to the SCU, so they can take care of threats." Why was she asking these questions when she knew the answers?

"To humans?" Val persisted.

"Yes, to humans and to demons in the Underground."

"So if you're all about sharing threats and helping people, why do people like David and Pia get hurt?" She sounded half-puzzled, half-belligerent.

Micah paused. He didn't know their full stories, and his father was no longer around to explain what had happened. Softly, he said, "That was very unfortunate, but I'm sure my father didn't know—"

"He knew," David said. "He knew trouble was brewing, and did nothing."

"I don't believe that," Micah said. But a niggling of doubt crept in. He didn't know for sure. Not really.

SORRY, DUDE, IT'S TRUE, Fang said, with regret in his voice. I REMEMBER. LUCAS UNDERESTIMATED THE THREATS. JUST LIKE YOU ARE NOW.

Could it be? Micah glanced uncertainly at David.

"And we're not the only ones," the scarred demon said. Before Micah could protest, David added, "What about Val?"

"What about her? Val can take care of herself, far better than I can."

"No, I mean, why didn't you take care of Val when she was growing up in that toxic household, raised by humans who treated her like crap? Why didn't you take her away from that bitch of a mother, let her know there were others like her, reassure her that she was not alone? Why would you let any one of us suffer isolation and doubt?"

Helplessly, Micah looked at Val to see how she was taking this.

"Yes, why didn't you come for me?" she asked softly.

Such a simple question shouldn't shake him so much, but it did. "I told you. We figured you were integrating into the human world so well, you'd be better off not knowing."

"Yes," David said sarcastically. "You're all about integration, about helping us 'pass' in the human world, when you should have been more concerned about keeping us *safe*."

"Val was never in danger," Micah protested.

"Really?" David challenged. "She didn't know how to use her powers—was that safe for her, or the men around her?" He answered his own question. "Hell, no. And when she stalked vampires, was that safe? How about when she got kicked out of her own house, tossed into the streets like yesterday's garbage? Do you think she was safe then?"

Stunned, at first Micah had no response. Damn it, David had a point. And what defense did Micah have? He'd blindly followed the guidelines his father had laid down, without questioning them. He'd taken the easy way out. Did that make him a bad leader? No. He'd done his job the best he could with the information he had. "I sent Fang to her."

YEAH, BUT I'M ONLY ONE SMALL HELLHOUND. I CAN'T HELP EVERYONE. AND SOON I'LL HAVE A LITTER FULL OF BABY HELLHOUNDS TO PROTECT. When Micah shot him a glance, Fang shrugged. DOESN'T LOOK LIKE I CAN COUNT ON YOU TO DO IT.

Micah flinched. So that was why Fang was on their side. From the expression on Val's face, it looked like she was, too. If Fang and Val didn't trust him, how could he expect the rest of the demon community to follow him? Could he have been wrong?

YEAH, DUDE. CONSIDER THIS YOUR WAKE-UP CALL.

Four sets of eyes stared at him. Hell, if they were right, he was responsible for some of Val's torment . . . and others' pain, as well. Micah thought he'd done the right things. But, looking into their unwavering gazes, he realized he'd done the convenient things.

An unaccustomed feeling of guilt niggled at him. "Okay, I'm listening," Micah said. "What do you want from me?"

The scarred demon snorted. "You're more concerned about feeding your incubus and running this club than you are about your own people." Intense now, David said, "What we need is for you to be a real leader. Research the old ways. I don't care about the mumbo jumbo. Find out what they used to do, how they used to keep us safe. You should be doing everything you can to ensure our existence remains secret. How many tormenters like Pia's father have met the Memory Eater lately?"

Val's eyes widened in surprise. "The *what?*"

And there it was—the one thing Micah had hoped to keep hidden. He closed his eyes. The Memory Eater was the Underground's dirty little secret, and he'd wanted to keep it that way. Opening his eyes, he said wearily, "Trust me. You don't want to know."

"Another damn secret, Micah? Seriously?" Val shook her head. "Tell me. Now."

"Better yet," David said, "show her."

Okay, maybe it was better. Better that Val see exactly what returning to the old ways meant.

Parker Blue

Chapter Four

Micah knew I hated secrets and here he was keeping even more from me. Maybe there was something to David's claims. "What's the Memory Eater, Micah?" I asked, my voice tight.

Micah looked down at the keys and weighed them in his hand, as if wondering what to do with them. "A remnant of the old ways David is so fond of. You sure you really want to see this?"

Damn betcha. I was tired of being kept in the dark. "Show me."

He led me to a cell around the corner, one you couldn't see from the door. The candlelight didn't penetrate well enough to see into the cell very far, but I could tell it didn't hold the same fixtures mine had. In fact, it seemed empty except for something—some*one?*—huddled in the far corner. What was it? I stepped closer to the bars to get a better look.

Big mistake. The huddle erupted and flew at me with inhuman speed. Grabbing me by the shirt, it jerked me hard up against the bars and shoved its face into mine. "Releeease meee," it whispered in a grating voice.

A skeletal face, its bone-white skin stretched tight against the skull, seemed to hang in the air, inches from mine, teeth bared, eyes reddened and glowing with madness. I slammed Lola into the creature, or at least I tried. No luck. Crap. I thought the drug had worn off. Desperately, I tried to shove him away physically.

Behind me, I felt Micah using his incubus to reach for the creature. "Stop," he said, his voice surprisingly gentle. "Release her and back away."

No wonder Lola hadn't worked—this, whatever it was, was a *woman.* She let go at Micah's command and took a step back.

I straightened my shirt and moved out of arm's reach, then stared at her now that she was revealed in what little light there was. Thin to the point of gauntness, she wore some kind of black unitard or something that made her look like a loose collection of knobby sticks topped by a barely fleshed skull, her breasts so small as to be almost nonexistent. Creepy.

Why didn't you tell me? I asked Fang.

YOU HAD TO SEE FOR YOURSELF.

"Sssheee is the one," the creature hissed, staring at me with her mad eyes.

I kinda hoped she meant Pia, but that was just wishful thinking. Unnerved, I asked, "The one for what?"

Micah shrugged. "Who knows? She's . . . insane."

"Fang? What does she mean?"

I DUNNO, Fang said with a shake of his head. AND NO WAY AM I GOING INTO THAT MIND TO FIND OUT.

Can't say I blamed him. "*This* is the Memory Eater?"

Micah nodded.

"Tell Val why she's called that," David said, stepping forward to stare intently at Micah. Until he said something, I'd almost forgotten he was there.

Micah sighed. "Because she can make anyone forget anything. A moment, an event, a person . . ."

"Or the existence of demons and the Underground," David added. "She plucks the memories out of your skull and they're gone for good."

Really creeped out now, I backed farther away, toward Pia, wondering how far away would be safe.

"Don't worry," David told me. "She only eats memories at Micah's command. Didn't you ever wonder why the soothsayers chose him as leader at such a young age?"

I'd never thought about it. "I figured it was because his father was leader before him."

David shook his head. "No, it's not a hereditary position. It's because incubi can control her, ensure she only eats the memories the Underground wants her to." He glanced at Micah with a raised eyebrow. "But when was the last time you actually used her abilities to help us?"

Micah grimaced. "She's a person, not a tool to be used at someone's whim."

"Is that what your father told you?" David asked, sounding sarcastic. "Is that why he didn't erase Pia's father's memories of her abilities *before* the monster cut out her tongue? Would that have been a whim or a kindness? For both of them?"

Micah's jaw firmed. "It would have been the behavior of a tyrant, who believes his choices are the only ones. Only a tyrant or a power-hungry dictator deploys the Memory Eater indiscriminately on impulse, on slim suspicion. These are people's lives we're dealing with, David. They deserve a chance before we rape their memories. In either way, yours or my father's, mistakes can be made. My father believed the future would be better if we tried to break from the old ways. That the mistakes would be fewer. I'm honoring his vision."

Whoa. They both had great points. I didn't know whose side I was on. Could I be on both?

YOU NEED TO MAKE UP YOUR OWN MIND ABOUT RIGHT AND WRONG, Fang said. I BROUGHT YOU HERE SO YOU'D HAVE ALL THE FACTS.

Micah continued. "Once I start using her whenever there's even the smallest threat of exposure, where do I stop?" He shook his head. "And do you really want me—or anyone—to have that kind of unbridled power?"

David looked unmoved. "What I want is for you to protect your own kind."

"I know my job," Micah said softly. "But I never forget that I'm dealing with people's lives, and that the Memory Eater is a person too. She doesn't really enjoy this, you know. Do you think this is what she wanted in life?"

I looked at the poor creature in a different light. If I'd eaten all those memories, maybe I'd be insane, too. She just stood there, her arms limp at her sides, her head lolling on her chest, as if she'd been hanged by the neck until dead, then stood upright.

"What's her name?" I asked.

Micah shook his head. "I don't know. She won't tell me."

How strange. Wouldn't she want him to know?

MAYBE SHE DOESN'T REMEMBER, Fang said sadly.

Maybe, but it made me wonder. "Why do you keep her locked up in an empty, dark cell?"

"I don't. There's a door in the back of the cell that leads to her apartment. She has all the comforts of home there. But sometimes, when the madness takes her, she prefers to stay in the cell."

PLUS, WHEN HE NEEDS TO BRING SOMEONE TO MEET HER, THE ATMOSPHERE OUT HERE SCARES THE BEJEEZUS OUT OF THEM, Fang said in a sardonic tone.

No kidding.

Micah shook his head, his expression sad. "We can't let her out into the world, and to tell the truth, she prefers it down here."

I glanced at her once again. She hadn't moved from that strange position. "What's your name?" I asked her.

She looked up. The madness in her eyes had dimmed, replaced by the murky light of understanding. "I am the Memory Eater," she said, her voice raspy. "It is who I am, what I do, until you release me from this existence." She sounded more sane now.

"Why me?" I asked.

"Because the soothsayer promised me."

"Which soothsayer?" I pressed. Maybe there'd be a record of it or something.

"In Ausssstin," she said vaguely.

I was beginning to get that uneasy feeling again. The one in which your life begins to unfold and force you into your destiny. You might still have a choice, but only after you were firmly on the path. I hated that feeling.

Before I could ask another question, her eyes unfocused again. We'd lost her to that world inside her head. I could only imagine what it was like to live with all of those memories fighting in her mind.

"There's a Demon Underground in Austin?" I asked Micah.

He nodded. "I was going to suggest you contact them when you get there."

Pia made rapid movements with her hands—sign language—and David translated. "You're still going to go with the vampires, after everything we've told you?"

"I have to. I gave my word." At their annoyed looks, I added, "That doesn't mean I'm going to help them do anything against our interests. My contract says only that I have to work for them until they come out." And David had just about convinced me that it was wrong for the Movement to reveal themselves if that action would eventually make the world aware of demons' existence as well.

"What if they never come out?" David persisted. "Are you okay with that?"

I shrugged. "If they don't come out within the next five years, I'm still released from the contract." But that meant five years in servitude to bloodsuckers. I could also be released if Alejandro chose to do so out of the goodness of his heart, but I didn't see that happening.

David said, "While you're there, you might want to be careful when dealing with the Austin Underground. I'm not hearing good things about them."

"Like what?" Micah asked, looking surprised.

"Like strange things happening, people gone missing, and Dina Bellama making the Underground into her own private playground."

DINA IS THE UNDERGROUND LEADER IN AUSTIN, Fang told me.

Exasperated, I asked, "You want me to fix them, too?" Ridiculous.

"No," Micah said. "But it wouldn't hurt for us to know what's going on, just in case it spills over onto us."

Turning to him, David challenged, "This mean you're going to step up and be the leader you should have been all along, or are you going to have the Memory Eater erase the memories of anyone who tries to make you do your duty?"

"I am ready to ssserve," the Memory Eater said.

I shivered. Would she really rip out my memories if Micah asked her to?

YOU KNOW IT, BABE.

Judging from the expression on his face, Micah was mighty peeved. "I wouldn't do that," he said, but a flicker of guilt in his eyes showed he'd at least thought about it. He glanced at the skeletal woman. "You can go back to your home, now."

She nodded, and moving as though the weight of the world was on her shoulders, left through the door at the back of the cell. The bright light on the other side blinded me temporarily until she shut the door behind her. The light cut off and I wondered if that's how she felt—severed from community and hope.

"Come on, Val," Micah said. "You know I have everyone's best interests at heart."

Until now, I'd considered Micah my hero, my guardian angel. But I had to admit his halo was tilting off its axis, looking a bit tarnished. I glanced at him and said thoughtfully, "I know you think you do. But I wonder, is your way—your father's way—what's really best for the Underground?"

He looked hurt. "I'll think about David's concerns, but why would you believe his judgment over mine, Val? They represent a bitter minority."

Pia stepped forward, glared at Micah, then signed at David.

David nodded. "Pia wants me to tell you that we may be in the minority, but it's a significant one. We're the lost, the maimed, the demons who counted on the Underground to protect us but were disappointed by Micah and his father. All we want is a chance to make it what it should be, so no one else has to suffer."

"I said I'd think about it," Micah said in exasperation. "Why are you even listening to them, Val? They locked you up."

It was a good question. I knew and trusted Micah, but I also trusted Fang's judgment. "They locked me up so Pia would feel safe," I told him. "And I understand why now."

"It's theater. They're just trying to turn you against me."

David started to protest but I stopped him with a raised hand and answered Micah myself. "No, you're not hearing what they've been saying. They want you, as leader, to help them feel safe."

David nodded. "That, or step down and let someone else lead."

"Who?" Micah challenged him. "You? You think you can do better? You haven't got a clue what I'm dealing with."

"I couldn't do worse."

Anger flared in Micah's eyes, but he didn't respond. Maybe he *was* listening.

YEAH, Fang confirmed. WITH YOUR HELP, DAVID HAS WEDGED IN SOME DOUBT AND GOTTEN HIM TO RETHINK HIS POLICIES.

David shrugged and continued, "But it's not up to me. By tradition, the soothsayer uses her abilities to choose the best person for the job. It might be you, it might be me, or it might even be someone else . . . like Val."

"Me?" He was kidding, right? He had to be kidding. "No way. I don't want to be a leader."

David smiled. "You are one, whether you realize it or not. Others are following your example, not waiting for Micah to give us permission to defend ourselves, but taking it into our own hands to clear the streets of undead scum who prey on humans."

"That's dangerous," Micah protested. "Val has training where most do not."

"And whose fault is that?" David shot back. "Besides, it's more dangerous to leave them out there."

Pia retrieved an envelope from one of the chairs along the wall and handed it to Micah.

David gestured at it. "That's a petition from a dozen members of the Underground, requesting a Naming Ritual to validate your position as leader. By tradition, it is our right to call for one."

"What you're really asking for is a vote of confidence," Micah said tightly.

Pia nodded, her intent gaze never leaving Micah's face.

Micah turned to me, his face grim. "And you, Val? Do you think the Underground needs a new leader?"

Oh, no, he was not going to put this on me. But since he asked, I was going to tell him the absolute truth. "I don't know. But this would answer the question either way, right?"

YES, Fang agreed. LET THE GROUP DECIDE WHAT IS BEST FOR THEM.

Micah's lips tightened. I guess that wasn't the answer he was hoping for. "All right," he bit out, "I don't think it's necessary, but you'll have your ritual."

"When?" David asked.

"After Christmas. I don't want to interrupt anyone's holiday plans. Will that work for you?" he asked David stiffly.

David and Pia both nodded.

"Good," he said, practically biting out the word. "I assume you can see yourselves out." Without waiting for an answer, he strode out of the room like he couldn't get away fast enough. Or like it hurt too much to stay.

I watched him go, disturbed that I might be the cause of his pain. *Did I do the right thing?* I asked Fang.

DON'T WORRY, Fang said. HE'S NOT MAD AT YOU. HE'S MAD AT HIMSELF, THAT HE DIDN'T SEE THIS COMING. HE PRETTY MUCH JUST GOT THE CRAP KICKED OUT OF HIS BELIEFS. HE FEELS A LITTLE GUILTY AND HE'S WORRIED THAT THE RITUAL WILL GO AGAINST HIM AND SHOW THAT HE'S BEEN SCREWING UP ALL ALONG.

And I'd just gone and said it was necessary. Crap. Why couldn't I have kept my mouth shut? No matter what happened with this ritual, I was afraid my easy, cousinly relationship with Micah had just changed forever.

Chapter Five

"So," I said, turning to David. "The least you can do is give me a ride home."

"Sure. Let me get my truck and I'll meet you out back."

As David left, Pia moved toward me. She gazed into my eyes then grabbed my hand and deliberately pumped it up and down. Her way of saying thanks, I guess.

RIGHT, Fang confirmed. SHE ASKED ME TO TELL YOU THAT SHE APPRECIATES YOU BACKING THEM UP. MICAH WOULDN'T HAVE LISTENED TO THEM WITHOUT YOUR HELP. AND SHE'S SORRY SHE HAD TO DRUG YOU AND LOCK YOU UP.

"You're welcome," I told her. I still didn't think the drug and cage were necessary, though I did understand why she wanted them. "And you're forgiven. But next time, just text, okay?"

She grinned and nodded.

As I followed her out of Micah's secret basement, Fang trotted alongside me. DO YOU FORGIVE ME, TOO?

He sounded uncharacteristically anxious. *I don't know. Why shouldn't I wring your neck for putting me through that?*

As we squeezed into the cab of David's beat-up pickup, Fang cuddled up in my lap. BECAUSE YOU LOVE ME? he asked plaintively, looking up at me with his big brown eyes.

Okay, I had to admit, he did cute and adorable really well. I couldn't help but scratch him behind his fuzzy ears. *That's beside the point.*

BECAUSE I WAS HELPING PIA AND DAVID . . . THEY'VE BEEN THROUGH A LOT. I FIGURED THEY DESERVED SOME SLACK. BESIDES, YOU NEEDED TO HEAR AND SEE WHAT MICAH HAS BEEN HIDING FROM EVERYONE.

You could have done that with words alone.

MAYBE. BUT WOULD IT HAVE BEEN AS CONVINCING?

Probably not. *You scared the hell out of me.*

I KNOW, AND I'M SORRY FOR THAT.

And why me? Why didn't David pick on someone else?

LIKE HE SAID, IT'S BECAUSE YOU CAN MAKE A DIFFERENCE. PEOPLE SEE YOU DIFFERENTLY. DAVID AND MICAH KNOW HOW INFLUENTIAL YOU ARE, JUST BY BEING YOURSELF, EVEN IF YOU DON'T.

Ridiculous. Why did everyone forget that I was still only eighteen? Sure, I felt years older in experience, but I was too young for all the responsibility everyone kept trying to shove off on me. And I sure didn't want it. But the Demon Underground didn't have the same social conventions tied up with arbitrary age numbers. They didn't see years. They saw something else. If I could figure out what it was, I'd darned well stop showing it to them.

WHAT ELSE ARE YOU GOING TO DO WITH YOUR LIFE? Fang challenged. DO YOU EVEN KNOW WHAT YOU WANT TO BE WHEN YOU GROW UP?

Maybe not, but I wanted to be the one to make the choice, not have it shoved down my throat. *Don't push me. This is not going to make me want to forgive you yet. And don't even think about getting pizza until I do.*

OKAY. He sighed heavily. I CAN LIVE WITH THAT.

We rode in silence the rest of the way home. When we arrived, David and I exchanged phone numbers and Fang and I got out of the truck. It was near dawn, but all the lights were blazing in the house. Guess my roomie, Gwen, was up.

Inside, two people and a hellhound sat in the living room, their postures tense. Gwen looked worried, her short red hair more tousled than normal, and Shade's general swirliness was an agitated mess.

WHERE HAVE YOU BEEN? Princess demanded. MY HUMAN WAS WORRIED ABOUT YOU.

Shade was seven-eighths human, but I always thought of him as demon. Apparently, Princess didn't. And I noticed that the part hellhound, part Cavalier King Charles Spaniel didn't say *she* was worried. She'd always been self-centered, but now that she was pregnant with Fang's pups, she was more demanding than ever.

At least Gwen and Shade looked relieved to see us. Gwen said, "When I got home from the ER, I found your motorcycle here and your cell lying next to it."

I patted my pockets. Sure enough, my phone was gone. It must have fallen out during the struggle.

"I called Shade," Gwen continued, "but when you weren't at his place, we both got worried."

That explained why he was here. "Sorry," I said. "But it wasn't my choice." Privately, I asked Fang, *You didn't tell Princess about this?*

No, he answered ruefully. YOU TRY REASONING WITH A HORMONAL HELLHOUND, SEE HOW FAR YOU GET.

I hear ya.

Shade moved around the couch to envelop me in his arms. Oh, my. Lola liked. Now finally free of the sticky web of the drug, Lola was able to reach out and touch. She wanted to drink up all the yummy goodness that was Shade, but I wouldn't let her. Not right now anyway. For now, it felt good just to be wrapped in his arms, feeling the warmth of his body against mine. Knowing someone cared enough about me to worry infused my being with a warm glow of happiness.

Sappy, I know, but Shade affected me that way. Home again with friends surrounding me—it didn't get better than this.

"What happened?" he asked, holding me at arm's length.

Since he was still touching me, the swirls were gone and I could see his face. That made me happy, too. Our relationship was still new, and I never got tired of his hot studliness. Didn't think I ever would.

GAG ME, Fang said, pretending to choke.

Ignoring him, I sat down on the couch and wondered how to explain. "I'm sorry, Gwen, but most of this is Demon Underground business. I'm not sure how much I can tell you."

"Doesn't matter," she said and rose to give me a hug. "I'm just glad you're safe." Sighing, she added, "Time to get some shut-eye." As she left the room, she tossed over her shoulder, "Oh, and don't let Jack eat *everything* in the kitchen, okay?"

Jack wandered into the living room, carrying a heaping platter of food, still looking like a lumberjack instead of the former keeper of the *Encyclopedia Magicka.* "I heard that," he said, waving a drumstick in Gwen's direction

"You were supposed to," Gwen called out, then shut her door firmly behind her.

"You brought Jack with you?" I asked Shade, bemused.

Shade, who sat next to me and snuggled close, shrugged. "He insisted."

HE LIKES THE FOOD, Princess, always bluntly honest, put in.

The former keeper had been imprisoned in a sort of pocket universe for decades. Since he'd come back to this world, he didn't seem to be able to get enough chow to make up for all his lost meals. He spent most of his time eating and watching television, which fascinated him.

Jack placed a hand over his heart. "I'm hurt."

I chuckled. "We might have believed you if you'd taken the drumstick out of your hand first."

He shrugged and set the plate on the coffee table. "I heard you come in, so I brought extra to share. I reckon you're hungry."

I was. And so were Fang and Princess, so we all chowed down on Gwen's scrumptious fried chicken, mashed potatoes, and corn on the cob as I told the demons about my night and what was going on in the Underground. Jack admitted he was disturbed that Micah hadn't kept some of the old ways, but Shade was unreservedly on Micah's side and seemed upset that I could possibly doubt him.

"I'm withholding judgment until the Naming Ritual," I told Shade soothingly. "Micah said he'll hold one after Christmas."

"And when were you going to tell me your plans for the holidays?" Shade asked.

I'd never heard that particular tense tone in his voice before. His expression was tight, like he was trying to hide his feelings. Surprised, I said, "You know I'm going to Mom and Rick's for their annual Yule and Christmas celebration. You're invited, too."

"No, I mean before that. With Alejandro and Austin."

"I just learned that tonight," I told him. "It's not like I was keeping it a secret. A few things have happened since then . . ." I glanced at Jack, who was still stuffing his face. "Micah told Jack, I take it."

Shade didn't relax much and I wondered what his problem was. He handed me my phone. "Yes, and Austin called you earlier. We thought it might be about you, so I answered."

"No biggie. What did he want?"

"He wanted to tell you he'll be picking you and Jack up here tomorrow evening, shortly after sunset." Shade still sounded stiff and defensive.

"Okay. Makes sense, what with luggage and stuff. Is there a problem?"

Princess filled us in. WE TOLD THE VAMPIRE YOU WERE MISSING BUT HE SAID YOU COULD TAKE CARE OF YOURSELF, AND MADE MY HUMAN SOUND LIKE A WHINY LITTLE PUP.

Shade didn't look happy that Princess shared that with us, but I laughed. "Well, to Austin, I guess we do seem like children. He must be at least a hundred years old, right? An old geezer."

Shade relaxed. "I told him I'm coming with you."

"Can you do that? I mean, will the vampires in Austin let Alejandro bring more people?"

"Who cares?" Shade said. "I'm going to be with you, not him. You need someone other than vampires by your side. I'll take the Ducati."

IN CASE YOU HADN'T NOTICED, HE'S JUST A WEE BIT JEALOUS OF AUSTIN, Fang said privately.

Now that was dumb. And strange. He was cool with my ex, Dan, who was fully human, but he was jealous of a vampire? There was no reason for it, but hey, if it meant Shade came with me, I was all for it.

Shade glanced at his hellhound. "Gwen agreed to take care of Princess while I'm gone."

SHE PROMISED TO PAMPER AND PET ME, AND GIVE ME A PINK BED OF MY VERY OWN, the pregnant diva shared with us.

I hid a grin, secretly glad we wouldn't have to deal with her drama. "Sounds good to me."

"Will you help protect Gwen, too?" Shade asked, sounding totally serious.

Princess tipped her head up. OF COURSE. I AM AN EXCELLENT HELLHOUND.

"Good," I said. "And I'll text Micah and ask him to check in on both of you."

Jack said mournfully, "Can we not bring Gwen along?"

"Don't worry," I told him. "There are plenty of places to eat in Austin. You won't starve." Heck, he'd be lucky if he didn't balloon up to twice his size, the way he'd been eating. "But that's not why you're going, remember? You're supposed to be teaching me how to use the books."

"I will," he said.

"When?" I pressed him. "You haven't taught me anything yet."

He swallowed a bite of mashed potatoes. "What's your hurry? We have a great amount of time."

Annoyed, I snapped, "Maybe, maybe not. I'm going to the capital to meet some strange vamps and demons and face unknown dangers. If the books can help me, I'd like to know how before I go."

HE DOESN'T WANT TO TELL YOU, Fang said.

I glanced at the hellhound and grinned. *Oh yeah, that's* why I keep you around. You can be handy sometimes.

DOES THAT MEAN THE PIZZA BAN IS LIFTED?

Don't push it. Turning to Jack, I asked, "What don't you want to tell me?"

He grimaced and set down his fork and paused for a long moment, as if wondering how much to tell me. "Well, you see, back in my time, they called me the keeper, but it was a misnomer. I didn't keep the books so much as they kept me."

"What you do mean?" I asked.

"The mage demon who created them did so with one clear imperative—protect themselves at all costs. He wanted to make sure they would be available for use by his descendants."

Shade swallowed a bite of chicken. "Trevor said only full mage demons can create new spells and use them. His descendants have to read them from the books. Was he telling the truth?"

Good question. Trevor, the SOB mage demon who'd tried to kill me and steal the encyclopedia, had been lying to us and manipulating us to find the books for him. Who knew what was the truth and what was a convenient lie?

"Yes, partially," Jack confirmed. "Each mage demon can be taught one spell, passed down from parent to child. But that's all. The others have to be read from the encyclopedia. Unfortunately for them, the books gained awareness and a mind of their own."

I nodded. I remembered feeling that. And that explained why Trevor had a shield but no other powers.

"Self-preservation is what drives the books now. They don't want to be used by anyone, because it endangers them. So they choose keepers who aren't hungry for power, with no reason to love mage demons, and who are willing and able to defend them tooth and nail to keep them out of mage demon hands."

"So, you're saying . . . what?" I asked. "That they're all take and no give?"

"Sometimes," Jack admitted.

Shade protested, "But you said Val could get her powers back."

Jack held up his hands defensively. "Not exactly. I said the books can grant her powers—other powers within their ability. And they can . . . if they want to."

"If they want to? What does that mean?" I wasn't sure I liked the sound of this.

"The books do what's good for *them*, though that may not necessarily be what's good for *you*."

"So what exactly did you plan on teaching me?" I asked indignantly. "Or were you just hanging around, making empty promises while you take advantage of Gwen's food?"

"No, I can help," Jack assured me. "I know things about the books, how to coax things out of them, and what happens when you do accept one of their gifts."

"Like what?"

"Well, for each new ability I gained, the power in my other ones lessened."

"You mean I'd lose Lola if the books gave me super strength or something?" I wasn't sure if I loved or hated that idea.

"You wouldn't lose your succubus powers, so much as you'd see them diminish. And the more abilities you accept and use, the more your others weaken." He shook his head. "I found out the hard way. You *can* regain your full succubus powers if you use them a lot more than the other abilities. It's a strange balancing act you have to learn."

Shade squeezed my knee reassuringly and asked Jack, "Now that you're no longer the keeper, do you still have all those abilities?"

"No, thank heavens. I'm back to the one I was born with. The ability to lasso with a rope of energy."

That made sense—I remembered him using it when we tossed Trevor back into that pocket universe.

"I can teach you the way of it," Jack promised. "How to balance the forces." He grinned. "You'll see. We'll have a great time in Austin."

Great. Now all I had to do was go to an unknown city where a strange bunch of vamps were in charge, spy on the demons there, stand by Alejandro's side *without* helping him come out, keep the fact hidden that the Slayer has lost some of her mojo, *and* learn how to convince the freakin' books to give me my powers back.

Yeah, right. Piece of cake.

Chapter Six

I didn't own a suitcase, so I packed what I thought I'd need in my duffel bag and put the books in a backpack, since Jack was supposed to teach me about them. I had no clue what we'd face in the capital, but it was best to be rested and alert, so I spent the remaining time catching some z's with Fang.

Shade and Jack had gone home to do the same, and by the time they came back to drop off Princess, we were ready. At about an hour after sunset, two shiny black luxury cars pulled up. As Fang and Shade said goodbye to Princess, Jack and I went out to meet them.

The passenger window glided down on one car and Alejandro smiled at me. "Good evening, Ms. Shapiro. Are you ready?"

I nodded and Alejandro said, "Excellent. Vincent will drive me, and you and Mr. Grady may accompany Austin in the other car."

Heaven forbid we'd crowd the vampires by taking only one luxury vehicle. I nodded at Vincent in the driver's seat. I remembered meeting the short, bald guy before, if you could call it "meeting" when I'd broken up a fight between him and fire demon Andrew.

Austin got out of the other car and opened the trunk so we could stow our stuff. He wore a snazzy business suit instead of his normal jeans, though he hadn't given up his Stetson and boots, I noticed. Shade and Fang emerged from the townhouse, and as Jack and Fang climbed into the back of the car, Shade took my hand so he wouldn't be all swirly. He nodded at Alejandro. "I'm coming, too," he said with a stubborn tilt to his chin.

Austin shut the trunk and lounged against it with his arms folded, looking as though he was fighting a smile. His boss, Alejandro, shook his head. "I'm afraid that is not possible. I agreed not to bring more than four to meet with the enclave in Austin."

"No problem," Shade said, almost belligerently. "I'm not going with you, I'm going with Val. I'll follow on my bike. It's my right to go where I want."

Austin lifted an eyebrow, expressing his amusement at Shade's expense. I'm not sure why, but it annoyed me.

BECAUSE HE'S MAKING FUN OF YOUR BOYFRIEND WITHOUT EVEN TALKING, Fang said. YOU'RE ANNOYED BECAUSE YOU CAN'T DEFEND SHADE WITHOUT LOOKING SILLY OR MAKING SHADE LOOK WEAKER TO AUSTIN . . . *AND* YOU WISH YOU COULD COMMUNICATE AS MUCH AS HE CAN WITH A SINGLE GESTURE.

Sometimes I hated it when the hellhound was right.

Alejandro shook his head. "You may have the right to go where you wish, but you cannot stay with Ms. Shapiro and the rest of us. That would violate the terms of my agreement."

Shade shrugged. "No problem. I'll stay with the Austin Underground. That way I can be available for her when she's free."

One corner of Austin's mouth quirked up and he looked even more amused, obviously not trying to hide it.

Shade must have caught it, too, because he stiffened. "I'll see you there," he said more to Austin than me, then grabbed me and kissed me passionately.

Normally, Lola and I had no problem responding to Shade's kisses, but PDA wasn't my thing and it felt kind of like Shade was staking a public claim. Not cool.

DUDE, Fang broadcast to both of us. LAY OFF. VAL IS NO ONE'S PROPERTY.

Shade broke the kiss, looking sheepish.

HE SAID HE'S SORRY, Fang told me. HE DOESN'T KNOW WHAT CAME OVER HIM . . . BUT I DO. A LITTLE CASE OF AUSTIN ENVY. JEALOUS MUCH, DUDE?

Shade looked mortified, so I squeezed his hands then gave him a swift kiss. "I'll call you later, when I know more about where I'm staying and what I'll be doing."

"Good," he said softly. "I'll look forward to it."

Austin's expression still held that infuriating smirk as he invited me into the front passenger seat with a flourish. Annoyed, I asked, "Shouldn't you be holding down the fort here? Why didn't Alejandro bring Rosa or Luis or someone else?" Anyone else . . .

"Alejandro didn't think it wise to bring Rosa, and Luis does well when he's in charge here. Besides, I asked to come," Austin said, getting behind the wheel and starting the car.

I grimaced. "To torture me?"

That damned grin popped out again. "Not everything is about you, Slayer. I am sire to someone in Austin and I want to visit him, that's all."

"You have a son?" Jack asked in surprise.

Fang snorted, but Austin answered, "Not genetically. Being a sire means initiating a human into the vampire community."

Austin's version sounded too pretty. "Exchanging blood-flavored Big Gulps, you mean." Then, translating for Jack who'd been out of the world for a while, I said, "Making them into bloodsuckers, too." The thought of Austin—or anyone—making more vamps kind of made me uneasy. "How many have you sired?" I probed.

He shot me a sideways glance as if to say my question was too personal, but answered anyway. "Not many, and each time it was with their full knowledge and consent. It is not something we do lightly. There are a great many responsibilities and duties associated with being a sire."

"Really? Like what?" Jack asked eagerly.

Glancing at the former keeper in the rearview mirror, Austin drawled, "I prefer to keep that to myself." When that killed the conversation, he added, "The drive takes about an hour. Perhaps you could use the time to teach Val about the books, so she doesn't have to rely on her succubus all the time. How far have you gotten?"

"Not far," I said.

"There's still a lot to learn," Jack added. "But I prefer to do that in private, if you don't mind."

HE DOESN'T WANT TO SHARE IN FRONT OF THE VAMPS, Fang translated.

Yeah, I got that, but sooner or later, Jack was going to have to give me some more details I could use.

Austin shrugged. "Suit yourself. I just thought she should learn more as soon as she could. Never know when another mage demon might come looking for the books."

Good point—one I'd been trying to make with Jack since we'd tossed those two mages through the portal and onto their keesters in another world.

When Jack didn't answer, Austin asked, "Is it true Trevor's father caused the 1906 San Francisco earthquake? I was there, too."

And that's all it took to get the two of them swapping war stories about an event that had happened long before I was born. *Yawn.* Thank goodness the drive to the capital wasn't longer.

When we passed Garlic Creek and Slaughter Creek on the outskirts of Austin, Jack chuckled and observed how appropriate it was for vampires. "I see why their slogan is Keep Austin Weird."

Cowboy Austin was not amused, so the rest of the ride was in silence until we arrived at an office building near downtown. The entrance had a sign with what looked like three red raindrops, and I realized I'd seen that symbol before on the Movement's establishments in San Antonio. Must be a universal vamp blood bank donation sign for those in the know, kind of like the green cross for medical marijuana dispensaries.

We followed Alejandro's car into the gated underground garage and the five of us plus Fang got out and stretched. Alejandro, Austin, and Vincent looked all dressed up in their business suits. When Vincent gave Jack and me a subtle up and down sneer, he managed to make me feel scruffy. Oh, well, I didn't have anything resembling a suit and wouldn't wear it even if I did. So, I smiled at him like it didn't matter.

Alejandro didn't seem to care. Gathering us together, he said, "We are the guest of another vampire, in her territory. Ms. Shapiro, Mr. Grady, I don't expect you to know our customs, and they won't expect you to, either. I would ask you, though, to keep quiet and follow my lead."

I shrugged. "Okay, I'll be good." But I didn't let on that when I'd gotten out of the car, I'd tucked a bit of wooden insurance in the back waistband of my jeans, just in case. It was covered with my vest.

We all piled into the elevator and Alejandro spoke briefly with someone on the intercom, then we took the elevator to the top. But instead of revealing a cubicle farm, the opening doors showed a sumptuous apartment that must have taken up the entire penthouse. The walls and floors looked like they were made of cream-colored marble with veins of gold, and there were gilded cherubs, scrolls, flowers and other gold crap all over the walls and furniture. The windows were draped in heavy, emerald-green silk, and the striped cushions on the carved and gilded furniture matched.

WHOA. IT LOOKS LIKE LOUIS THE FOURTEENTH THREW UP IN HERE, Fang said.

I had to agree. Not a style I'd go for. But it was a perfect frame for the woman I'd just noticed. She lounged on a settee in the middle of the room, her long flowing red hair, creamy complexion and emerald slip dress beautifully complemented by the carefully designed room. She was stunning, and she knew it. Even the four hunks surrounding her, in skin-baring black leather vests and pants, seemed to have been chosen for their ability to complement her and the room. Though to me, they resembled rejects from an erotic romance cover shoot.

Cliché much?

"Alejandro," she crooned and languidly raised one milky-white arm toward him, her wrist limp.

Alejandro apparently knew his duty, for he glided over to her, dropped to one knee and kissed the outstretched hand. "Lisette, how good to see you again."

Gag me.

GUESS WE KNOW NOW WHY THEY LEFT ROSA AT HOME, Fang quipped.

Yeah. I couldn't suppress a grin and Austin shot me a warning look. I shrugged and tried to cultivate a serious expression. It was difficult, though, with this silly farce playing out before us. Jack didn't seem to think so, though. He appeared fascinated by it all, especially Lisette.

Her four attendants, good-looking blonds all from the same cookie cutter, didn't look so happy. I privately labeled them Tweedledee, Tweedledum, Tweedledumber and just plain Twee. Mr. Dum, especially, looked as though he wanted to rip Alejandro's throat out for touching Lisette. Twee looked more interested in Austin.

Speaking of Austin, he became the object of Lisette's attention now. She slinked up off the lounge and undulated toward him with a predatory gleam in her eye, looking like a real-life version of Jessica Rabbit, the sexy cartoon bombshell from *Roger Rabbit*.

SHE'S NOT BAD, SHE'S JUST DRAWN THAT WAY, Fang said with a snicker.

Yeah, right.

Lisette didn't spare a glance for the rest of us. Her eyes were all for Austin as she unnecessarily straightened his tie then caressed his chest. His blond studliness certainly fit her type. "Have you come to serve . . . under me . . . finally?" she asked, her lips a breath away from his.

Whoa. No wonder they called it vamping. And she was apparently an expert at it. Lola could take lessons from this chick. Not that Lola needed to—all she needed was her innate power. And speaking of Lola, she was getting quite interested in the four hunkalicious hotties over there. I figured it wasn't cool to snack on your hostess's flunkies, so I reined her in.

Austin removed Lisette's hands gently from his jacket and took a step back, straightening his lapels. "No, I must refuse your flattering invitation once again. I am very happy serving under Alejandro." His flat tone refused to recognize the innuendo.

She pouted but let him go and glided back to Alejandro and the Tweedles. "Too bad," she said over her shoulder. "We could have such . . . fun."

"Sadly," Alejandro said, "we are not here to have fun."

She pouted again, but swept an arm invitingly toward the chairs around her. "Please, have a seat."

I perched on an ornate chair that was as uncomfortable as it looked. Tweedledumber stood behind me, and the others in our party had guards, too, except for Alejandro who sat facing Lisette. She, on the other hand, chose a chair that looked more like a throne.

Seriously? My mouth twitched and Fang nudged me with his nose, giving me a warning look. I bit my lip and controlled my expression. Okay, if she wanted to play queen for a day, I'd go along.

Lisette gave Alejandro a regal, condescending nod. "So, tell me, why have you brought the Slayer into my abode?"

I didn't think she'd even seen me, much less known who I was. Tension suddenly ratcheted up as her minions focused intently on me. Hey, Lola was up for a little showdown, but I hoped it wasn't necessary.

"I brought her here to help," Alejandro said, his voice and gestures soothing.

"Help destroy us?" Lisette challenged, her nostrils flaring.

Sheesh. Did the woman always act as if some hidden camera was filming her every move?

"Not at all," Alejandro said. "A soothsayer told me that if I led with Ms. Shapiro by my side, I would achieve my heart's desire."

Well, Tessa hadn't actually mentioned my name. That was Alejandro's interpretation.

"And your heart's desire is . . . the New Blood Movement?" Lisette asked.

"Of course," Alejandro said smoothly.

She nodded. "That is my desire as well. She will . . . behave while she is here?"

Alejandro smiled at me. "She has given her word to help me. And her word is her bond."

Unfortunately, true—that darned contract. I gave her an innocent smile and tried to look like an obedient little Slayer. I guess it worked, because Lisette deigned to give me a glance, then apparently dismissed me from her thoughts. Tension eased and she seemed to relax.

Alejandro continued, "You say our friend in the government no longer wishes to help us?"

"That is correct. He doesn't feel the timing is right."

"But the legislature doesn't convene again until January," Alejandro protested. "How does he know the timing isn't right?"

She shrugged. "I'll let him answer for himself. Boys?"

Tweedledee evidently took that as a signal, because he crossed the room to another door and beckoned to someone beyond it. A man—a definite suit type with a photogenic face—came in, straightening his tie. It seemed everyone knew who he was but me and maybe Jack, because they didn't introduce him.

Alejandro shook his hand and Lisette gestured him to a seat. Alejandro turned to face him. "I thought you were spending the holidays talking to the legislators and working on our behalf to convince them to legalize the Movement."

The man shook his head. "I planned to, but this is a bad time. Haven't you heard the news?"

"What news?" the vampire leader asked.

"There are reports of *chupacabras* terrorizing Austin."

Huh? What was a *chupacabra*?

Fang shrugged. BEATS ME.

"*Chupacabras?*" Alejandro repeated, his eyebrows raised. Turning to us, he said, as if he couldn't quite believe it himself, "In English, that means goat-sucker."

I couldn't help it. I let out a choke of laughter.

The legislator glared at me. "It is no laughing matter. Goats, deer, dogs . . . they have all been found drained of blood on the outskirts of the capital. We're lucky the media is blaming a mythical creature instead of vampires, but if you reveal yourselves to the public now, the attention may shift to you . . . and not in a good way."

Oh.

"Has anyone actually seen one of these chupacabras?" Alejandro asked in distaste.

"Not a reliable account. Just a midnight encounter. If we are to believe the witness, the creature is ten feet tall, grotesque, faster than lightning, and all fangs and claws. Ridiculous."

"What have you done about it?" Lisette asked.

The man shrugged. "We are investigating, and I am subtly encouraging belief in this creature to turn attention away from you. But unless this threat is dealt with, public hysteria cannot be far behind." He paused, then said, "I know it wouldn't be anyone in the Movement, but do you think it could be some rogue vampires?"

Very politic of him, but rogues would go for humans, not animals.

"Very possible," Lisette said. "With Alejandro's help, we shall take care of this threat for you."

The suit stood and smiled. "Thank you." He leaned forward and they held a furtive whispered conversation for a few moments, then he nodded and left.

Wonder what that was all about?

HE PROPOSITIONED HER FOR TONIGHT AND SHE POLITELY DECLINED, Fang told me. At my startled look, he added, NO, HE'S NOT A DEMON. I CAN'T READ HIS MIND. I JUST HAVE GOOD EARS.

Once the suit had left, Alejandro said, "You know it is unlikely to be rogues. What do you think it is? Do you believe in this cartoon monster?"

Lisette shook her head, then glanced away, looking pained. "We have . . . three members who have gone missing, right around the time of the 'chupacabra' attacks. I don't think they would do such a thing, but it cannot be discounted."

Yep, three crazed vamps would account for it.

"Who?" Alejandro asked.

"Etienne, Ronald, and . . ." she glanced apologetically at Austin, ". . . Wes."

"No." The single word exploded out of Austin like a gunshot. "I sired Wes. I know him. He would never do such a thing."

"Nor would Ronald and Etienne," Lisette said. "But the fact remains, they are missing, and we cannot find a sign of them."

"Are you certain?" Jack asked. "People can change—"

"Highly improbable," Alejandro confirmed. "Once they are turned, people become more of what they were as humans, not less."

"Yes," Austin added. "Wes was a kind, gentle man as a human, and no less so as a vampire. I can't see him draining livestock."

"Nor can we," Lisette said.

Jack shrugged, seeming unafraid of the bloodsuckers. "Perhaps someone is forcing them to hunt, or is imprisoning them so the blame will fall on them later. There could be other reasons."

Lisette nodded. "That is why we allowed you to come. Perhaps between us, we can learn what this creature is and stop it before it ruins things for all of us." She glanced at me. "You seem to enjoy killing things. Perhaps you would assist us in tracking these creatures down and eliminating them?"

Now that was just insulting. All they ever wanted from me was lust or death. If they were going to treat me like this, I wanted something out of it, too. And I knew just the thing. "It's not in my contract," I told her with a fake smile.

TAKE *THAT*, YOU BLOODSUCKER, Fang exclaimed.

Austin made an abortive movement, like he wanted to grab me but restrained himself. "Val, please, you must help us. She's right—you and Fang are very good at this sort of thing."

Fang nudged me with his nose. HE'S GOT YOU THERE.

Alejandro gazed at me sternly. "The contract states that you agree to help us reveal ourselves. We won't be able to do that until the menace is abated. Surely, you see that this is related, an integral part of our agreement."

Exactly what I thought he'd say. "That's open to interpretation. Shall we have our lawyers get together and discuss it?"

"Val—" Austin began to protest, but I cut him off.

"Never mind. Tell you what—I'll make you a deal. If I find this so-called chupacabra for you and kill it, you terminate the contract."

OH, GOOD PLAY.

Alejandro frowned. "I may need your services in the future, too."

I shrugged. "And if you ask real nice and don't treat me like a filthy assassin, I might even say yes."

PLUS THE MONEY, Fang said. DON'T FORGET THE MONEY.

Don't worry, I won't.

Alejandro regarded me gravely for a moment, and I could see Lisette and Austin urging him silently to take the deal. "Very well," he said reluctantly. "You have my word."

"Good." I turned to Lisette. "And if the chupacabra happens to be one of your people? Do you still want me to kill it?"

She looked uncertain for the first time since I'd met her. "I am not comfortable with you making that choice. You will take the boys with you—"

"No way. I work alone or not at all."

She bristled, and Austin said, "Maybe a compromise?" When we both turned to face him, he added, "You've worked with a partner before, Val, so how about you take me on? You know how well we spar together."

He gave me one of those raised eyebrow looks, and I knew he was reminding me that my powers were gone and that I could use someone with his speed and strength. Dang it, he was right, too. But I still hesitated, not wanting to give in too soon.

"I would consider it a personal favor," Austin said softly, almost formally.

Several sharp intakes of breath alerted me to the fact that something significant had just happened. Unfortunately, I had no idea what it was. From the puzzled expression on his face, Jack didn't seem to have a clue, either.

I THINK IT MEANS AUSTIN OWES YOU A FAVOR IN RETURN, Fang said.

Okay, having Austin owe me a favor couldn't be a bad thing. "All right then, you have a deal. I'll even throw in tracking down your missing vamps for free." After all, if it was the last thing I was forced to do for Alejandro, it was worth it.

Chapter Seven

Once I made my promise, Lisette seemed to have no more use for me. We retrieved our luggage from the cars and the Tweedles showed us to our rooms. Alejandro, Austin and Vincent got sumptuous guest suites right below the penthouse, while Jack and I were given adjoining rooms on a lower level apparently reserved for us second-class citizens who didn't suck blood.

Fine with me. Though it resembled a bland beige hotel room, it had a bed, bath and desk, which was all I needed. While Fang nosed around, investigating the space, I called Shade.

He answered, but all I could hear was loud music. "Hold on," he yelled. Soon, I heard a door close and the noise became muffled. "So, you made it all right?"

"Just fine. How about you? Find the Underground okay?"

"Sure. It's on Sixth Street."

My eyebrows rose. No wonder the music was so loud. I'd heard Sixth Street was party central for the college students. "In a bar?"

"Yeah. It's called Club Purgatory, too. Kind of like a Demon Underground franchise across Texas, I guess."

Weird.

"Where are you staying?" he asked.

"I'm not sure. Somewhere downtown. Probably not too far from you."

"So, Alejandro have you working hard?"

"Kind of." I filled him in on the chupacabra thing. "How's it going there?"

"Okay, I guess. I'm still waiting to meet their leader. She's busy with club business and performing, so it might be awhile."

"Performing?"

"Yeah. She's a succubus like you, and I guess she does some kind of sexy song act to feed on the audience. Like Micah does with his dancing."

Another succubus? I didn't like the sound of that, and Lola sure didn't. She considered Shade her own personal snack. Alarm spiked in me. "Hey, they have some kind of vamps-only meet and greet thing going on now, so we unworthy demons have a few hours free. Want to get something to eat?"

"Sure, but I can't exactly go out in public."

Oh, yeah. Sometimes I forgot his swirliness kept him limited. If it wasn't for other demons providing a space where he could be his own swirly self, he'd never be able to get out. "Okay, how about I grab some food and bring it to you? Is there a place there where we can sit and eat?" Besides, I should probably meet the Underground here, too, especially after what David had said about there being something a little off with them.

Fang perked up at the mention of food and wagged his tail. DINNER?

"Yeah," Shade said. "They have a staff-only section we can use. It's quieter. I'll let the guy at the door know you're coming."

"Will they let Fang in?"

"I don't think so."

I looked down at the hellhound.

NO BIGGIE, he assured me. GET ME A PIZZA AND I'LL BE HAPPY. I COULD USE A NAP.

"Okay, thanks." We compared notes and figured out the Underground was within walking distance, so I didn't need the car, even though Austin had given me the keys.

A card on the nightstand gave instructions on how to have food delivered, so I made arrangements with the concierge to have a pizza delivered to the room, telling him to open the door and leave the box on the floor.

DOES THIS MEAN YOU FORGIVE ME? Fang asked.

"Somewhat. It's just that pizza is the easiest thing to order right now." I tried not to think of what else the concierge would order in.

Jack tapped on the door and stuck his head in, looking hopeful. "Some dinner would go down mighty fine right now."

I grinned at him. "I just ordered something for Fang, but I'm planning on getting some food to take to Shade. Want to come?"

"Of course."

I started to walk out the door, then paused for a moment, considering. We were in vamp territory and I had to leave the room unlocked so Fang could get out. I didn't care about any of my stuff, but . . . "I should probably take the books with me."

Jack nodded. "Yes, you should."

So, I slung the backpack over my shoulder and headed toward Sixth Street. We located a take-out Mexican restaurant, then found the seven-block party that was Sixth Street. There weren't as many people as I expected, but that could be due to students going home for Christmas break.

This Club Purgatory was right in the middle of the nightlife. I nodded to the guy at the door who was dressed like a Goth version of Santa Claus, with black and gray where red and white should be, and fake blood trickling down from one of his "fangs" into his scraggly beard. Ick. Some things were just in poor taste.

I raised my voice above the music so I could be heard. "Shade told you we were coming?"

Dark Santa nodded and gave us directions to get downstairs. The basement at this club seemed bigger than the one in San Antonio, and thankfully none of the *Purgatory* theme showed up here. Instead, there was a bright, clean break room where Shade was waiting for us. I kissed him, feeling kind of shy in front of Jack, and since no one else was there, we grabbed a corner table in the large room. We ate, then I pulled out the books and thumbed through the first volume.

"What are you looking for?" Jack asked.

"I want to see if there's any mention of chupacabras in the listing of demons, see what we can find out." I checked and even had Jack double-check, but there was no mention of them anywhere.

"I'm not surprised," Shade said. I touched his hand so I could see his features and he added, "I looked them up on my cell while I was waiting for you. I don't think they're real. The first sighting was in the midnineties and seems to have come from a woman who watched too many horror movies."

I nodded. "So, if they're not real, the goat-sucker is either a vamp or some other demon we're not familiar with."

Shade grinned. "I'm going with vamp."

"Yeah, Lisette said a few were missing. She didn't seem to think any of them would go rogue and suck on livestock though."

"It could be rogues who aren't affiliated with the Movement," Jack said.

Could be. We'd had some trouble with them in San Antonio. "That's what I thought at first, but rogues would more likely snack on people. I hear they taste better."

"Maybe Lisette's people drank some demon blood?" Shade

suggested. "That made some of Alejandro's people go crazy."

"Maybe," I said doubtfully. "But if the blood banks were tainted, Lisette would know by now. I don't know of any demons who would volunteer to be dinner for a vamp, and the members of the Movement wouldn't take it from anyone who is unwilling."

"Are you sure about that?" Jack asked, looking skeptical.

I thought about it for a moment. "No, not really. Lily rose to become a trusted lieutenant in the New Blood Movement, and she didn't think 'willing' was a necessary adjective for a snack."

"Who?" Jack asked.

"Lily Armstrong. She was Dan's ex-fiancée who turned vamp and tried to take over Alejandro's organization by leading the rogues."

"What happened to her?" Jack asked.

Shade grinned. "She lost her head. Literally."

Decapitations-R-Us. I shrugged. "She was holding Dan, Fang, my stepfather and my sister captive and was going to kill one or more of them. I had to stop her."

Jack nodded as if it were a completely reasonable thing to do. Thank goodness for demons who understood the world I lived in. "We cleaned out most of the rogues from the Movement in San Antonio," I added, "but there could be some in Austin. So, no, I wouldn't trust Lisette's judgment on this."

"Okay," Shade said, tapping the screen on his smartphone. "Let me see what I can find out about these sightings so we can track them down."

I pretty much used my phone for talking and texting only, but Shade used all its capabilities. This was the kind of stuff he loved—playing with electronics and researching stuff. Yep, he was totally hot *and* a geek. Who said they couldn't coexist in one body?

While Shade surfed the Internet and took notes, I asked Jack to tell me more about being a keeper.

"What do you want to know?" he hedged.

"Tell me more about these powers the books gave you. How does it work?"

"You know they can't actually talk? The voice you heard was me when I was trapped inside, and the voice urging others to do evil was the mage demon I'd imprisoned with me."

I nodded impatiently. "But can you communicate with them?"

"I can't anymore, but you can, since you're the new keeper. The books know what you're thinking, so you can ask them for certain abilities."

"So I could get my strength and fast healing back?" I asked eagerly.

"Maybe, if the books want you to have it." He shook his head. "But remember, those abilities are no longer part of you, so if you are granted those and use them, your succubus abilities will weaken."

Would that be a bad thing? Sure, I'd come to rely on Lola, but the thought of never again having to keep my distance from men, or fend off advances from those who got too close and got sucked into Lola's lustful energy field . . . well, it was very appealing. I had always yearned to be normal, but was it even possible now? Everyone in the vamp and demon communities knew me as the Slayer, and many wanted to kill me because of it. Giving up the best defensive weapon I had to gain more strength didn't seem like a good idea.

Besides, having a normal life was little more than a pipe dream. The only way I could possibly lead a normal life was to go far away from everything I knew and everyone I loved *and* lose all my special abilities. I wasn't desperate enough for that. Not yet.

But one thing I did want, was out of the contract with Alejandro. And to do that, I had to find this so-called chupacabra. If the books could offer help with that, I needed to use them. "Okay, the books know what I'm thinking, but how do they communicate back to me if they can't talk?"

"Like that," Jack said, nodding at the table.

The second volume of the *Encyclopedia Magicka* was actually *glowing*. "Whoa, I didn't know it could do that."

The book started vibrating like a cell on mute. "Go ahead," Jack said. "Open it. It's all right."

What was this? A cosmic telephone? Tentatively, I opened the glowing book. It trembled in my hand, then flipped pages rapidly on its own until it came to rest on one page where words seemed to burn themselves in fire across the paper.

Wow. Cool. When they dimmed to glow softly, I started to read them. "It says—"

"No, don't read it aloud," Jack cautioned. "It's a spell that will give you a new ability, so don't voice it unless you really want it."

"You mean I'd lose part of Lola right away?"

"No, you wouldn't lose any of your current abilities until you actually say the activating words of the spell with intent to use it," Jack explained.

"What is it?" Shade asked, trying to read the book upside down.

I read through the spell silently. "It looks like it would give me the ability to locate mage demons within a certain range. Why would I want to do that?"

Shade snorted. "Maybe because a mage demon and his son tried to steal the books and rule the world with them?"

"Well, yeah, there is that," I conceded.

Jack gave us a rueful grin. "This is the first ability the books offered me, too. That self-preservation thing I told you about. The only problem is, if you use a spell from the books, a mage demon can sense them. Remember, the books know they're safe in the hands of a keeper. But in the hands of a mage demon . . ."

". . . not so much," Shade said. "They'd have access to every spell in the book."

"Exactly," Jack said with a decisive nod. "And some of them are *very* dangerous. You don't think Trevor and his father were the only mage demons in the world, do you?"

I hadn't thought about it at all, to tell the truth. And that was a real Catch-22. Use them to detect a mage demon and they could detect *you.* "I think I'll pass for now."

"Mage demons?" I heard a woman say behind me. "What do you want with mage demons?"

I turned around to see a voluptuous woman with long corkscrew blond curls in the doorway. She wore a curve-hugging red dress that slinked halfway down her calves . . . and only barely covered her rather impressive chest. From the stage makeup and the light succubus hold I felt she had on the two rather innocuous-looking men with her, I gathered this was the Underground leader here in Austin. Sheesh—she was seduction in one neat package. Unlike me, she'd inspire lust just by the sight of her—no succubus needed. And the men with her seemed utterly smitten.

Lola bristled at the appearance of another succubus, and I didn't object as Lola reached out to lightly grab onto Shade and Jack's chakras. If Lola had them, *she* couldn't get them. "Dina Bellama, I presume?" I said, attempting to be polite.

I could feel her trying for my guys, but she wasn't able to get hold of them. Lola had them too tight. "The Slayer, I presume," she mocked me, apparently annoyed at being balked of her prey.

But if I was any judge of succubi, I'd say her tank of lusty energy was pretty well topped off for the night. She positively oozed sensuality. She didn't need anything from Shade or Jack—she just wanted to assert her domination. Already, I didn't like her. And Lola positively hated her.

Aloud, I said, "Yes, I'm Val Shapiro and this is Jack Grady and Shade."

Shade and Jack had both stood up politely. Shade was doing his swirly thing and Dina, apparently fascinated, sauntered over to touch his face in wonder. Her eyes widened when his face came into view. "Well, well, what have we here? No wonder you're holding on tight to this one. I wouldn't let him get away either. But what kind of demon has that kind of mask?"

Shade, looking annoyed, backed away from her hand so he became one big mass of roiling ropes of energy again. I raised an eyebrow at her, silently reminding her it was rude to ask that in the Underground.

"He's a shadow demon," one of her two pets told her, glaring at Shade. "He can bring full demons into this world through a portal."

Well, yes, that was technically true, but Shade was so much more than that.

She whirled on me, eyes sparking with anger. "And you're looking for mage demons, too? Are you *trying* to destroy the world?"

Jack stepped forward with a frown. "Your assumptions are incorrect. Just because he *can* bring demons through a portal doesn't mean he *will*. And this shadow demon is the reason we were able to shove two mage demons in San Antonio through a portal and lock them away forever." He paused, then added, "In answer to your second question, we aren't looking for mage demons. We're looking to avoid them."

I suppressed a smile. *Go, Jack.* He said it much better than I could.

Dina looked down her nose at him. "Who the hell are you?"

"I'm the former keeper of the *Encyclopedia Magicka*. Val is the new keeper."

"Yes, Micah mentioned something about the books." Dina's gaze flicked to the table. "Those?"

"Yes," Jack said.

Darn, I wish he wasn't so fast with the answers. I wasn't so sure I wanted her fondling anything that belonged to me. I moved to block her way to the table.

Instead of pushing past me, she looked down at me with amusement. "Selfish, are we?"

"Just protective. After all, the books can have a bad effect on anyone who isn't a keeper."

"Well, I'm afraid I can't let you run loose around my town with dangerous books or a shadow demon. You'll have to leave them both here while you play with the vampires." Her eyes narrowed and she added, "I insist."

Leave Shade and the books? Not a chance in hell.

Chapter Eight

My first instinct was to attack Dina and her two henchmen, then grab Shade and the books and get the hell out of here. But that would tick off Micah and defeat the whole purpose for coming here in the first place. David had said there was something hinky going on in the Austin Underground, and I had a feeling he was right. I just needed to stay on their good side long enough to find out what.

So, I beat my first instinct into submission and tried reason first. "Don't be ridiculous. They're not a threat, especially in my hands. Didn't Micah tell you that?"

Dina slinked back to her two henchmen. "Micah said a lot of things. I prefer to make my own judgments."

Jack took a step forward. "You can't have the books. Val's the keeper."

Dina shrugged. "So? If I have the books, I'll be the keeper."

"It isn't that easy," Jack protested. "The books choose who protects them. They chose *her*, not you."

"Oh, I don't plan to protect them," Dina assured him. "I plan to destroy them."

"No." Jack and I yelled simultaneously.

When she took a surprised step back, I added, "Destroying them would be much, much worse. You'd obliterate half of Texas, release wild magick into the world, tear a hole between our reality and the demon world, and let full demons through." Or so Trevor had claimed. Personally, I didn't want to test it.

"Well, we have to do *something* with them," Dina said. "A mage demon came through here looking for those books."

"*What?* When?" Sure wish I had Fang here right now to pick her brain free of everything she knew.

"A couple of days ago."

"What did you tell him?"

Her gaze narrowed. "Do you think I'm an idiot? I lied to him, made him believe they were in New Orleans." She fondled a large teardrop crystal in her décolletage, bringing attention to her impressive cleavage again, and smirked. "I can be *very* persuasive."

Yeah, the Lola kind of persuasion. More calmly, I asked, "Why didn't you tell Micah?"

"I planned on it, but a few things came up since then."

"Like what?" I demanded. What could be more important than that?

"Like missing members of the Underground. A number of people have vanished, two in the past few days, and we can't find any trace of them." To her credit, she looked worried.

"I'm sorry about that," I said, "but didn't you think it might be the mage demon doing this?"

"Of course I did," she snapped.

"Then why didn't you call on us for help? You knew we'd contained one mage demon already."

"Because I took care of it. And if he comes back again, I can control him long enough to feed him to Micah's Memory Eater. But what if a female mage demon I can't control comes looking for them? Apparently, the Slayer blasted the damn books into wakefulness enough so any mage demon in the country knows they're active."

"That's not how it happened," Shade protested and reached forward to lightly clasp my arm and bring his features into view. "Besides, mage demons are pretty rare. I've done some research in the Underground records across the country. There's only one other mage demon in the country, and you just sent him to New Orleans."

Dina cut him off with an upraised hand. "Doesn't matter. The books are dangerous. If we can't destroy them, they need to be neutralized somehow."

"What about me?" Shade asked softly. "You think I'm dangerous. Do you plan to destroy me, too?"

"Don't be ridiculous," Dina said, caressing him with her gaze. "You're one of us. I just want to keep an eye on you, keep you happy, ensure you have no reason to lose your temper and bring an army of full demons into our world."

Did Micah tell her *all* our secrets? Exasperated, I said, "I'm the keeper. I keep the books neutralized *and* I keep Shade happy." Shade gave me an odd look and I wished I'd phrased that differently. Before she could protest again, I added, "We don't need you or your permission to be here."

"Then why did you all ask to see me?"

"Because we hoped you would have a place for me to stay while Val is working," Shade explained. "It's easier if I can stay around people who understand so I don't have to hide my skin. But I can make do at a hotel if I have to."

"Of course I have a place you can stay," Dina assured him. "But, why don't you stay with Val?"

"Because the vampires won't let him while she looks for the chupacabras," Jack told her.

Exasperated with Jack's loose lips, I explained the whole thing all over again.

Dina looked worried. "You think one of my people is responsible for killing animals?"

"Actually, no," I said. Not until she mentioned it, anyway. "I think it's rogue vampires. But this so-called chupacabra might have something to do with your missing people."

She nodded. "That makes sense."

Good. We were getting somewhere. "So we'll just go and—"

"No," Dina said, interrupting me. "You're like a loose cannon. I'd be foolish to let you roam free." I started to protest, but she held up a hand. "Yes, I understand you're here to help, but to ensure you're careful with where you point your weapons in my city, you can either leave the books or Shade with me. I'll take good care of them until you finish your business and are ready to leave Austin for good."

Yeah, I just bet she would. "And if I don't agree?"

"Then we'll personally escort you all out of town and keep track of you to ensure you don't enter uninvited again."

Suddenly, there were a lot more men in the room—and every single one of them was controlled by Dina. I didn't know what abilities these demons had, so fighting my way out could be a problem, especially given my weakened strength. But since I wasn't willing to leave either Shade or the books in her clutches, I tensed, ready for action. I didn't know what the hell I was going to do, but hoped something would come to me.

"Can we have a moment to talk this over?" Shade asked Dina in the tense silence.

She looked amused. "Be my guest. You can use the phone room." She gestured toward a small room, barely big enough for the three of us. It held a small table, chair and phone—must be used for the demons to make personal calls in private.

I grabbed the books from the table and stuffed them into my

backpack. Shade, Jack and I squeezed into the room and shut the door. To keep Jack from getting too touchy-feely so close to Lola, I leaned into Shade and told Jack, "Hands off," reinforcing the order with Lola. Come to think of it, I should have done some ordering before. "And don't tell Dina anything more about our business. Got it?"

He nodded wordlessly, and I asked Shade, "What is there to talk about? You have an idea how to solve this stalemate?"

"Yes," Shade said earnestly, his hands grasping my shoulders. "Leave me here."

"What? Are you delusional? You do realize she's a succubus? Give her the slightest opening and she'll be all over you." The thought of that woman putting her hands on Shade totally made me see red.

He shrugged. "She said she'll take good care of me."

"How do you know she'll keep her word?" I didn't trust her as far as *he* could throw her.

He seemed unconcerned. "She knows that if she breaks her promise, she'll have the entire San Antonio Underground to deal with. And if she tries it anyway, then that will tell us something, too, won't it?"

But then Shade would be violated. I couldn't stand that, even if she *could* make him enjoy it. "No," I said with finality. "You return to San Antonio and take the books with you. That way she doesn't have to worry about either one." And neither would I.

Shade froze, then raised an eyebrow. "Is that an order?"

Oh, crap. I hadn't meant it to sound like that. "No, of course not."

"Good. I can take care of myself, you know. I don't need you to babysit me."

Oh, geez, I was really messing this up. "I know, but—"

Shade squeezed my shoulders reassuringly and cut me off. "You don't need my help to track down rogue vamps. This way, I can do what I'm good at. Scout out the organization, see what's really going on here."

That would be helpful, but not at this price. "No." Oh, hell. That probably came across as an order, too. "I mean, it's too risky. She could make you do anything."

"She would be foolish to risk the Slayer's wrath," Jack said. "I'm sure she's aware of that. And she has to sleep sometime. Shade will be free of her influence then."

Shade nodded. "If I think it's too dangerous, I'll get out."

"But what if Lola needs you?" I asked, looking at him pleadingly. I was trying to find any way to change his mind, short of using Lola to force him to do as I wanted.

"Lola can feed on Jack," Shade said firmly. "Or Austin. I bet he'd like it."

Was jealousy prompting this attitude? "Look—"

Shade interrupted me. "I don't need your permission, Val. And I'm not your boy toy. I'm a trained watcher, and I know what to look for. I'm going to do my job whether or not you agree. Micah obviously needs to know more about how this place runs."

Crap. He'd pulled out the big guns. How could I protest without being overly possessive or implying he was weak or incompetent? I couldn't.

"Okay," I gritted out. But I sure as hell didn't like it.

Chapter Nine

Micah finished his dance at the club and eluded the women's groping hands to exit the stage. He needed their lust to feed the incubus part of him and keep it quiescent, but sometimes he felt like nothing but a piece of meat. Or maybe it was because everything seemed to annoy him after his discussion with David and Val. Having someone question everything you were proud of in your life would do that to you.

He wasn't even sure what exactly they expected of him. Except for one thing. He'd agreed to watch over Gwen and Princess while Val and Fang were away. He checked his watch. Gwen should be getting home from the ER about now. He could call—

No, wait, he'd do better than that. He'd go by and check on her, take a break from all this noise and need. He showered quickly and let his assistant, Tessa, know he'd be gone for a bit, then headed over to Gwen and Val's townhouse.

Gwen answered the door in blue scrubs, looking tired. "Hi," she said, looking surprised to see him. She backed away a couple of steps, then looked embarrassed. "Sorry, but I know getting too close—"

"It's okay." He smiled. It really was. In fact, it was refreshing to know a woman who tried to avoid the incubus lure instead of getting up close and way too personal. "Val asked me to stop by and check on you and Princess while she's gone."

"Oh, sure. Come in."

Micah followed Gwen into the living room and sank down onto the couch. Their place was small but comfortable, and with Gwen's bright, whimsical Christmas decorating, it was a nice place to spend time. Gwen went to the kitchen and came back with a glass of iced tea for him. He smiled again. She even knew what he liked to drink.

Settling on the chair across from him, she cocked her head and said, "You know, they've only been gone a few hours. You don't really need to check up on me."

He chuckled. "Yes, I know, but I also wanted to bring you something." He pulled out his wallet and handed her some cash.

She looked at the money in her hand. "What's this for?"

"Groceries."

"You do know I have a job, right?"

"Yes, but I also know you're constantly feeding my people in the Underground. And I can't imagine what Princess is like now that she's pregnant. She's probably demanding filet mignon and escargot three times a day."

I HEARD THAT, Princess told him mentally from somewhere outside the room.

Gwen chuckled. "Maybe, but I can't hear her. And, as a nurse, I'm making sure she eats sensibly. In fact, she's eating in the kitchen right now."

I'M FINISHED NOW, the part hellhound, part Cavalier King Charles Spaniel said and came trotting into the room. CHICKEN AND RICE AND YOGURT. BLEH. TELL HER I WANT SOMETHING GOOD.

You're lucky you're not getting store-bought dog food, Micah told her silently. *Be grateful.* Aloud, he told Gwen, "Princess says to thank you for taking care of her."

Princess actually rolled her eyes.

Gwen laughed. "Nice try, but I know her expressions. She's miffed that I didn't give her lasagna, isn't she?"

Micah chuckled along with her. "Probably."

Petting the dog's silky head, Gwen told her, "Well, you're getting what's good for you and the puppies."

Princess *hmphed* and laid down with her head on her paws, looking dejected.

Micah nudged her with his foot. "Hey, didn't I hear Gwen got you a pink satin bed? And what's that you're wearing? A new pink collar?" It was all blinged out with rhinestones and glitter.

IT'S A NECKLACE, Princess said, sounding indignant. Then, grudgingly, she added, YES, SHE HAS BEEN VERY NICE TO ME. UNLIKE SOME PEOPLE I COULD MENTION. The hellhound glared at Micah then licked Gwen's hand.

"Now she really is saying thank you," Micah told Gwen.

Gwen kissed the dog on top of the head. "She's so sweet."

Micah almost choked. "You wouldn't say that if you could hear her."

HMPH, Princess said. I'M GOING TO TAKE A NAP. She trotted off to the bedroom, her nose held high.

"I don't mind taking care of her, really." Gwen put the money down firmly on the coffee table in front of him. "I don't need this."

He pushed it back toward her. "Consider it hazardous duty pay."

HEY, Princess protested from the other room.

Micah grinned. "Or consider it Fang's salary and use it to buy Princess whatever she needs. You'd know what that is better than I would."

Gwen laughed. "Okay. That I'll do."

Gwen's cell rang. "Excuse me," she said, then went into the kitchen and had a brief conversation. When she came back, she said, "That was my brother. He was checking up on me, too." Placing her hands on her hips, she added, "And I told Dan the same thing I'm going to tell you. I'm a big girl now. I don't need men to take care of me or to check up on me. I can take care of myself."

"I know you can," he soothed. "But Val will hand me my head on a platter if I don't do as she asked."

"Okay, then—"

The doorbell rang and Gwen glanced at the door, looking exasperated. "Who else did she send to check up on me? The vampires?"

"I don't know." Micah rose. "You want me to send them away?"

"No, that's okay. I can do it myself." Gwen opened the door. "Can I help you?"

Micah moved so he could see past her. A middle-aged woman stood under the porch light—stocky, hard faced, with scraggly red hair. "Does Val Shapiro live here?"

"Yes, but I'm—"

Without waiting for Gwen to finish, the woman pushed her way into the house and kicked the door shut.

Gwen backed away, holding up her arms.

What the hell? Micah took a threatening step forward, then noticed the woman held an odd-looking gun with a long, slender muzzle. *Was that a silencer?* Micah reached out to snag her with his incubus and force her to drop the gun, but couldn't get a hold on her. It was as if someone else had her in thrall already. *What the hell?*

His adrenaline spiked. "What do you want?"

"Don't move," the woman said, swiveling to point the pistol at both of them. "And don't try anything funny, or I'll shoot both of you."

Micah's mind worked furiously, as he considered and discarded options. What was the best way to get out of this alive? Keep her talking. "Who are you?"

"My name's Carla. Not that it matters. What does matter is what my boss, Asmodeus, wants."

Ridiculous. That couldn't be her boss's real name. Mythology said Asmodeus was the king of the demons. At least now Micah knew Carla was probably a demon, though wasn't sure exactly what kind.

"Who are *you?*" she asked, waving her pistol in his direction.

"Micah Blackburn, the leader of the Underground here in San Antonio." Maybe his position would earn the demon's respect. "Val's not here."

Carla snorted. "Yeah, right. Nice try." She waved the gun again, this time toward Gwen. "She already admitted she's Val. And since you're the so-called leader of the Demon Underpants, I'm sure one of you can help me. Just give me what I want and I'll be on my way. Or . . ." She held out her other hand and a small fireball the size of a cherry tomato appeared in it.

Fire demon. Damn. So why did she need the pistol? Because she didn't trust her puny talent?

Gwen was a lot calmer than Micah expected. It must be her ER training. She lowered her arms a little. "I'm not Val, really. I'm Gwen, her roommate. I can show you my license—"

"You think I'm a fool?" Carla bit out. "I'm not falling for that."

Micah exchanged a glance with Gwen. Maybe they'd get out of this unharmed if they played along. "What do you want?" he asked.

"The books."

"What books?" Gwen asked. "I—I have a lot of books."

The woman snarled. "Don't play games with me. You know what books—the *Encyclopedia Magicka.* They're mighty powerful."

She'd probably heard how Andrew's fire ability had grown much stronger when he had the books. But evidently she hadn't heard how they'd almost driven the fire demon mad as well. Why did everyone assume *they* were immune?

"The books are dangerous," Micah said. "Not many people can handle them."

"Yeah, right. Me and the boss aren't worried about that."

Okay, he'd try a different tack. "Why do you think Val has the books?" Micah countered, trying to look puzzled.

"I *know* she has them. A demon told me right before he died. Too bad, so sad," Carla mocked. "Seems the rumors about the Slayer and the books were too juicy to stay quiet."

Damn. If this woman had already murdered another demon, that didn't say much for their chances.

"They're not here," Gwen said quickly.

"Then where are they?" Carla snarled. "Tell me or you'll regret it."

Micah didn't get a chance to find out what Gwen had in mind because a ball of furious fur came charging from the other room. Princess yelled, DON'T HURT MY FRIENDS! She clamped onto the woman's ankle and bit down hard.

Carla yelped, but shook off the hellhound, then flicked the fireball at her. Micah snatched Princess out of the way just in time and beat out the flames on the rug before the idiot woman killed them all.

Gwen gasped. "Don't hurt her, she's pregnant."

LET ME AT HER, Princess said with a snarl. I'LL TEACH HER—

"Quiet," Micah told her, holding her tight despite her struggles. "The bad lady has a big nasty gun." *And she'll kill you as soon as look at you. Think of your puppies.*

That made Princess stop struggling, but she didn't stop growling.

"Did that dog just talk in my head?" Carla asked, looking surprised.

OF COURSE I DID. I'M A HELLHOUND.

For once, she hadn't insisted on being a purebred spaniel.

The woman's face split in a nasty grin. "Well, well. Would you look at that? I thought it was a rumor, but there really are hellhounds left in this world. We could use those puppies."

I'D KILL THEM BEFORE I'D GIVE ANY TO YOU, Princess growled.

Watch it, Micah warned her. *She might decide she doesn't want a puppy after all. Then you'd be one dead hellhound.*

Princess sniffed mentally. I ONLY SAID THAT TO YOU.

Good thing.

"Please," Gwen said, "we don't have the books."

Carla scowled. "So it's going to be the hard way, huh?" Almost nonchalantly, she shot Gwen in the chest with a quiet *pfft*, then before a horrified Micah could react, she shot him, too.

Stunned, Micah fell to the floor and everything faded to black.

Chapter Ten

I arrived back at my room still ticked off at having to leave Shade behind. Jack, wisely, hadn't said anything as we'd headed back to the blood bank, and I'd worked myself up into a good head of pissiness. Unfortunately, there was no one to take it out on.

Jack hurried to his room, and when I opened the door to mine, I saw Fang asleep on his back on the bed, all four fuzzy paws hanging limply above his distended belly. The almost empty pizza box on the floor told the story. He'd pigged out, the little mutt. I slammed the door and dumped my backpack on the bed.

Fang jerked and scrambled upright, looking frantically around the room. HUH? WHAT? WHERE'S THE DANGER?

"Me. I'm the danger," I spat out. "I want to kill something."

He backed up a step. THAT SOMETHING WOULDN'T BE YOUR FAVORITE FOUR-LEGGED FRIEND, WOULD IT?

"Maybe. I'm leaving my options open." I paced around the small room, feeling caged and wanting to claw something.

But he could read my mind and knew I didn't mean it. He relaxed and scratched his ear. WHAT'S GOT YOUR KNICKERS IN A TWIST?

"Dina Bellama and Shade."

I didn't have to say any more as I let Fang read my mind to learn what had happened.

Fang snorted in surprise. YOU LEFT YOUR HOTTIE BOYFRIEND WITH ANOTHER SUCCUBUS? WHAT WERE YOU THINKING?

"I was thinking I didn't have a choice. He wanted to stay and I couldn't force him to leave." Well, Lola could have, but that would have been wrong. Not that I hadn't thought about doing just that. For a brief moment. Then sanity had reigned as I'd realized I'd no longer have a boyfriend if I forced him to do what *I* wanted.

WHAT ARE YOU GOING TO DO ABOUT IT?

Good question. One I'd wrestled with on my stomp all the way back to the room. "I tried to call Micah to see if he could reason with Dina, but he didn't answer. How can I get Shade out of there without pissing anyone off?" Or keep an eye on him so I wouldn't worry. I stopped pacing for a moment. "You think David would help keep an eye on Shade?" I figured he owed me after that kidnapping stunt.

MAYBE. YOU COULD ASK.

Good thing we'd exchanged phone numbers. I called David and explained what was going on.

"You were right," I told him. "There's something odd going on here. This Bellama chick seems to have a tight hold on all the men in her group."

"That's new," David said. "She didn't before."

"I wonder why she thinks she needs it?"

"Whatever the reason, it can't be good. What's Micah doing about it?"

I sighed. "I haven't been able to get hold of him yet, but I left a message. I'm sure he'll get back to me soon."

"Hold on, let me talk to Pia." After a few moments of silence, David came back on the line. "We'll ask around, see what we can find out . . . and keep an eye on Shade for you. He's one of the good guys. I'll let you know if I learn anything."

"Okay, thanks."

I hung up and Fang flopped back down on the bed. SO, WHAT DO WE DO NOW?

I continued pacing, thinking. "The best way to get Shade out of her clutches is to find what's really causing those attacks so we can go home."

I'M IN. WHERE DO WE START?

I halted abruptly and made a decision. "We start with Austin." The cowboy, not the city. "Hopefully, he'll be through with his party." It was still a long time until dawn.

I grabbed the backpack and took the stairs up.

Fang followed, complaining. EVER HEARD OF THIS NEW INVENTION CALLED AN ELEVATOR?

"Too slow," I told him. "Besides, you need to burn off some of that pizza, chubbo."

Fang burped but came along anyway, grousing the whole time.

I could use some way to work off this mad, so I pounded on Austin's door as Fang collapsed on the floor with a groan.

Austin opened it with a jerk, wearing low-riding jeans, no shirt, and toweling his damp hair. Dang. Lean, yet muscled, and wearing nothing but those jeans, he could've been a male model in a Calvin

Klein ad.

Lola liked.

In fact, she wanted to reach out and touch . . . real bad. She even sent a few tendrils that way, but no way was I giving that cowboy any more ammunition against me. I reined her in, tight. It was tough to do since I stupidly hadn't let Lola top off her tank lately. I'd hated to take advantage of Shade by feeding on him too often, but now I was paying the price.

"Geez, Austin, put a shirt on," I snapped.

He raised one eyebrow and a corner of his mouth quirked up as he leaned against the door frame. "I just got out of the shower. You're lucky I put on pants. Where's the fire?"

Annoyed by his amusement, I said, "I thought you were all hot to find these chupacabras and your friend Wes. Let's go."

"Did you have some place particular in mind?"

I averted my gaze so Lola wouldn't be tempted by the eye candy. It was disturbing feeling this way about a vampire. "Uh, the scene of the crime. Maybe we can learn something the police didn't. Fang has an excellent nose."

Fang belched again. SO LONG AS FANG DOESN'T HAVE TO WALK.

I ignored him.

Austin nodded. "Good. Lisette gave us information on where the attacks took place. Let's see what we can find out." He put on his shirt, boots and hat, and we headed out the door.

Now that we were actually doing something, I felt my anger fade.

I navigated using the map Lisette had provided, and Austin drove northwest of the city, out into hill country. Fang, the big load, commandeered the backseat to take another nap.

"So, how's the boyfriend?" Austin asked.

I winced. Trust him to find a sore spot. "Fine," I replied in a tone that didn't encourage further discussion.

It didn't stop Austin. "Had a fight, did you?"

"No."

"Then what's put you in this foul mood?"

I sighed heavily. "I visited the Demon Underground in Austin. Let's just say they didn't exactly welcome me with open arms."

"Is that all?"

"No. Their leader, Dina, wanted to take the books from me, saying there was a mage demon in the area and she wanted to 'protect' them." I shook my head. "There's something hinky going on there, but

I don't know what."

Austin was silent for a moment, then said, "You think she might have something to do with this chupacabra scare?"

I thought for a moment. It would tie things up very neatly if she were the bad guy and I could stop her and take Shade back all in one fell swoop, but . . . "I doubt it. There are demons missing as well."

We were silent for the rest of the drive to Bull Creek District Park. The parking lot was deserted at this time of night, and as I got out of the car and peered into the dark woods, I asked, "Got a flashlight?"

Austin closed the driver's door. "Nope, don't need one. Don't you carry one around in your handy-dandy slayer kit?"

All I had in my "kit" were the extra stakes I tucked in the back of my waistband, plus the books and other odds and ends in my backpack. I resisted the urge to punch him and just stared at him, my jaw set.

He shrugged. "Let's check the trunk."

Luckily, the trunk held a few tools, including a flashlight, so I grabbed it. "Okay, where to now?"

He consulted his notes and pointed to a trail. "Take that one down to the creek."

Fang took off in that direction, his nose low to the ground. "Smell anything?" I asked.

LOTS OF THINGS. TOO MANY. HUMANS, DOGS, DEER . . . THEY'RE EVERYWHERE. THIS MUST BE A POPULAR PLACE.

I relayed his comments to Austin, who nodded. "Very popular. During the day, lots of hikers, dog lovers, kids."

"And at night?"

"Let's just say there's an unsavory element at night."

"Like vampires?"

He chuckled. "Or demons."

WHY DO YOU EVEN TRY? Fang asked, his nose still to the ground. YOU CAN'T EVER GET THE BEST OF HIM.

I let that pass and glanced around. "I don't see anyone."

Austin shrugged. "Maybe because of the news reports of chupacabras in the area."

That made sense, but I was going to keep a wary eye out just in case. We followed Fang down to the creek. It was cooler here, and I wished I'd worn a heavier vest. The area around the gravel path was dense with juniper and oak, the darkness making it creepy. I heard the water before I saw it, and though some rocks in the creek dripped with icicles, the water still flowed. I bet this was gorgeous on a balmy spring day. Now, in the darkness with only a flashlight for illumination . . . not so much.

Austin stopped to consult his notes again. "A coyote was found drained of blood over there."

I went in the direction he pointed, toward a huge oak tree. I shined my light on the area, but the coyote had been removed. I couldn't see much except trampled brush. Austin could see better in the dark, so he bent down to examine the area.

"Find anything?" I asked.

"No. Too many people and animals have been in this area to distinguish any prints."

Just what Fang said.

Speaking of Fang, where was he? He'd evidently followed his nose elsewhere.

I SMELL SOMETHING OVER HERE. TO YOUR LEFT.

"Fang smells something," I explained to Austin. "What is it?" I asked Fang.

SOMETHING DEAD.

Oh, fabulous. Sure, I made bloodsuckers dead on a regular basis, but I didn't have to stick around long enough to actually smell them. And, as we shoved our way through the brush, the closer we got to Fang's find, the more I got a good whiff. Make that a bad whiff. *Phew.*

"A deer," Austin said unnecessarily, gazing down at the dead animal.

He bent down to examine it while I played my flashlight over the body in the trampled brush. It looked as though it had been dead a week or so. Too bad this winter hadn't been cold enough to freeze it. As Fang sniffed the deer, I remembered what I'd heard about dogs.

"Don't go rolling in that smell," I warned him.

He cocked his furry head to look up at me. PUHLEEZE. I'M A HELLHOUND. I DON'T HAVE THOSE PRIMITIVE CANINE INSTINCTS.

"Well, excuse the heck out of me. How would I know that?"

They both ignored me as Austin continued to examine the deer and Fang wandered away.

Austin rose, dusting off his hands. "Three bite wounds, all different."

"Vampire?"

He settled his hat more firmly on his head. "Yep."

There was pain in that simple word. "Different? You mean three separate vampires?"

He nodded.

Carefully, I asked, "Do you think your buddy Wes and—"

"No," Austin said fiercely, interrupting me. "Wes wouldn't deliberately hurt anyone, not even an animal."

Oookay. Not going there again. "Then who?"

He shook his head. "Some of the rogues, I suppose."

"Doesn't make sense. The reason they don't join the Movement is because they want to snack on humans. Why would they resort to animals?"

Austin didn't say a word, just stared down at the dead animal.

HEY, Fang shouted mentally. COME HERE. YOU NEED TO SEE THIS.

"Fang's found something else," I told Austin.

It was difficult to follow a mental voice, so Fang darted out to lead us to his discovery. I followed more slowly, using the flashlight to find my way, and he led us to a small open space. I glanced around, but didn't see anything remarkable. "What is it, Fang?"

He pawed at the ground. LOOK DOWN HERE.

I crouched to see what he was talking about, and Austin did the same. I shone the flashlight along the ground and didn't get it for a moment. Then I realized what I was seeing. Black ash.

YEP, Fang confirmed. FRIED VAMP.

Austin knelt down and sifted his fingers through the residue. What the heck? Then I realized what he was doing as he pulled an old-fashioned gold pocket watch from the ash, blackened and cracked by unholy fire. He was looking for identification.

"Do you know who that belongs to?" I asked softly.

He nodded.

I was almost afraid to ask. "Is it Wes's?"

"No," he said, rising and placing the watch in his pocket. "It belonged to Etienne, one of Lisette's missing. He was very proud of this watch."

Crap. "Do you think he . . ." I waved vaguely in the direction of the dead deer.

"I don't know what to think. I can't imagine what would make Etienne do such a thing." Austin glanced down at the ash, all that was left of Lisette's vampire. "Or why he was out in the open like this. He was too smart to let the sun catch him unaware."

"Maybe he was wounded and couldn't get to safety," I suggested.

As I said that, I wondered what prompted me to want to make Austin feel better. After all, he'd been nothing but snarky to me.

"Maybe," Austin conceded. He looked at me. "You think he caught the perpetrators and was wounded in the fight?"

I could see he liked that scenario. I shrugged. "Maybe. I don't know."

Fang jerked up his head. WATCH OUT. INCOMING.

Chapter Eleven

Micah woke, feeling stiff and sore. He blinked his eyes open, trying to figure out where he was and how he got here. As best he could see in the scant moonlight filtering into the dark room, he lay sprawled on his side on a bare mattress, his wrist manacled to a radiator.

Blearily, he remembered the demon who'd demanded the books, then shot them when they denied they had the encyclopedia. Strange, he didn't feel as if he'd been shot. What he'd thought was a silencer must have been a dart gun with a sedative. He wondered how Gwen—

A surge of adrenaline shot through him. Gwen. Where was she? His incubus abilities should help him find any woman. He felt around mentally for her. Or at least, he tried. Something was blocking him. Perdo. Damn it, the demon had shot him with Perdo.

He bolted upright to a sitting position and found Gwen beside him on the other side of the mattress, also manacled to the radiator. She was breathing, thank heavens. And, because of the Perdo, his incubus powers wouldn't affect her when she did wake. One little ray of sunshine.

Now, how could he get them both out of here?

Something blunt poked his leg, and he looked down. Princess. Ah, another advantage to the Perdo—he couldn't hear her demands.

"Chill, dog. If you're talking to me, I can't hear you," he said. "We were drugged."

Princess flopped down on the mattress with a huff, and Micah looked around the space, hoping to spot something, anything that would get them out of here. Unfortunately, it was a small, stark room empty of furniture except the mattress. Narrow windows were set high on the concrete wall—this must be a basement.

So what? What could he do with that information?

Nothing, unless he could get loose. Mentally, he ran through the contents of his pockets, wondering if there was anything he could use to pick the lock. A stray paperclip, maybe?

Wait—his phone. Had Carla taken it? He could call 9-1-1 and ask for help. The police could find them with the GPS. Especially when they learned Detective Dan Sullivan's sister was one of the kidnappees.

With his right hand manacled and useless, he used his left to fumble the phone out of his right pocket. He punched in 9-1, but that was as far as he got before Princess bit his hand.

He dropped the phone and shook his hand. She hadn't broken the skin, but why the heck did she do that? The hellhound rolled her eyes frantically toward the door, then Micah heard footsteps coming. Damn it, no time to call. Princess sat on the phone just as the door opened.

Carla again. The fire demon switched on the light and it stabbed through the fog in Micah's brain. He closed his eyes against the pain, but had to see what the demon was doing, so he opened his eyes a slit.

Gwen stirred, groaning, and Carla said, "Good. You're both awake."

Gwen scrambled to a sitting position. "What do you want?"

The demon pointed a gun at them again. Micah wasn't sure, but it looked like the same dart gun she'd used on them earlier. That explained why a fire demon needed a gun.

"It's simple," the demon said. "You tell me where the books are, Slayer, and I don't hurt you or your boyfriend."

Princess growled a warning. DON'T HURT MY FRIEND.

If Micah could hear the hellhound again, the Perdo must be wearing off. Too bad his headache wasn't.

Carla laughed. "That's up to her. If she tells me where the books are, I'll let you all go."

Is she telling the truth? Micah asked Princess silently.

YES. BUT SHE THINKS IT WON'T MATTER. WHEN THEY GET THE BOOKS, NO ONE WILL BE ABLE TO STOP THEM.

Not good. With those books, she'd be able to wreak total havoc.

DO SOMETHING, Princess insisted.

The only thing he could do was convince Carla she had the wrong woman. "We told you before, she's not Val. She's Val's roommate, Gwen."

Carla snorted. "Nice try. Do you think I'm an idiot?"

"No, I think you're mistaken." How could he convince her? "Look, she's wearing hospital scrubs because she's a nurse. Do you think the Slayer would wear scrubs?"

"Maybe." Carla looked doubtful for the first time.

Micah searched for something else that might convince her. "You shot us with Perdo. In demons, you know that the aftereffect is one hell of a migraine when the eyes are exposed to light, right?"

"Yes. So?"

"So that's why I'm squinting. But what's she doing?"

Gwen stirred. "My eyes are wide open. No headache."

"That's because she's *human*," Micah said. "You kidnapped the wrong girl. Gwen is Val's roommate."

"The boss ain't gonna like this." Flames flickered on Carla's hand for a moment before she closed her fist and punched the wooden door. It left quite a dent.

BAD LADY ANGRY, Princess said.

No kidding. But at least she believed what Micah said.

Too bad Micah's incubus powers wouldn't work on her. Unfortunately, Gwen was inside his personal field, and now that the Perdo was wearing off, she was feeling the effect and cuddling up against him. Not that he minded, but it felt as though he was taking advantage of her, even if it was inadvertently. He tried to pull his personal field in close to his body, but because of the drug and the lack of practice, it wasn't easy.

Though his head felt as though it was about to split, Micah attempted to follow up on the advantage. "So, now that you know Gwen isn't Val, you can let us go."

Carla let out a bark of laughter. "Not gonna happen. And now that we know she can't control the boss, he can talk to you himself. But I'll make you a deal. You tell me where Val is, and once I squeeze the books out of her, I'll let you both go."

AND ME, TOO, Princess declared.

"Will Asmodeus agree to that?" Micah challenged. Where was this shadowy boss, anyway? Did he even exist?

Carla ignored him. "What's it gonna be?"

"Val went out of town," Gwen said.

"Where?"

Val could take care of herself, but there was no reason to send this demon after her. "We don't know," Micah lied. "Some kind of family problem."

Carla turned to Gwen, flames flickering along her hands again. "She woulda told her roommate where she was going."

Micah felt Gwen tremble. "No, she ran out real fast, saying it was an emergency. She took the books with her."

"You're both lying," Carla said flatly. "You gotta be. So, how about I give you a little incentive?" She walked over to the mattress and glared down at them. "What do you think would happen to the bitch's pups if I kick her real hard in the stomach?"

NO! Princess yelled, and jumped up to scurry away from her. DON'T HURT MY PUPPIES.

Carla grabbed for the hellhound and missed.

A tinny voice came from the mattress beside Micah. "9-1-1, what is your emergency?"

Damn. Princess must have butt-dialed the last number when she was scrambling away. Micah tried to grab for the phone and muffle it before Carla heard it.

Too late.

The fire demon whirled and snatched it out of his hand, saying into the speaker, "I'm sorry, my kid accidentally dialed your number." She hung up without waiting for a response, then hefted the phone, smiling. "Well, well. What else have you got in your pockets?"

She came toward him, and Micah's hands curled into fists. Though his right hand was immobilized by the manacle, his weaker left hand could still deliver a punch.

Carla paused. "I wouldn't do that if I were you, bub. For every punch you land on me, the girl and the dog get two just as hard."

Micah bit back his anger as Carla roughly rifled through his front pockets. If she'd forgotten to search them, she must not be very good at this. Or maybe this was her first kidnapping. And maybe she'd make another mistake Micah could exploit.

The fire demon tossed Micah's keys across the room, but left the coins behind. She turned Micah over and slid his wallet out of his back pocket. Grinning, she opened it. "Nice. Whatever kind of work you do, it must pay real well." She pocketed the cash, then tossed the wallet and the rest of its contents into the corner.

Next, she searched Gwen. Since Gwen only had her scrubs on and her purse had been left behind, the only thing Carla found on her was her hospital badge.

She backed away from them and squinted at it. "Gwen Sullivan. Huh. Guess you were telling the truth about that, anyway." She dropped the badge to the floor. "Congratulations, chickie, Asmodeus can use you as a bargaining chip." She turned to grin at Micah. "But you, why would I need you?"

"Don't hurt him. He's Val's cousin," Gwen blurted out.

Not strictly true, though since they had the same type of power, they were probably related somehow. They considered each other family, anyway.

"Okay," Carla said. "Two hostages. Even better. Now, tell me where Val took those books, or I'll kick the dog."

NO, Princess cried out.

Don't tell her anything, Micah shot at her. *Or I'll kick you.*

Unfortunately, Princess could tell he was lying, so she ignored him. DON'T HURT MY PUPPIES, she cried. SHE WENT TO THAT BIG CITY ABOVE US.

"Big city above us? What does that mean?" Carla asked.

Princess, having a smaller percentage of hellhound in her than Fang, wasn't quite as articulate. She seemed to have problems with grammar and using some proper nouns like the names of cities. Good thing in this case.

YOU KNOW. THE BIG CITY WHERE PEOPLE MAKE RULES.

"Rules? You mean laws?" the fire demon asked.

"Washington, DC," Micah blurted out.

Carla looked surprised. "Now why would you give up the name of the city so easily? Could it be you're trying to throw me off track?" She thought for a moment then smirked. "Tell me, dog. Did she go to the state capital—Austin?"

YES, YES.

Micah closed his eyes. If his head didn't hurt so much, he'd bang it against the wall.

"Good dog," the demon said. "For that, I won't kick you. Especially since their expressions just confirmed it."

I'm an idiot, Micah thought. Then again, it wasn't like he had much practice at being a kidnap victim.

"New plan," Carla declared, looking down at Micah's phone. "Looks like you have Val Shapiro's number saved. How about I take a picture of the two of you and we send it to her with a little message?" She grinned and tucked the gun into her belt, holding up the phone. "The boss is gonna like this. Say cheese."

Micah bared his teeth, and Carla snapped a picture, then laughed and pulled out the dart gun and shot the two of them.

Everything went fuzzy. *Damn. Here we go again . . .*

Chapter Twelve

The attack came out of nowhere. Something hit me from the side like a freight train, smashing me up against a tree. I bounced off and whirled to face my assailant, noticing Austin fighting off his own attacker.

I scrambled for my stakes behind me, but the backpack and the tree were in the way. Fang had hold of the guy's ankle and was trying to pull him off me.

"Don't hurt them," Austin yelled, still fighting the other guy.

Don't hurt them? Was he kidding? The guy slavering over me had his gaze locked on my carotid like it was dessert. No way was I going to let him get his incisors anywhere near me. I managed to push him away a little and slammed my knee into his groin. He let go of me and bent over in pain.

"They're . . . Lisette's," Austin panted out, between blocking punches.

Okay, I hadn't hurt him permanently. But I couldn't believe my eyes. The guy who'd attacked me rose up and went for me again. Dang. That should have kept him down longer.

Austin yelled, "Use—" The other vamp cut off what he was about to say by slugging him in the mouth.

But I'd already had the same idea. I shoved Lola into the bloodsuckers with all my force. "Stop!" I hadn't been able to be selective, so I caught Austin in that as well. Fang was still worrying the guy's ankle. "You can stop, too," I told him. "Lola has them." At least I'd remembered to use her a little earlier this time.

The hellhound let go with a final shake of the guy's pant leg. YEAH, I KNOW. THEY JUST PISSED ME OFF.

I grinned. "Thanks for the help." I reached down to pick up the flashlight, which had been knocked out of my hand during the assault.

Now, what to do with the others? Lola was chomping at the bit to suck up some of that lovely energy through the invisible tendrils that connected me to them, but I wasn't so sure I wanted it. It seemed tainted somehow. These guys weren't normal, that was for sure. Maybe

Austin could shed some light on it.

Slowly, I disentangled Austin's strand from the others and released him.

He rubbed his jaw, then leaned down to scoop up his hat. Settling it on his head, he said, "You've got to make that an immediate instinct or you're gonna get killed some day."

Yeah, he was right, but there was no way I was going to admit it. "You're welcome," I shot back.

"For what?"

"For not killing your buddies." Though one of them was gonna have a real sore crotch for a while. "Is one of them Wes?"

He nodded at the one who attacked me. "Yes, that's Wes. And this is Ronald." He didn't look at all happy about the fact.

"Okay, that accounts for the rest of Lisette's missing vamps. But why did they attack us?"

He shrugged, his shoulders tight, as if he was trying to hold in some undefined emotion. "I don't know. Ask them."

Easy enough. I shined the light on one of the vamps. "You, Ronald. Why did you attack us?"

Ronald opened and closed his mouth several times, but no words came out, as if he wanted to obey me but couldn't figure out how to make his mouth work.

I turned to the other vamp. "Wes, why did you attack us?"

Same response.

UH, I THINK THEY'RE JUST A FEW BRICKS SHY OF A LOAD, Fang said.

Yeah, I'd come to that conclusion myself. And I remembered where I'd seen that mad look in the eyes before.

Austin said it. "Demon blood. They drank demon blood."

"Afraid so. I guess they didn't get the memo that demon blood makes vamps go crazy."

"They did. Alejandro made sure Lisette was warned about the threat."

"Then why would they do such a thing?" I asked. "Maybe Lisette didn't warn them?"

"Maybe. Let's go ask her," Austin said, sounding pissed off. He turned and headed back toward the clearing, then glanced over his shoulder at me. "You coming?"

What was I? His servant? "What about your friends?"

"Bring them, too. We'll help them," he said curtly, and kept on walking, sure I'd follow.

GIVE HIM A BREAK, Fang said. HE'S JUST FOUND HIS PAL HAS ALL THE INTELLIGENCE OF A TURNIP.

Okay, I could cut him some slack. I told my two lust-struck puppets, "Follow Austin to the car."

They did, and I had them get in the backseat and go to sleep.

Fang refused to go back there with them, so he curled up on the seat between Austin and me. Now that we were closed up in the car, I noticed something else—a distinct aroma coming from the back seat. Apparently, crazy vamps didn't care that much about personal hygiene. Combine that with spilled blood and dead deer, and the smell was enough to make anyone hurl.

"*Phew*," I said, clamping my fingers over my nose and trying to breathe through my mouth. "Can you open the back windows?"

YOU THINK YOU HAVE IT BAD, Fang complained. YOU OUGHT TO HAVE MY NOSE.

Right now I was really glad I didn't. I rolled my window down as Austin hit the buttons for the others, and we took off. Fang climbed into my lap and stuck his head out the window.

Better? I asked him.

MUCH.

I glanced at Austin. His jaw was clenched and he kept his eyes firmly on the road.

"Hey, look on the bright side," I said. "At least we found the so-called chupacabras. Alejandro should be happy." So was I. I suddenly realized I'd be free of the contract and could do what the heck I wanted.

Austin made a noncommittal grunt.

I DON'T THINK HE WANTS TO TALK, Fang said, his eyes squinted against the wind.

So we didn't, all the way back to Lisette's.

When we arrived back in the parking garage and Austin turned off the engine, I finally spoke. "So, what do you want me to do with these two?"

"Take them with us."

Oookay. Easier said than done. I pushed Lola into their chakras again and had to yell to wake them. Once they were conscious, I was able to easily control them. "Lead on," I told Austin.

We went to the elevator, and when the doors opened, we ran smack into the bear-like Jack Grady. "Where the hell have you been?"

he asked. "I've been worried and was just going to go hunting for you."

"Sorry, we went looking for clues." I gestured at Ronald and Wes. "We found them."

Jack dismissed them with a glance. "Didn't it occur to you to leave a note?"

I glanced at Austin. No help there. "Uh, no. It's not like we're joined at the hip or anything." And I wasn't used to having to tell someone where I went or what I did. I wasn't sure I liked it. "Sorry, I didn't know I had to keep you informed of my whereabouts."

He muttered something under his breath that I didn't catch.

I DID, Fang said, sounding amused. WANT TO KNOW WHAT HE SAID?

I'll pass. To Jack, I said, "Come on, we're going upstairs to return Lisette's lost sheep to the fold."

Austin used the intercom to identify us, and the elevator rose smoothly toward the penthouse. There must have been hidden cameras, too, because as the doors opened, I could see a small crowd had gathered, waiting for us. Lisette took center stage, looking gorgeous in a flowy electric blue dress.

"Austin, how wonderful. You found them." Lisette moved forward, her arms outstretched in welcome, then she must have gotten a whiff of our odorous friends because she recoiled. "What's wrong with them?"

I shot a glance at Alejandro, who was standing beside Lisette. "Maybe we could do this privately?" I suggested. I didn't know how Lisette or her minions would react to the knowledge that I was controlling these two and that they'd most likely gotten this way by drinking demon blood.

"Yes, let's," Alejandro said.

Lisette frowned but said, "Very well. Everyone, go away." She made shooing motions and the other vamps melted away, shooting curious glances over their shoulders and murmuring to each other as they left. Only Alejandro and Lisette remained.

Jack wandered over to sit down and Fang trotted after him. I'LL JUST WAIT OVER HERE WITH JACK. LET ME KNOW WHEN THE DRAMA'S OVER.

Lisette gestured at Ronald and Wes. "But where is Etienne? Is he still missing?"

Austin pressed his lips together. "I'm sorry. We did find Etienne, but . . ." He pulled the watch from his pocket and handed it to Lisette.

Her mouth rounded in an O and tears spilled from her eyes as she cradled the watch and gently brushed ash away. She even looked pretty when she cried. "*Mais non.* How can this be?" She whirled on me, fists clenched. "Did you do this?"

I held my hands up and backed away a step. "Not me. The sun did that. And there hasn't been any sun since I left you."

"She's right," Austin confirmed.

Lisette must have realized the timing was wrong, because she nodded and looked toward the two I had in my control. "Why do they act so strange?"

"Because they're your so-called chupacabras," I told her.

"Absurd," she declared. "They are staunch supporters of the Movement. Why would they drink animal blood when the blood bank has so much to offer?"

"Because they aren't exactly in their right minds," I explained, trying to break it to her gently.

"What?" Lisette turned to Austin. "What does she mean?"

Austin tipped his hat to her. "Val is a succubus, Lisette. She is keeping your men under her control because they attacked us in the park."

"What? Nonsense. Let them go," she insisted with an imperious gesture.

"I don't think you really want me to do that," I drawled.

"She's right," Austin told Lisette. Then, to Alejandro, he said, "They seem to have the same problem Lorenzo and Carina did."

Alejandro sucked in his breath. "Then please do not release them, Ms. Shapiro, until we have them somewhere safe."

Lisette looked back and forth between the two vampires. "What does this mean?"

Alejandro and Austin seemed reluctant to explain, so I did. "It means they've gone insane. They weren't in their right minds, so they attacked us." I glanced at them and noted their condition. "It looks like it happened a while ago."

Austin spoke up. "Val is keeping them from harming the rest of us. We suspect they drank demon blood."

This wouldn't have happened if they'd known the danger of combining demon and vampire blood. "Didn't you tell them about the danger of drinking demon blood?" I asked her. "And what happened to the poor demons they drank from?" They must be the ones Dina was worried about.

Lisette glared at me. "Yes, I told them. I told everyone. And no one in my house would dare drink from another without their permission. You must be mistaken."

Austin made a calming gesture. "Lisette, the demon blood came through the blood banks in San Antonio. Are you sure yours aren't contaminated?"

Her hand flew to her mouth and her eyes widened. "I don't know."

Alejandro patted her reassuringly on the arm. "If it did, we would have more cases by now. They must have come across it some other way."

Yeah, by sipping directly from a vein. But I kept my mouth shut. We were outnumbered here, and I didn't want to get them pissed off at me.

"I can't think how," Lisette said. "*Mon dieu.* How could this have happened? Perhaps the demons forced them to drink?"

I couldn't help it. "Oh, yeah. I can just see demons grabbing vamps and forcing them to bite their necks and suck out all their lifeblood."

"You aren't helping," Alejandro said sternly.

"Okay, okay. I'll be quiet. But you need to come up with a more likely scenario."

Lisette frowned. "We have another who hasn't checked in yet. You think . . . ?"

"It's possible," Austin said reluctantly.

"Then we must check all the supplies, *tout suite.*" Lisette turned, and with a regal move of her hand, picked up a bell on the side table and tinkled it.

One of the Tweedles came on the double.

"Wait," I said. "What do you want me to do with these two? I can't hold them forever."

Lisette glanced at Alejandro. He bowed smoothly. "With your permission, I will take charge of them. We have had some success in restoring sanity to our afflicted ones. But I'll need the help of some of your people."

Lisette nodded, and as she gave instructions to her minion, I followed Alejandro back into the elevator with the two mindless vamps. Austin, Jack and Fang joined us, and we rode down together, my two charges stinking up the elevator. We stopped at the basement where Alejandro gestured us toward a room that looked like an old-fashioned hospital ward, with neat beds, boasting crisp white sheets, lined up on both walls down the entire length of the room. All of the beds were empty.

Was this where the vampires slept during the day? Darn. I'd had visions of silk-lined coffins in my head.

I DOUBT IT, Fang drawled. IT'S PROBABLY JUST WHAT IT LOOKS LIKE—A HOSPITAL.

Too bad. I really wanted to see where they slept someday.

Alejandro gestured toward two beds. "If you wouldn't mind asking them to lie down and go to sleep?"

"Of course. Wes, Ronald, lie down on the beds." I went even further. "And do anything Alejandro asks you to."

"And Lisette as well," Alejandro reminded me. "This is her house."

"Okay, do whatever Lisette asks you to, too. Now, go to sleep."

With them taken care of, I said, "So, now that the chupacabras have been caught and identified, how are you going to spin this?"

"Spin?" Alejandro asked in confusion.

Austin translated. "She means, what story are you going to tell the press?"

The vamp leader frowned. "I don't know yet, but we will think of something. Wild dogs, or coyotes perhaps. Those with mange have been mistakenly identified as chupacabras before."

"So, your chupacabras are identified and caught. That means I'm free of the contract," I said, grinning.

"Not quite yet," he said. "There seems to be the possibility of another afflicted one. I would appreciate it if you would help us find him."

"Can't you do that on your own?"

Austin turned to look at me. "You are the best person to handle them without hurting them. And you seemed so concerned earlier about the demons they drank from. Don't you want to know who the demons are and if they're all right?"

HE HAS YOU THERE, Fang said.

Like I needed to be reminded that Austin always had the upper hand. Dang it, I really wanted out of that contract. But he was right. The demons here weren't close family like the ones in San Antonio—more like distant cousins you didn't really want to hang out with but still felt akin to. I didn't care about Dina, but I owed it to Micah—and

David and Pia—to find out what was going on.

I sighed. "Of course I do." I gazed down at the two we'd caught, remembering how mindless they'd appeared. "Austin, did they seem more out of it than the ones in San Antonio to you?"

Austin nodded. "You have a theory about that?"

"Yeah. I think they drank a lot more demon blood than the others." If the demons in question even had any left. "I'll go back to the park tomorrow in the light of day and see what I can find. We didn't get a chance to look around much."

"I appreciate it," Alejandro said. "I'll ask Lisette to send a clean-up crew after nightfall tomorrow to get the deer and anything else you find." He paused for a moment, then added,

"It is close to dawn and we have much to do here. We'll see you tomorrow at sunset."

Oh, good. Free time. I headed for the elevator before he could change his mind, with Jack and Fang following. What should I do? Call Shade? No, he could call me for a change. Besides, he was probably asleep. The question was, who was he sleeping *with*? Not that I distrusted Shade, but Dina's succubus could force him.

I winced. No—don't go there. That place hurt.

How about feeding your favorite hellhound? Fang asked plaintively. And Jack is hungry, too.

Jack's stomach growled, right on cue. He shrugged, looking sheepish.

Thankful for the distraction, I said, "Okay, let's get something to eat."

A diner was open nearby, so I grabbed some breakfast and took it back to the room so Fang could eat with us.

While we ate, I decided to grill Jack some more about the books. "So, what else can you tell me about the books?"

"What do you want to know?" he countered.

Sheesh. Squeezing info out of Jack was like trying to take pizza away from Fang. Even if you could eke out a little, what was left wasn't worth much.

Very funny, the hellhound said.

"If I want a particular ability, can I ask the encyclopedia for it, or do I have to look through the whole thing to find it?"

"You can ask." Jack shrugged. "But whether the books respond or not is up to them. And only the second two volumes have spells. The first is merely an encyclopedia of demons and other nonhuman species."

I knew that. "So, if I decide to read one of the spells to get an ability, do I lose some of the succubus abilities right away?"

"No, not until you use the new spell or ability."

"Then how much succubus power do I lose?"

Jack paused, then said, "It depends."

COME ON, DUDE, Fang said. IF YOU DON'T TELL HER, I CAN READ IT FROM YOUR MIND, YOU KNOW.

From the widening of his eyes, I gathered Jack hadn't thought of that. And didn't like it much.

"What does it depend on?" I asked him.

With a sidelong glance at Fang, Jack said, "It depends on how difficult the ability is and on how long and how intensely you use it."

GO ON, Fang said. TELL HER THE REST.

I raised my eyebrows at Jack. "Give."

"Some spells you can use all the time, like the shield Trevor used. Others, once you use them, you have to wait a period of time before you can use it again."

Oh, wonderful. "How do I know which is which?"

"There's usually an indication on the page, at the bottom."

In other words, read the fine print. Mage demon lawyers . . . just peachy. "What else aren't you telling me?"

He hesitated for a moment, and Fang said, HE'S WORRIED IF HE TELLS YOU EVERYTHING, YOU WON'T HAVE ANY MORE USE FOR HIM. HE ISN'T FAMILIAR WITH THIS TIME, SO HOW CAN HE SUPPORT HIMSELF?

"It's okay, Jack," I told him. "Micah will find something for you to do. That's what the Underground is for, remember?"

He nodded, but the tight expression around his eyes showed he didn't quite believe me.

"It's all right," I told him. "There's time." And now that I'd finished eating and relaxed a little, I suddenly felt all of the day's aches and pains clamor for my attention. And that wasn't even taking into account how tired I was. "How about we get some sleep and do some more searching in the morning?"

"Good idea," Jack said, and left for his own room.

I cleaned up the debris from the take-out and checked the windows. Since this was a vampire establishment, they had excellent black-out metal blinds that completely cut off the light. I made sure they were closed and asked Fang, "Need anything before I take a shower?"

He settled down on the bed. NOPE. JUST SLEEP. YOU NEVER KNOW WHAT VIOLENCE AND MAYHEM TOMORROW WILL BRING.

I chuckled. "Maybe it'll be uneventful."

Fang snorted. AROUND YOU? I DOUBT IT.

Chapter Thirteen

I woke around two in the afternoon, and by the time I roused Fang and Jack and fed them, it was almost three.

I stood up from the table outside the diner. "C'mon, guys, daylight's burning." The sun set around five thirty this time of year. Luckily, someone had left keys to one of Alejandro's cars hanging on my doorknob with the license plate number on a tag.

I drove back to the park and there were a few cars around, but not many. I hadn't noticed it last night, but now I saw a sign saying, "All pets on leash." I read it aloud to Fang.

I'M NOT A PET, he said stubbornly.

"I know, but no one else does." And there was a Parks and Recreation truck parked in the lot, with a man inside watching us. "Don't worry, I won't keep hold of it unless I have to." I rummaged in the backpack for the leash, carried for times like this when Fang had to pretend to be a real dog, and snapped it on him.

"You lead the way," I told him, trying to make him feel better.

He set a brisk pace that Jack and I had a hard time following, until we got to the place where the coyote had been killed. "Okay, let's search."

"What are we looking for?" Jack asked.

Good question. This was Dan's area of expertise, not mine. "I don't know. Any kind of clue. Another pile of ash, a scrap of fabric or any sign of where the vampires may have holed up during the day." A big sign with a pointing arrow saying, Clue Here would be nice.

I dropped the leash and we investigated the area around the ash pile that had been Etienne. We didn't find anything, so we went to take a look at the areas where the animals had been killed. Jack headed for the deer and Fang took off in his own direction, trying to sniff up some identifiable scents, I guess. I took the coyote kill, checking every square inch around it.

I was bent over, peering at a bush, when I heard a voice behind me. "Didn't you have a dog earlier?"

Startled, I spun around to see a fit middle-aged man with a Parks and Rec logo on his shirt. Pressed pants, short haircut, very straight arrow. "Sorry, you scared me. What did you say?"

He smiled, the kind of smile that didn't reach his eyes. "I said, didn't you have a dog earlier?"

From the expression on his face and the book in his hand, I gathered he was about to write me a citation.

"Yes," I said carefully.

"You know they're supposed to be leashed."

"Oh, he is. My friend has him." I turned in the direction Jack had gone. "Jack, can you come here?"

Fang, I called mentally. *Find Jack, tell him what's going on and have him bring you here on the leash.*

Fang grumbled, but knew it was necessary. I heard some rustling through the underbrush, then Fang bounded out, with Jack behind him holding the leash. Fang sat down beside me, his tongue lolling out, making him look innocent and goofy.

Nice touch.

I THOUGHT YOU'D LIKE IT, Fang snarked.

"What is it?" Jack asked, looking at the guy and acting dumb. He was almost as good at it as Fang.

I nodded at Mr. Straight Arrow. "He just wanted to be sure we had . . . Snookums . . . on a leash."

SNOOKUMS? Fang said indignantly. COULDN'T YOU COME UP WITH A BETTER NAME THAN THAT?

Sorry. Not on such short notice. I didn't want to get into a whole conversation about Fang's name.

Jack nodded, saying heartily, "Of course we do, sir. We'd never break the law, would we, love?" Jack grabbed the man's hand and pumped it. "Thank you, sir, for everything you're doing to keep our parks safe and clean."

Fake much? *Tell him to tone it down a notch, willya?* I asked Fang.

ALREADY DONE. HE'LL KEEP IT ZIPPED.

"Call me Ben," the guy said. Then, "What were you doing there?"

"What? Where?" I asked, stalling for time. I could use Lola to force him to do what I wanted, but I didn't see any need for that yet.

"You were looking very closely at that bush. Did you lose something?"

"No, I uh . . . I'm just doing some research."

"Research on what?"

"On the area. For a book." Then in case he didn't get what I was trying to say, I added, "I'm a writer."

NICE SAVE, Fang complimented me.

"Really?" Ben's face lost its tension and he looked more interested. "What kind of book?"

"Oh, a novel. A horror novel." My life certainly resembled one.

"Have I ever heard of you?"

How the blazes would I know who he'd heard of? "No, I'm sure you haven't. This is my first book and I need to do some more research on exactly what kind of foliage and stuff are in the park." There. That ought to explain why I was examining the bush.

"Maybe I can help," he said, grinning. "What do you need to know? I know a lot about the park."

Maybe he *could* help. "Well, you see, I have this girl who's been kidnapped right here and dragged away by a monster."

"What kind of monster?"

"A vampire."

Jack made an abortive movement, evidently out of surprise that I'd said the *v* word, but kept his mouth shut.

"Like Dracula?" Ben asked.

Sheesh, was that the only vampire he'd heard of? "Kind of, but this one is scarier and meaner." Trying to keep him on my track, I said, "So, picture this. It's nearing daylight and the vampire has to find somewhere to hide away from the sun. Are there any caves nearby where he might hide out? I want to get the details right."

Jack looked at me like I'd just grown a brain he didn't know I had.

Fang said, GOOD ONE.

I thought so.

The guy thought for a moment. "Couldn't you put the story near Bee Cave or the Inner Space Caverns?"

"No, it has to be right here—the book is almost done so I can't change it. And the cave needs to be close."

He scratched his chin. "I don't know of any caves near here, but do you think he might be able to hide under a rock overhang?"

"Good thinking. Do you know of such a place?"

"Maybe. Most people come here for the swimming, hiking and biking in this part of the park, but a few get off the path. You think a vampire would?"

"Absolutely."

"Okay, then follow me."

We followed Ben and thrashed our way through the brush as he led us toward an outcropping of rocks. "On the other side," he said.

So, we clambered over the boulders while Jack and Fang went to find a way around. Fang wasn't made for climbing rocks, and since Jack had the leash, he had to follow the hellhound.

Ben jumped down on the other side of the rock and grinned, gesturing at the area underneath. "Will this work?"

"It just might."

WHAT DO YOU SEE? Fang asked.

A big gray rock with an overhang, I told him. *The area underneath is tall enough for several men to crouch under. And it looks like it goes back a ways.*

"Think a vampire could hide out here?" Ben asked.

"Yes, I do." Several, in fact. "If you don't mind, let me go in alone to get the feel of the space." And keep him out of Lola's proximity.

"Sure. Do your thing."

I wasn't sure what kind of *thing* writers did, but Ben probably didn't know either. I crouched down and went as far underneath as I could, trying to look like a writer taking note of all the details. Crap. I just hoped there wasn't a vampire there now.

There wasn't, but there was enough space farther in for several people to lie down where the sun wouldn't reach them. And I recognized the smell. Wes and Ronald had been here, all right. I felt around for clues, but the only things under this rock were dirt, twigs and dead leaves.

My backpack bumped against the rock above, making it difficult to go farther, so I slipped it off and felt around in the dark. Wait— there was something. Two somethings. One felt like a piece of fabric and the other was something small, smooth and flat. I wanted to get a good look at it, but if I took it into the sunlight, Ben might see it and take it away from me.

So I stuffed it in my backpack and made my way out of the space.

Jack and Fang had evidently found a way around, because they were waiting there.

WE FOUND SOMETHING, Fang said.

So did I. What did you find?

ANOTHER PILE OF ASH. AND A BELT BUCKLE.

Maybe the other missing vampire?

"Well?" Ben asked. "Did you get what you were looking for?"

I brushed the debris off my clothes. "Yes, I did. Very spooky. Perfect for my book. Thanks so much for showing it to me."

"No problem. Anything else you need to see?"

"No, that's it." He might get suspicious if we hung around, and I wanted to get rid of him so I could get a good look at what we'd found. "You ready to go, Jack?"

He nodded wordlessly, apparently taking Fang's zipping instructions to heart.

We went back to the stream, Ben following us all the way. He'd turned from being a hard-ass into a burr I couldn't shake. On the way back to the parking lot, he asked me tons of questions about my story, and I made things up with Fang's help. The hellhound watched a lot of television, so he gave me a plausible plot.

When we got back to the parking lot, I dumped the backpack in the back seat. "I know it sounds confusing, but it makes sense when you read it. Thanks for your help, Ben. I appreciate it."

"Sure, no problem," he said genially. "Say, what's the title? I'll be on the lookout for it."

I opened the door and sat in the driver's seat, hoping to give him a hint. "I don't have a title yet."

"Oh. Well, then, I'll just look for your name. What is it? You didn't tell me."

My inventiveness was tapped out. What was a good horror writer's name? "It's Steph—Stephanie. Stephanie Queen." I closed the door in his face so he couldn't ask me any more questions.

He took it in stride and waved as I started the car and pulled out of the lot. "I'll watch for it," he yelled to my retreating car.

"You do that," I muttered.

STEPHANIE QUEEN? Fang asked, snickering. HOW ORIGINAL.

I shrugged. *Hey, it worked, didn't it?*

Jack reached down to unhook Fang's leash. "Fang said you found something. What is it?"

"I don't know, but when we get far enough away so I'm sure Ben isn't following us, I'll take a look."

A couple miles later, we went through a drive-through for some drinks, then parked in the back of the lot. "Let me see the buckle you found."

Jack handed me a metal belt buckle that looked like a skull with a cowboy hat being choked by a snake. It was certainly distinctive. Maybe it would help identify someone. "Let me see what I found." I pulled the pack out from the back seat and rummaged inside, then came out with the two things I'd found under the rock—a wallet and a scrap of fabric. "Well, well. You think this might be a clue?"

DON'T GLOAT, Fang said. OPEN IT.

I did, and the young face that stared back at me from the driver's license was one I'd never heard of. "Adam Bukowski. Do you know that name?" I asked Fang.

NOPE.

I rifled through it, but it contained only the normal stuff you'd find in a wallet. Nothing saying "Member of the New Blood Movement" or "Bloodsuckers-R-Us." Though he did have an expired University of Texas student ID.

"Nothing," I complained. "What was it doing under the rock?"

"What about that?" Jack asked, pointing at the fabric.

Ah, now it made sense. The scrap of fabric was denim, with the imprint of the wallet outlined in faded white where it had rubbed against the material. "He must have ripped his pocket off on the rock without realizing it."

"You think it belonged to a vampire?" Jack asked.

MAYBE. OR MAYBE IT BELONGED TO SOME GENERIC SCHMUCK FOOLING AROUND WHERE HE SHOULDN'T BE. Fang snorted. WOW. SOME CLUE YOU FOUND THERE, BABE.

But I wasn't ready to throw in the towel yet. "Maybe. Maybe not. Let's do some checking."

By the time we got back to the blood bank, it was almost sunset. I waited until the sun was fully down, then knocked on Austin's door, leaving Jack and Fang-the-Cynical behind.

This time, Austin was fully dressed, thank goodness. "Hi," I said brightly. "Have a computer?"

He raised his eyebrow but ushered me in. "In the corner."

Of course. Lisette would provide her special guests with all of the latest toys. I crossed the room to the laptop and switched it on. Right about now, I sure wished Shade was with me. He was a real whiz with electronics.

"Why do you need one?" Austin asked, sitting down near me. Thankfully, not too near. Didn't want to get Lola all riled up.

I told him what I'd learned and showed him what we'd found. "Do you know if Lisette has a vampire with this kind of belt buckle, or one named Adam Bukowski?"

"I don't know, but I'll ask."

Austin went into the other room to call and I sat down at the computer. I might not know as much as Shade, but I could do a simple search. I found several people named Adam Bukowski on social networking sites, but I didn't belong to any so I couldn't check them out. I tried a few other search words along with it, but nothing seemed to pop up. And he no longer lived at the address on his license.

Austin came back in. "Any luck?" I asked him.

"No, she doesn't know anyone by that name. How about you?"

"No, but I'm not very good at this," I admitted.

"Move over," he said, careful not to come too close. "Let me try."

He tried the same things I did, and had a few tricks more, but didn't turn up anything useful.

I tapped the wallet against my chin. "Hmm. Is it normal in this day and time to have nothing on the Internet about you?"

Austin shrugged. "It is for someone like me. You, too, I bet."

I nodded. "Good point. Maybe Adam's a demon."

"Just what I was thinking."

"How's Lisette's relationship with the local Demon Underground? They know each other well enough to share membership rosters?"

Austin shook his head. "I doubt it. They tolerate each other but don't socialize. How about Micah? Would he know?"

"Maybe. But I know someone who definitely would." Tessa, as Micah's assistant, had all of the information on the Underground at her fingertips. "I'll call her."

I pulled out my phone and noticed that I had a voice mail from Micah. I rarely turned the ringer on since I didn't want my *Thriller* ringtone belting out my location to any baddies looking for me.

Well, Micah could wait. I needed to call Tessa first.

"Hi, Tessa. Can I ask you a favor?"

"Uh, sure," she said, sounding distracted. "What is it?"

"Do you know of a demon named Adam Bukowski in Austin or San Antonio?"

"Not offhand," she said. "But I can look it up and call you back if I find out anything."

"Okay, good. Or you can text me if I don't answer."

"Sure, sure. Say, Val, do you know where Micah is?"

"No. Why?"

"It's probably nothing," the soothsayer said. "He left last night to check on Gwen, but he didn't come back to do his last set."

"I have a voice mail from him. It probably explains everything. Let me call you back."

"Okay, please do, right away."

"You got it."

I hung up and hit the buttons to listen to Micah's voice mail. Only, it wasn't Micah's voice. "Hello, little Slayer," the man said, almost playfully. "This is Asmodeus. I have your cousin and your roommate. If you ever want to see them alive again, meet me at Club Purgatory in Austin at noon, with the books in hand. We'll trade." He paused, then his voice turned more serious. "Oh, and in case you're wondering if this is a hoax, take a look at the attached picture."

Fear chilled me. Frantically, I thumbed through the necessary buttons to see the picture. Sure enough, it showed Micah looking angry and Gwen scared. Both were handcuffed to something behind them, Princess huddled beside Micah's leg. This was real.

Oh, crap. What time had he called?

I checked the time and froze. He'd left it this morning. Noon had come and gone. What was I going to do?

And how was I going to tell Fang?

Chapter Fourteen

Micah closed his eyes against the light's onslaught. He had another pounding headache, thanks to that second shot of Perdo. The fire demon and her boss apparently found it easier to move them when they were drugged, because she'd dumped them in another basement on another mattress. Or it could be the same mattress, for all he knew. But the basement was different.

This basement was only partially finished, with skeletal stud walls framing the space with sketchy rooms. At least it had what passed for a bathroom—a rudimentary one with just a toilet and sink. The chain linking Micah and Gwen together was a lot longer this time, hooked over a pipe in the ceiling near the bathroom so they could use the facilities.

Micah rose and tried to yank the pipe down with the chain, but it was too big, too sturdy to budge. And the high windows were too narrow to escape through. So, after they exhausted all the potential escape possibilities, they exchanged life stories. And when that got old, they told each other stories.

"I don't get much time to read," Gwen admitted. "Mostly, I just remember the fairy tales I heard as a child. You probably know all those."

Micah nodded. "We demons probably had different bedtime stories than you did, but some of the ones you're familiar with really happened, only they featured real demons or vampires in the starring roles."

She stood and stared down at him. "Seriously?" At his nod, she said, "Don't tell me which ones. I don't want to know. What's your favorite demon story?"

He regaled her with the story of the magickal talisman that could extend the power of an incubus or succubus indefinitely. The brave incubus used the talisman to rescue the girl, save the village, and let everyone live happily ever after.

When he finished, she said, "I see why you liked that one. Was that one of the true ones?"

Micah shrugged. "My father said it was, but I always assumed it was wishful thinking on his part."

She nodded. "Wishful thinking . . . I know how futile that is."

Damn it, Micah thought he'd distracted her for a while, but now she was sad again. "Gwen—"

She made an abortive gesture. "Not now, Micah, please. No platitudes. And, uh, I need to use the bathroom. Can you . . . ?"

"No problem." He gave her the slack she needed to reach the facilities. Then, to give her as much privacy as he could, he turned his back and closed his eyes. His mind drifted to the upcoming vote of confidence. Talk about wishful thinking. After this mess—if they ever got out of it—the Underground would probably vote unanimously to kick him out altogether. Not that he'd blame them right now.

But he hadn't been a bad leader. Maybe he'd relied too much on using the only role model he'd had as a guide, but who wouldn't? His father had done a great job of keeping the Underground together—everyone said so. He'd made a lot of improvements to help demons and keep tabs on the vampires. And he'd done a lot of good for the community. If his father had failed to keep his people safe, surely it wasn't intentional.

The chain attached to his handcuff jingled as Gwen flopped down on the mattress again. Micah opened his eyes a fraction. Gwen sat huddled at the opposite end, hugging her knees and rocking.

"Are you all right?" he asked. She'd held it together far better than he'd expected. Then again, she was an ER nurse, accustomed to dealing with horrible things on a daily basis.

"No," she said in a small voice. "I'm scared."

"It's okay," he reassured her. "I'm scared, too."

"He's been gone a long time, and Val was supposed to meet them at noon." Gwen checked her watch. "It's way past that now. What do you think is going on?"

"I have no idea." Though he did have plenty of guesses, none of them good.

"What if Val doesn't show up? What if she doesn't give that monster the books?"

He'd run that scenario through his mind many times, and he didn't like it at all. "Hey, look at me." She turned to face him, worry on her face. "It's okay. I'm sure Val and Fang are doing everything in their power to find us."

MY HUMAN, TOO, Princess said.

"Yes, Shade, too," Micah repeated for Gwen's benefit. "Probably the whole Demon Underground." He wanted to hug Gwen, comfort her, but that would bring her inside his personal field, and he knew it disturbed her when his incubus made her feel an unwanted pull toward him.

"Do you think he's going to kill us?" Gwen whispered.

"No." He toed the burger bag Asmodeus had brought them earlier. "Why would he bother to feed us and give us access to a bathroom and water if he intended to kill us?" Gwen had refused to eat, though Princess had no such problem, claiming she needed to eat for her puppies. Micah shrugged. "Maybe he gave Val the address and it's taking her awhile to find us."

"Which do you want?" Gwen asked.

"What do you mean?"

She paused, raising her head to study him intently. "Would you rather Val give in to his threats so he'll release us and put the whole world at risk, or refuse him?"

Micah noticed she left off the obvious corollary—that their chances of living through this would be drastically reduced if Val refused to trade the books for their lives. He gave Gwen's question some serious thought. Put the whole world in jeopardy or save the three of them? He'd come to respect and admire Gwen as he'd listened to her talk, and he had no desire to die, but . . . "I'd have to choose the rest of the world."

Gwen sighed. "Yeah, me too."

The question was, would Val see it that way?

NO, Princess declared. THEY WILL SAVE ME AND MY PUPPIES.

Maybe. "When he shot us the last time, why didn't you run and get help?" Micah asked Princess. She could have saved herself, which was what he'd expected her to do.

Princess snuggled up to Gwen and licked her hand. MY HUMAN SAID TO PROTECT HER.

The mothering instinct, probably. Micah suppressed a sigh. Running away probably wouldn't have done any good anyway, since she wouldn't have been able to tell anyone where they'd been moved to. Micah assumed they were in Austin, since Carla and Asmodeus would want to be near the books and Val.

He relayed Princess's thoughts, and Gwen stroked the hellhound's ears. It seemed to make Gwen feel better. How could he help?

Platitudes wouldn't help, but maybe a viable alternative would. "Knowing Val, she'll probably try to save everyone."

"How?" Gwen asked.

Micah leaned his head against the wall and sighed. "I don't know. Maybe give Asmodeus the books so he'll release us, but follow him and stop him before he can use them—or they use him."

Gwen gave him a crooked smile and raised her hand. "I vote for that plan."

He tried to smile back, though he wasn't sure how genuine it appeared. "Yeah, me too." Her stomach growled and he picked up the burger bag and tossed it to her. "Here, eat something. It might make you feel better."

She shook her head. "No. My stomach is churning so much, I don't think I could keep anything down."

How could he help her? There was one way. "Would you—" He stopped, not sure if he should ask this question. "Would you like a hug?"

She cast him a wary glance. "You mean you want to use my energy?"

"No, nothing like that. I can inspire desire in you, but I can also use my ability to make you feel calmer."

She hugged her knees harder and darted a glance at him.

"I would never do anything to harm you," Micah assured her softly. Then, hoping humor would help, he added, "Val would kill me if I did."

Gwen hesitated for a moment longer, then said, "Okay, why not?" and scooted close.

He drew her under his arm, firmly controlling the incubus urge to draw on all that tempting feminine energy beside him. "Go ahead, relax."

She sighed and put her arms around him, laying her head on his shoulder. He caressed her chakras with his power, sending calming energy through her body. He felt her tension ease, and was grateful he could do something to help her. Princess cuddled up against them, partially on his lap, partially on Gwen's. The little spaniel had her own kind of calming influence.

They stayed that way, sharing each other's warmth and comfort without saying a word until Micah heard footsteps upstairs. He jerked upright.

"What is it?" Gwen asked, looking besotted.

Princess scrambled off his lap and he untangled himself from Gwen's arms, getting his personal field as far away from her as he could. "Someone's upstairs."

She rose to her feet and hugged herself. "Who? Val? Or *Carla?*"

"I don't know."

Micah heard someone start down the stairs. Hope and dread warred within him. *Who was it?*

BAD MAN, Princess declared.

Damn. Hope faded. Maybe he could wrap this chain around the demon's neck and—

"Don't try any funny business," someone bellowed outside the door. "Or the girl and dog will regret it."

The door slammed open and a large, powerful man stood there, glaring at them, pointing that damned dart gun.

"As—Asmodeus?" Gwen asked on a shaky breath.

"You got it, lady. Carla won't be back. I don't need her anymore, and she failed me too many times."

Damn. Unlike Carla, this guy didn't look like he had any weaknesses. Micah stood there, tense and ready for action if the opportunity presented itself.

"Guess the Slayer doesn't think much of you two," Asmodeus bit out, looking thoroughly pissed off. "She didn't show up for the meeting."

Gwen backed away and Princess stayed with her, growling a warning.

Fear for them surged through Micah, sickening and searing. "Maybe she didn't get the message." Micah needed to keep the guy talking and convince him not to do anything rash.

"I stayed for an hour," the demon spat out. "She didn't show."

"Val sometimes forgets to charge her phone," Gwen said, sounding frantic.

"Or she leaves it behind," Micah added. "Or turns the ringer off so it won't distract her. She hasn't had one for very long so she forgets about it."

When the demon frowned, Micah said, "Try calling her again. You wouldn't want to miss out on trading us for the books, would you? Or I'll give you the names of other demons who could track her down."

Looking suspicious, Asmodeus said, "I don't think so."

Damn. How could Micah convince him. "Maybe—"

"Shut up," the demon said. "Let me think."

Well, if he was thinking, maybe he'd be smart enough to see that dead captives weren't good bargaining chips. Micah exchanged a worried glance with Gwen.

Finally, Asmodeus raised his head, grinning. "I know what I'll do."

"What?" Micah dreaded the answer, yet needed to know.

Asmodeus laughed. "Give the Slayer more incentive."

"What does that mean?" Gwen asked.

He paused, obviously playing with them.

OH, NO. Princess said, whimpering. HE'S A MAGE DEMON.

Not good. Not good at all. Jack had told them mage demons had only one power without the books. Trevor's was a mind shield. *What's this guy's power?* he asked Princess.

I DON'T KNOW. Broadcasting to Asmodeus, Princess asked, WHAT'S YOUR POWER, MAGE DEMON?

He scowled. "So you figured out what I am, huh? It doesn't matter now." He gave them a tight smile that looked deadly. "I have the ability to reach into another dimension and pull back a damned soul and anchor it in a person's body in this world." He crooked his finger at Gwen, beckoning her to him. "I think you'll do."

Micah wasn't sure what that meant, but it couldn't be good. "No," he said, holding back rage and fear. "You can't." How could he stop this?

Though she looked scared to death, Gwen asked, "Is it permanent?"

Asmodeus smiled. "Oh, yes, quite permanent. Unless I free you."

"If I do this, will you let them go?" she asked and took a step toward the demon.

Micah couldn't let her sacrifice herself. "No," he said firmly and reached out with his incubus powers to grab hold of her. "Gwen, don't move." His power wasn't at full strength, thanks to the double shots of Perdo, but he could hold on to one woman.

She froze obediently.

Just in case, he grabbed the chain binding him to Gwen, pulling it until there was no slack on Gwen's side and she couldn't move without him letting go. Princess moved to put her small body protectively between Asmodeus and Gwen. But the Perdo still hadn't worn off—how long could he hold her? Right about now, Micah wished he had that mythical amulet.

"Don't be stupid," the demon snapped at him. "Why would I accept her deal when I hold all the cards? I don't need her permission.

Or yours."

Having nothing to lose, Micah rushed him, intent on wrapping the chain around his neck. But Asmodeus was too fast for him. He backed up the stairs quickly, and Micah came to an abrupt halt, knowing the chain would keep him from reaching the demon.

Asmodeus laughed. "I also don't need to touch her." Tucking the dart gun into his belt, he closed his eyes and raised his hands palms out, muttering something.

A spell?

Damn it, no. Micah rushed back and grabbed Gwen in a fierce hug, hoping that if he held her tight enough, if he held her fast in his own thrall, Asmodeus wouldn't be able to subvert her soul to a damned one.

As Princess snapped and snarled, Asmodeus's chant suddenly came to an end. And the woman in his arms changed. She still looked the same, still clung to him, but there was a vast difference. She didn't feel the same and her expression turned sly, her hands aggressive. Worse, his incubus powers had been abruptly cut off from her.

"Gwen?" he asked uncertainly.

She looked up at him with a wicked smile. "I'm afraid not. You can call me Lilith."

Chapter Fifteen

"What's wrong, Val?" Austin asked.

I explained quickly, then called the kidnapper back at Micah's number to tell him why I'd missed the meeting, hoping the guy hadn't done anything rash. I never dialed so fast in my life. Crap. No answer.

"He's not answering," I told Austin. I dialed again, frantically, hoping I'd somehow misdialed the first time. Same result. This time I left a voice-mail message. In a rush, I said, "Please, please don't hurt them. I didn't get your message until now. I'll go to the club right away. Or call me again, tell me where to meet you. I'll be there, I promise. Don't hurt them."

I stared at the phone, willing it to ring, then realized how stupid that was. But I needed to do something, anything, "I have to tell Fang," I told Austin.

"Okay, I'll come with you."

I didn't wait for him or the elevator, but took off down the stairs as fast as I could. I burst into the room, and Jack and Fang looked up from their television watching, startled. I knew Fang could read it from my mind, but for some reason, I had to say it out loud anyway. "Micah, Gwen and Princess have been kidnapped."

"What?" Jack said, leaping to his feet as Austin arrived more calmly than I'd managed.

"I'm so sorry," I told Fang.

NO, I DON'T BELIEVE IT, Fang said, shaking his head.

Denial wasn't going to help get them back. Sighing, I let him listen to the voice mail.

Fang's lips pulled back away from his teeth in a snarl, his hackles rose, and his eyes turned feral, like he was about to go Terminator on someone's butt. PLAY IT AGAIN, he demanded.

What good would that do? But I played the voice mail again anyway. It was just as chilling the third time around.

I DON'T KNOW THAT VOICE, Fang said, his voice in my head coming in hard, rapid spurts. DO YOU?

I shook my head.

IF HE HURTS EVEN ONE OF THEM—

I didn't hear what Fang would do because his mental voice deteriorated into nothing but snarls and growls.

I stared at the phone again, then noticed the charge was getting low. What if he called back and the phone was dead? I found the charger quickly and plugged in the phone. "We're going to the club, just as soon as the phone is charged." And hope like hell he'd meet us there.

Jack sank down on my bed, looking stunned. "Do you think they're still alive?"

"Yes," I bit out. They had to be. I wouldn't consider anything else. "He wants the books." I couldn't help but pace. "He'll keep them alive to trade."

"I hope you're right," Jack said.

OF COURSE SHE'S RIGHT, Fang snapped. AND WHILE SHE WAITS AT THE CLUB, WE'LL FIND MICAH, GWEN AND PRINCESS AND SAVE THEM.

Sounded like an excellent plan, with just one teensy flaw. "How?" I asked. "We don't know who it is or where they are."

Austin moved closer to stare down at the phone. "Think. He wants the books. Who could it be?"

Frustrated, I snapped, "It could be anyone."

"Not just anyone," Austin corrected me. "Only those who know what the books are and what they can do."

He was right. That narrowed it down a little. "Then it's either a demon or a vampire. Humans wouldn't know about the books." Except for a few—some of my friends in the Special Crimes Unit. And Gwen. But none of them could even use the books if they had them.

"This doesn't sound like one of us," Austin said. "Alejandro prefers you control the books, and Lisette thinks they're too dangerous to have around."

"Then it must be a demon," I concluded, pacing. "Someone in San Antonio or here." I glanced at Jack. "Unless you told the Los Angeles Underground."

He shook his head. "I don't know anyone there anymore."

IT'S SOMEONE IN AUSTIN, Fang snarled. HE WANTED TO MEET YOU AT THE DEMON HEADQUARTERS HERE.

He was right. "Dina Bellama," I said with disgust. "She's mixed up in this somehow, I know it."

Austin lounged against the door. "Think. Are you sure you're not just saying that because she's playing footsie with your boyfriend?"

I don't know how, but he managed to make the word *boyfriend* sound childish. My mouth tightened, but I refused to let Austin get to me. He had a point. "No. I'm saying it because she wants the books, she can control any man she wants, and he asked us to meet at her hangout. Isn't it interesting that they were kidnapped after Dina found out I had the books? Who else could it be?"

"She has a point," Jack said.

Yeah, several of them. All nicely sharpened and ready to plunge into a heart. I'd only used my stakes on vampires before, but they'd make a demon just as dead.

"So what's your plan?" Austin asked.

KILL DINA, RESCUE OUR FRIENDS AND GET THE HELL OUT OF THIS TOWN, Fang snarled.

"You need proof first," Jack protested. "You can't just kill people because you suspect them of doing something."

The voice of sanity. I hated sanity.

Austin looked confused, so Jack filled him in on what Fang had said. The cowboy didn't say anything. He just looked at me with his eyebrows raised, as if silently asking me if I was really going to do this thing.

Crap. They were both right. I couldn't stake her without proof. That would make me just as bad as those I fought. But what could I do?

"What can we do if he doesn't show up at the club or call you?" Austin asked.

I didn't even want to think about that. "We grab Dina and force her to tell us what's going on." I suddenly remembered something very important. "Wait. Maybe we *can* find them on our own."

Fang's head snapped toward me. HOW? he demanded.

I smiled. "Erica. She's a finder and she owes us big time." Shade had cured her inability to have children, and I'd been instrumental in making that happen. "She'll help," I said with certainty.

GOOD IDEA, Fang said. CALL HER.

I didn't have her number, but Tessa probably did, and I had to break the bad news to her anyway. I dialed her number.

"Hi, Val," Tessa said. "I was just going to call you. That guy whose wallet you called about, Adam Bukowski? He belongs to the Underground there in Austin."

Everything bad seemed to point back to Dina's organization. "Thanks, Tessa, but that's not why I called. I have bad news." I explained about the phone call and waited for Tessa to calm down. "I'm sure they're still alive," I assured her. "I just need Erica's help to find them. Can you give me her number?"

"Sorry," Tessa said. "But she's not in town. She and her husband went on a cruise to celebrate her cure and make a baby. She didn't take her cell and won't be back until next week."

I shut my eyes in frustration, then I remembered *her* ability. "You're a soothsayer. Can't you get a prophecy to find out where they are?"

"My gift doesn't work that way."

I knew she had no control over it, but . . . "Can't you at least try?" I was desperate here.

She sighed. "Okay. I'll let you know if I have any luck. Call me as soon as you know something."

We hung up and I checked my phone to see if the kidnapper had called while I'd been on the phone. Nope. Now what? I glanced around and my gaze fell on my backpack. The books.

I dumped them onto the bed and grabbed one of the volumes, clutching it tightly. "Please, please, please, for your sake as well as mine, give me a power that will help me find them."

Light glowed on one of the pages and I opened it, my hope rising. I read the page eagerly, then threw the book back on the bed with disgust. That again. "Paranoid much?" I asked the books, knowing it was useless and petty, but not caring.

"What is it?" Jack asked.

"It's the spell to locate mage demons," I bit out. As Jack had mentioned before, the books were more concerned about protecting themselves than about helping me. "No help there."

BACK TO MY PLAN, Fang insisted.

"Okay," I said. "We find a way to go after them after my phone is charged. I want to make sure it's fully operational in case someone calls back."

"You can't just show up at the club with the books," Jack protested.

I couldn't stop pacing. "Yeah, I know. I have to leave them behind, so I'll have something to trade once he assures me Micah and Gwen are safe."

AND PRINCESS, Fang added, a dangerous edge to his voice.

"Of course, Princess, too." I thought it went without saying.

Fang seemed mollified, so I added, "Jack, you'll have to stay here."

"Why?" he protested. "I can help. Give me something to do."

I didn't have time right now to worry about his need to be useful. "You can help by safeguarding the books. You said it yourself—I can't take them with me."

Jack looked annoyed. "You need some muscle beside you. You can't do this alone."

SHE HAS ME, Fang informed him.

"I'll go with you," Austin said.

I glanced at him in surprise. "Don't you want to follow up on the chupacabra thing, find Lisette's missing vampire?"

He shrugged. "I'll text Vincent and ask him to do that. You need my help."

I hadn't expected that, but I did appreciate it. "Thanks."

"They don't know me, so I can blend in, help when needed."

Austin, blend in? With his good looks and cowboy drawl, he was more likely to cause a stampede . . . in his direction. But there was no way I was gonna feed his ego by saying that aloud. I glanced at Fang, expecting some kind of snarky remark, but he was too wired to banter.

"Good idea," I said. "But Dina is a succubus as well. To make sure she doesn't grab you in her chakras, I'll have to hold you in my thrall."

A slow grin spread across his face and he looked up from his phone. "If you think you can handle me."

Annoyed, I shot back, "Of course I can."

He leaned back in the chair and crossed his booted ankles. "So, what do you plan to do if he doesn't show?"

HOW ABOUT WE CATCH US A SUCCUBUS AND TORTURE HER UNTIL SHE TALKS? Fang said.

Whoa. Remind me not to get you pissed at me. And if he was going in looking for blood, I was afraid this wasn't going to go well. Aloud, I said, "If necessary. But let's try something simpler first. Fang can overhear demon thoughts. If anyone knows anything about them or the demon who kidnapped them, he'll hear it and let me know."

Fang snorted. MY PLAN SOUNDED LIKE MORE FUN.

Good, a little snark. Maybe he wouldn't be as much of a loose cannon as I feared. "If we don't find out anything that way, we'll corner Dina and make her talk." Somehow. "More backup would be good, too. No more vamps—they'd stand out. And if too many San

Antonio demons show up, it'll make Dina suspicious." But I did need to let Shade know what was going on with his dog.

"How about David?" Jack asked.

Yes, of course. He was watching Shade for us so he should be nearby. I called him and filled him in, and he was glad to help. "He'll meet us there," I told the rest of them.

We stashed as many hidden weapons on us as we could, and, once the phone was charged, we left Jack and the books in our adjoining rooms, then headed out. When we got there, Club Purgatory was rockin', and with a few *don't look* nudges from Lola, Austin was able to sneak Fang in under his coat. But we changed our minds about Austin blending in, figuring it would be better to have him close by. We grabbed a corner table on the main floor, and Fang slid into the shadows under the table. I ordered a Coke—all they'd let me have since I was underage—and Austin ordered a beer. He was way over-age.

"Make that two beers," David said as he joined us, a ski cap pulled down over his head to hide the majority of his scars.

The server nodded and I introduced the two guys. They nodded at each other, and David reached down to scratch Fang's ears. "Hey, buddy."

When Fang didn't respond, I explained, "He's listening in to demon conversations, to see if he can catch a hint of who the kidnapper is or where they're holding our friends."

David nodded, and the four of us resorted to searching the room with our gazes, looking for clues and watching for trouble. Plus, I had to admit, I was also looking for Shade. I kinda wanted to see him, but kinda didn't. I was afraid he'd still be ticked off at me, but I had this fantasy that he'd spot me in the crowd, run to me in slow motion, and we'd kiss and make up.

Insert flat buzzer sound here. Wasn't gonna happen. I'd be lucky if he wasn't Dina's personal love slave by now. I winced at the thought.

No, you can't blame this on Dina. He'd find a way to get free if he needed to.

After a couple of hours of sitting there, doing nothing but drinking and getting on each other's nerves, I asked Fang, *Anything yet?*

NO, FOR THE FIFTIETH TIME. IF I LEARN ANYTHING, YOU'LL BE THE FIRST TO KNOW.

I knew that, but I hated waiting. Doing was my thing. Standing, I said, "I'll be right back. Bathroom." After all that Coke, I really did need to visit the ladies'. And that would keep the guys from coming with me.

After I used the facilities, I was too antsy to sit still again, so I wandered off down the hallway and through a door that said Staff Only. No one seemed to be paying attention to me back here amongst the bottle storage and dishwashing equipment. I snooped around a bit, but didn't find anything useful, so I slipped down the back stairs to the underground lair where I'd met Shade and Dina before. I heard voices in the break room, so I stopped outside the door to listen in.

"Snooping, are you?" a voice asked behind me.

I whirled and there was Dina with two boy toys in tow. Unfortunately, I knew one of them all too well—Shade. There went my dumb fantasy. I reached for him with Lola, but Dina already had control of him. It figured.

Backup, I yelled to Fang, *I'm in the basement and I need backup.* I hoped he was close enough to hear me.

ON OUR WAY, came the faint thought.

I relaxed and shrugged nonchalantly, pretending it didn't bother me that Shade was slobbering all over her. I had to remind myself that she'd probably ordered him to do that and he had no choice to obey her. "Just thought I'd visit again because, you know, last time was so much fun."

"Oh, really? I thought you'd come back to tell me you were leaving my city."

Wishful thinking, bitch. "No, I just have a few questions for you. Like why did you enthrall Shade? You promised not to."

She shrugged. "Actually, I promised I'd take care of him. And I have been." She leaned her forearm on Shade's shoulder. "Haven't I, sweet thing?" He pulled her close and planted a slow kiss on her neck.

I wanted to scream, throw things, or cut out her black heart, but none of that was acceptable. "Try that without your succubus thrall and see how far you get," I challenged. Shade wouldn't do that on his own. Would he? I forcibly tamped down my simmering anger, refusing to let it overflow and show her that she'd gotten to me.

"No, thank you," Dina said. "I rather like having a shadow demon around."

Austin, David and Fang arrived then, pelting down the stairs. Fang let out one explosive *humph* when he saw Dina, then settled down.

I felt a little better with my friends behind me. "I was just telling our hostess that we have a few questions for her."

Naturally, Dina reached out to try and seduce them into being her slaves, but I already had hold of Austin. And I couldn't even reach David. Huh. Well, if I couldn't, she couldn't either.

"Micah's missing," David said. "What do you know about that?"

"Missing?" Dina repeated, then fondled her crystal teardrop again, drawing the guys' attention to her cleavage. "I don't know anything about that."

Fang growled. SHE'S TELLING THE TRUTH, BUT SHE'S HIDING SOMETHING. FIND OUT WHAT IT IS.

How was I supposed to do that? "Have you heard from him lately?" I asked.

"No, not since he called to tell me about you and the books. Why? Have you misplaced him?"

"No, he's been kidnapped."

"Kidnapped?" she repeated in surprise. "You think I had something to do with it?"

"The thought had crossed my mind," I said dryly.

"Well, I didn't."

TRUTH, Fang confirmed.

Dina gasped, looking suddenly apprehensive. "You think I might be next?"

I thought about relieving her mind, telling her that the kidnapper wanted the books, but I felt like being petty. "I don't know. Maybe."

GEE, THANKS, Fang said. NOW ALL SHE CAN THINK ABOUT IS HOW TO PROTECT HERSELF.

I shrugged it off. She probably didn't have any information anyway.

"What else can you tell me?" she demanded. "My security detail has to know everything to protect me."

Aha, I had something she wanted. I smiled. "I'll make you a deal. I'll tell you what I know about the kidnapping if you release Shade."

"I don't want to leave," he said.

Was that Shade talking? Or Dina forcing Shade to want to stay?

Dina crossed her arms and glared at me. "No deal."

"Okay, then give me five minutes alone with him—without him under your control—and I'll tell him what I know. He can tell you." When she hesitated, I added, "It's the only way you'll learn anything."

Her eyes narrowed, then she spat, "Fine. Five minutes." She whispered something in his ear, then drew away from him. Dina gave me a confident smile. "Not that it'll do you any good," she murmured.

We'll see about that. I grabbed Shade's hand and tugged him through the door and into the phone room again. Once we were alone inside, Lola reached for him. It wasn't conscious on my part, but Lola hadn't fed in a while and was getting edgy from lack of energy. She was accustomed to feeding on Shade whenever she liked . . . and she liked right now.

But his chakras felt different, tight and closed off. Was that from having another succubus in them for so long?

"Stop it," he said, drawing away from me to the limits of the room.

I could see why he was tired of being controlled. "It's not me," I protested. "It's Lola. She likes you."

"You have control of her," Shade said, his voice uncharacteristically terse. "You can stop it."

Why was he so angry? "Already done. But let me touch you so I can see your face." I reached out to cup his cheek, but he jerked away. He did let me touch his hand, though. I clutched it hard. "I'm so sorry she's controlling you."

"It's part of my job." His expression was tight, uncompromising.

Okay, he was pissed. I got that. But he had to get over it soon. "She can't maintain control of you twenty-four hours a day. Can't you stay awake? Leave when she sleeps?"

"You don't get it," Shade said. "I have a job to do and I'm doing it. I don't need the Slayer's help or to be rescued by a vampire. I can handle this without you."

Was I coming on too strong? Too controlling? Suddenly uncertain, I asked, "Has Dina brainwashed you?"

"No, I finally came to my senses. Here, I'm treated like I'm somebody. Not just the Slayer's boyfriend or Micah's watcher and healer. Here, I matter."

"You matter to me," I said in a small voice.

"Not enough. You don't see me, Val. You don't see what's right in front of you."

I wanted to cry or throw things, but that wouldn't help. How could I convince him that I didn't see him as weak? That I needed him? "Shade—"

He drew away from me. "Enough. You've had your say. Now, tell me what Dina wants to know about the kidnapping."

"Okay, but you need to know something else." I swallowed hard, and wished I didn't have to reveal the rest. "Two others were kidnapped along with Micah."

"Who?"

"Gwen and Princess."

"Damn it, Val. You couldn't even protect my dog?"

Why was he being so unreasonable? This wasn't like him. "I'm sorry, I didn't know—"

He cut me off with an impatient gesture. "Tell me what you know about the kidnapping."

Confused and upset, I let him listen to the voice mail and see the picture. "That's all I know. I didn't get the message until it was too late to meet him. But he told us to meet him here, at the club. Doesn't that imply Dina is involved?"

"No, why would it? Demons often use Club Purgatory as a meeting place because we all know about it." He handed back my phone. "What are you going to do about this?"

"We're trying to find out more information, to learn where they are. Don't worry, I'll bring Princess back to you."

"You'd better." Shade frowned. "The important thing is that Dina doesn't have to worry. He obviously just wants the books."

That was the important thing? I shook my head. This was no longer the Shade I knew. He was different now, had turned into someone I wasn't sure I liked anymore. I couldn't even pretend it was thrall. He wasn't under thrall, he'd just changed. Blinking back tears, I ignored the gaping hole in my heart and went on about the business of saving my real friends.

Chapter Sixteen

I stomped out of the club, the guys right behind me.

"What's wrong?" Austin asked. "Did you learn anything?"

I couldn't answer right now, for fear I'd lose it completely.

DINA DIDN'T KNOW ANYTHING, Fang told David. TELL HIM TO LEAVE VAL ALONE.

At least Fang cared about me. I blinked back tears as I reached Austin's car, jerked open the back door, then got in and waited just long enough for Fang to clear the opening before I slammed it shut.

David whispered something to Austin. They both got in the front, giving me a wary glance. "What now?" David asked softly.

I had no freakin' clue. I was fresh out of ideas and worried to death the kidnapper would hurt my friends. I checked my phone for messages again. Nothing. Crap. Only one thing I could do. "Back to the blood bank," I snapped. "I'm gonna force those damned books to help me or dump them in a deep, dark hole somewhere."

The three of them were wise enough to keep quiet all the way back. I rushed up the stairs to my room and opened the door. No Jack. He must be in his room. I jerked the adjoining door open, but he wasn't there either. Crap. Where was he when I needed him? If he followed his normal pattern, he'd probably gone to get something to eat.

"There's a note," Austin said, and reached down to pick a piece of paper up off the bed.

I snatched it from him and read the old-fashioned spidery handwriting quickly.

Val, I'm sorry, but I can't sit and do nothing. While you look for Micah, I'll help Vincent with the vampire problem. Don't worry, I'll keep the books safe. Jack.

I crumpled the note and threw it against the wall. "Jack went with Vincent." The idiot couldn't believe Micah would help him find work, he had to go out on his own and prove himself. I turned to Austin. "Can you find out where they are?"

"Sure. I'll call Vincent." Austin called, but it went straight to voice mail. "He must have turned it off. I'll try Alejandro."

He held a short conversation with his boss, then said, "They went back out to the park to look for Lisette's missing colleague." He glanced at me apologetically. "Jack thought his ability might come in handy, given they aren't sure what they're dealing with. He took the books with him in the backpack."

I closed my eyes in disbelief. Sure, his ability to lasso someone with a rope of energy would be useful, but did he have to be so helpful *now?*

"Don't worry," Austin said. "Vincent will protect him."

That was the least of my worries. "Let's go get him and the books."

Austin drove as fast as he could without getting a ticket, but it still wasn't fast enough for Fang and me. When we got to the park, I saw a car just like the one we were in—Vincent's. Good. They were still here.

I opened the car door for Fang. "Do you hear them?" I asked.

Fang froze, one paw lifted, and sniffed the air. NO, BUT THEY MUST BE IN THE PARK.

"It's huge," David protested. "How will we find them?"

"Jack probably took Vincent back to where we found the others," I said.

Austin handed me the flashlight from out of the trunk and we took off down the dark trail.

Suddenly, Fang sprang ahead. I HEAR THEM. IT SOUNDS LIKE FIGHTING.

I just hoped it wasn't with each other. "They're fighting," I yelled at Austin, and we took off after Fang.

Austin was much faster than the three of us, so he outpaced us swiftly. David and I were handicapped by the brush and the miniscule illumination provided by the flashlight, but Fang didn't slow down. When I got to the small clearing, it was hard at first to figure out what was going on. Someone was down on the ground and four men were fighting each other wicked fast. Fang was chasing another through the bush.

A cowboy hat went sailing as a fist plowed into Austin's face.

I knew the drill by now. I whipped Lola into all four of them as David went to check out the guy on the ground. "Stop fighting," I ordered them through the ropes of energy connecting us. They obeyed, and I added, "Turn toward me so I can see you."

Austin and Vincent stood alongside two other vamps I'd never seen before. Carefully, I separated their strands and released the two vamps I knew.

Vincent rubbed his jaw, his face looking battered. "Thanks. They caught us off guard."

Austin didn't say anything. His mouth set, he walked over to me, yanked two stakes out of my back waistband, then before I could do or say anything, he tossed one to Vincent and they slammed the stakes right through the hearts of the other two.

The tie to Lola snapped as they died and the backlash threw me off balance. Whoa. "Guess neither one was your friend," I said, startled. So that's what happened when someone died under Lola's control. Good to know.

"Nope," Austin said. "Don't know either of these scum."

Oookay. "What makes you think they're scum?"

Austin answered. "Between us, Vincent and I know all of the members of the New Blood Movement. These two don't belong. Ergo, they're part of the ragged mob randomly killing people and animals." He stared me in the eyes, his jaw tight. "Scum."

That didn't surprise me as much as his use of the word *ergo*. Who talked like that?

AUSTIN WASN'T ALWAYS A COWBOY, YOU KNOW, Fang said as he came trotting back. SORRY, THE OTHER ONE GOT AWAY.

I glanced at Vincent. "Was the one who got away Lisette's missing vamp?"

"No. I'm sorry, they jumped us. I couldn't—" He broke off, rubbing a hand over his face.

Us? Where was Jack?

Oh, crap. I whirled to look at the man on the ground. David stood above him, looking down. "I'm sorry, Val."

What was wrong? I stumbled over to Jack's side and knelt down beside him. Blood covered his face and his neck. "Jack?" I shook his shoulder and his head lolled to the side. "Jack, wake up."

Fang rubbed up against me and licked my hand. HE CAN'T, BABE.

Okay, so he was unconscious. "We have to get him to Shade. Shade will heal him." Surely he would, no matter how angry he was at me.

"Shade can't heal this," David said softly.

"What? Of course he can." Look what he'd done for Erica.

Austin grasped my arms firmly and pulled me to my feet, holding my shoulders as he stared into my eyes. "He's gone, Val," he said simply.

Gone? I gazed back stupidly. No. It couldn't be. "You mean . . . dead?"

"Yes, I'm afraid so."

I pushed Austin away, not needing Lola's distraction right now. Jack couldn't be dead. He was one of the good guys. The good guys didn't die—only the bad ones.

THAT'S ONLY IN FAIRY TALES, Fang said sadly.

"He wanted to do this," Vincent said. "He was proud to be able to help you out. He was a good man."

I knew that. And I regretted all the horrible things I'd said to him, how I'd joked about him pigging out all the time. Right now, I wished he was back. I'd stuff him full of food until he couldn't eat any more.

HE KNEW YOU DIDN'T MEAN IT, Fang said, trying to console me.

"There is one thing you can do for him," David suggested.

"What?"

"You can find out who's causing this. I don't think those vamps were sane, either."

"They weren't," Vincent confirmed.

I nodded slowly and took a deep breath. I couldn't stand one more thing going wrong today. I just couldn't. I had to get back to the work at hand. Life was a bitch, but I could be a bigger one.

"Okay," I said. "That's the next order of business, right after we rescue Gwen, Micah and Princess." I was determined that no one else was going to die on my watch.

No one.

"What do you want to do about them?" David asked, nodding toward the dead vamps.

"Leave 'em," Austin said. "The morning sun will take care of them."

Yeah, but what about poor Jack? I looked down at him, and Vincent said, "Let me."

Gently, the short vamp picked up Jack like he weighed nothing. "Lisette will help us take care of him properly."

"No," David said. "The demons will take care of it. We have our own rites and rituals for this."

We did? I had no idea. The only other demon I knew who'd died was Shawndra, and I'd been unconscious during her funeral.

"As you wish," Vincent said. "We can hold his—hold *him* at the blood bank until you're ready for him. We have facilities down in the infirmary."

"Okay, good," David said, and we walked in silence back to the cars.

Vincent gently laid Jack in the backseat of his car, then handed me the backpack Jack had been wearing—mine, with the books inside. Strangely, I felt more complete with them near me once again.

The rest of us followed in Austin's car, in total silence, and Fang cuddled up close to me on the back seat. Even though he must be worried to death about Princess, he still worried about me. I didn't deserve friends like this.

DON'T BE STUPID, Fang said, poking me in the side. YOU'LL ALWAYS BE MY BEST FRIEND.

I buried my hands and face in his fur and the tears flowed then, silent and unseen in the dark recesses of the backseat. I'd take this brief time to mourn, then get back to work.

We arrived back at the blood bank, and Austin parked while Vincent kept on going. "He'll take care of Jack for you until David picks him up," Austin explained.

I wiped my face and said, "Okay. Thank you both very much, but I can take it from here."

Austin and David turned around to stare at me in surprise.

"Are you crazy?" David asked. "You can't do this alone."

"Sure I can. I don't want to get anyone else killed, not even Austin."

The vamp didn't even smile at my lame attempt at a joke. "The hell you go it alone," Austin said. "This concerns us, too. Where do you get off telling us what we can and can't do? You're not Superwoman anymore, you know."

"Gee, thanks for reminding me of my limitations," I snarked back.

"Someone has to," Austin said.

FACE IT, BABE, Fang put in. YOU'RE NOT GETTING RID OF ANY OF US. AND YOU DO NEED THE HELP.

Damn it. I might be able to do this without them, but it would be a whole lot easier with them. "Okay, okay. But if you get yourself killed, don't blame me." I grabbed the backpack and got out of the car, ignoring them.

I checked my phone again. Nothing. Crap. But I did know one thing I could do. I called Tessa and told her about Jack and that we were no closer to finding Micah. She hadn't learned anything helpful either. "I need a favor," I said.

"What is it?" she asked. "Anything to help."

"I need to bring the Mem—" I glanced at Austin then changed what I'd planned to say. "I need you to bring the woman in the basement here."

Tessa gasped. "You know?"

"Yes, I know."

"You don't know what you're asking," she protested.

"Yes, I do. We need all the weapons we can get, and she's a formidable one."

"No," Tessa said. "Micah is the only one who can control her."

"Micah's not the only one," I said, staring pointedly at David. "David's an incubus, too, so he can control her. He'll come by tonight and pick her up. Along with anyone else who wants to help find Micah."

I hung up and David sighed and shook his head. "How did you know I'm an incubus?"

"I figured it out when I tried to control you at Dina's club. I couldn't. Just like Micah."

"Yes," he said, "But I don't like to use my ability. It's what caused this." He made a sharp gesture toward the burned half of his face.

"But you'll do it to help us." It was a statement, not a question.

He closed his eyes. "Don't make me do this. Can't you find something in the books?"

"I tried, believe me, but they were no help."

"Try again," he insisted.

I sighed. "Okay, I'll try again. Can we do it in your room?" I asked Austin. I didn't want to go back to the adjoining rooms I'd shared with Jack.

"Of course."

We rode up to the elegant suite and David looked around appreciatively. "So this is how the other half lives," he murmured, making me wonder what kind of home he and Pia had. Did they live together? I didn't even know that much about the two of them.

THEY DO ALL RIGHT, Fang said. STOP STALLING AND THREATEN THE BOOKS SO WE CAN GET MOVING.

For some dumb reason, that made me smile. But the smile faded when I swung the backpack up on Austin's pristine table and saw the stains on the strap. Blood. Jack's blood.

Austin whipped it away from me. "I'll get you another one," he said and unzipped the bag to dump everything out on the table.

At once, one of the books vibrated and glowed—my cosmic messaging device again. Austin and David backed up, looking a little freaked out.

"It's okay," I assured them. "It's for me."

I grabbed the book and glared at it. "If you dare show me that same damned spell, I'll . . . I'll . . ." I couldn't think of anything bad enough that wouldn't take me and half of Texas out with it. "I'll stake you." That might hurt it a little anyway.

I opened the book and watched as it flipped pages until it landed at the glowing one. I leaned down to read it. "Huh." It was very simple. For some reason, I'd expected it to be more complicated.

"What is it?" Austin asked as David moved forward eagerly.

"It's a spell for exorcising demons." Now that might come in handy.

David backed away abruptly. "What does that mean, exorcise a demon? Would it just take out the demon part, leave us as a vegetable, kill us?"

"I don't know." I read through it silently at first. "It doesn't say, but there are no time limitations listed. Shall I take it?"

"I don't know," David said. "It sounds dangerous."

Yeah, it did. Good. "Dangerous for the creep who kidnapped my friends," I said with satisfaction. I began to read aloud.

"No," David said. "Stop. You don't know what it'll do to you."

"It's okay, Jack read from the book and it didn't hurt him." Someone else had done that. "And it won't affect my abilities until I actually use the spell."

"Leave her be," Austin said, grasping David's arm and pulling him away. "Let her do what she has to do."

SMART MAN, Fang said approvingly.

So you think it's okay to take this spell?

I THINK IT'S THE ONLY SHOT WE HAVE.

Yeah. I read the spell aloud, each word making the hairs on my body stand up and tingle, as if tiny ants ran up and down my body. "Demon thou art, demon thou shalt not be. Say it times three, I exorcise thee."

I felt a great swell of . . . something . . . as the hair on my head lifted and blew wildly in an invisible wind. Then the spell settled somewhere beneath my breastbone. The tension and wind vanished, but the spell burned in my gut like a case of magickal indigestion.

Strange. Now all I had to do was say "I exorcise thee" three times, and the spell would work.

"The words are gone," Austin said in wonder.

Sure enough, they were no longer on the page.

"So, you don't need me to bring—go to San Antonio," David said, sounding relieved.

"Sorry, David, you still have to go."

"Why?"

"Because I don't know how this power works exactly, and I'd rather use something I know and save this one for backup." Besides, two aces in the hole were better than one. "Please, David, help me save my friends. Save Micah. Isn't that why you came to me, to protect us? Micah's one of us."

He scowled, but said nothing. Did that mean he agreed?

HE DOESN'T WANT TO, BUT HE'LL GO, Fang told me as David pulled out his phone to text something.

Austin nodded at the books. "That spell. What if you don't use it? Can you give it back?"

"I don't know. Jack never—" I stopped and swallowed hard, fighting back tears. "Jack never told me how to get rid of one." But he'd done it, somehow, when I became the keeper.

David backed away, looking frightened. "Then whatever you do, don't say that three times."

"Can it be as simple as that?" Austin asked.

"I don't know," David said, "but I don't want to test it."

Neither did I.

JACK TOLD US SPELLS LIKE THIS REQUIRE NOT ONLY THE WORDS, BUT A FOCUSED WILL ON THE SUBJECT IN QUESTION, Fang reminded us.

Yeah. I'm sure that made us all feel better. Except for one thing. I could feel the spell deep inside, lying there like a dark blot on my soul, waiting to be invoked.

And oh so willing.

Chapter Seventeen

Micah groaned and woke with another pounding headache. This time, it wasn't Perdo. Asmodeus had caught him off guard and whacked him in the back of the head. Just after Gwen—

He winced from the memory.

SHE IS NOT GWEN ANYMORE, Princess said sadly, curled up beside him.

"I know," Micah said, glad of the spaniel's presence. "She's now . . ." What was it? Oh, yeah. "Lilith."

Why did it have to be Gwen, of all people? She was the poster child for good human-demon relations, proof that they could coexist, that he'd been right not to use the Memory Eater when he learned she knew of the Underground. And, on a more personal level, she was a good person. Kind, warm, funny—a real sweetheart. How could he get her back?

SHE CAME BACK AND LEFT YOU SOMETHING, Princess said and dropped a small object in his lap.

Aspirin. Thank God. He picked up the bottle and noticed that Asmodeus had fastened Gwen's cuff on his other wrist, still linked to the chain. He looked up. And it was still looped over the pipe in the ceiling, damn it. It was dark, too, the room lit only by the light above the sink.

He staggered over to the sink, and with chains clinking against the porcelain, took great gulps of water, as well as some aspirin. Gwen was a nurse, a caretaker. Did that mean she was still in control part of the time? Or did they share the body?

NO. SHE SAID SHE NEEDS YOU WELL, Princess explained.

Well, that was ominous. He plopped back down on the mattress. What did they plan for him? And Princess?

I CAN'T READ HER, BUT I KNOW THE BAD MAN WANTS MY PUPPIES. Princess sighed and nosed a bag near the bed. SHE BROUGHT FOOD. I SAVED YOU SOME.

He needed it so the aspirin wouldn't burn holes in his stomach.

"Thanks." He peered inside. Burgers again. And cold fries. Well, it was fuel. He couldn't be picky and needed to keep up his strength, so he ate the fast food.

After a little while, his headache began to recede, so Micah wondered how he could get out of this. What would his father do? Disgusted with himself, Micah shook his head. No, he had to stop using his father as his benchmark and think for himself. He had good instincts—he just needed to trust them.

So, what were his options? As he saw it, there were only two: lie here like a slug and wait for things to happen, or escape and save Gwen and Princess. Or the hellhound, at least. He didn't know what to do about Gwen and her predicament.

ESCAPE? Princess said, sounding hopeful.

It was worth a shot anyway. Micah glanced around the room, looking for options. Maybe the windows. He hadn't considered them an option before, because neither he nor Gwen could fit through the narrow space. But maybe Princess could.

He checked them out. Nope. They were boarded up tight on the outside. Even if he could break the glass and the boards, it would be noisy. "Are they still upstairs?" he asked the hellhound.

YES. I HEAR THEM WALKING.

All right. He'd save that for later, then. For now he'd consider every other option available. What could he do? Knock out the bulb and use the glass to slash the demon's carotid? Tear out a stud and use protruding nails to bash in Asmodeus's head? He liked that idea, but admitted it wasn't realistic. Asmodeus would probably send Lilith down again, knowing Micah wouldn't dare hurt Gwen's body.

He daydreamed about several other fantastic scenarios, but all of them depended on a miracle occurring and none of them were feasible. So, what could he use to his advantage? His incubus power wouldn't work on Asmodeus or on Lilith. And there weren't any other women around—or were there?

He sat bolt upright. Wait a minute. He didn't actually have to see a woman to control her. "Do you know where we are?" he asked the hellhound.

NO.

"You had to see something as he brought us into the house. Are we out in the country in an isolated house, or in a city neighborhood?"

CITY, Princess said.

Good. Then maybe he could do something.

YOU WILL SAVE US? the spaniel asked plaintively.

"I'm sure gonna try." He laid back down and shut his eyes. "But please be quiet." This was going to take some concentration.

Micah hadn't gone this long before without feeding on female energy, and he needed to take the edge off. With luck, that hunger should make it easier to find what he needed. He centered himself, then sent out thin, questing tendrils, seeking a woman, any woman. The tendrils brushed against Gwen/Lilith upstairs, but bounced off. Asmodeus still had her firmly under his control.

Concentrating harder, Micah wafted them out farther, hoping they would go beyond the bounds of the house. This was farther than he'd ever tried to go before, but it seemed to be working.

There. He found a woman. He reached for her energy, but she moved too fast and the energy was torn from his grasp. Damn. She must have been in a car.

So, if that was the street, there should be houses on the other two sides. He reached in both directions with his hands and mind, willing the strands to find someone who could help. Up on the right, he felt something. A woman asleep?

He jumped up and ran to the wall, flattening his hands against it, and concentrating all his effort on that one spark of life. Could he wake her? Hell, he couldn't get a hook in her. *Work, damn it.*

No use. He paused to gather more of his strength.

STOP, Princess said.

"Why?" he bit out, his concentration broken.

SHE IS COMING.

Sure enough, he heard footsteps on the stairs. Quickly, he moved back over to the mattress and laid down on it.

Gwen peeked around the door. No, it was Lilith, Micah reminded himself. That must make Asmodeus the serpent, though this was no Garden of Eden. Or was it Lilith? She raised a finger to her lips and walked over on tiptoe toward him. She'd changed out of the scrubs and was now in a low-cut green dress.

"Gwen?" he whispered. "Did you break free of their control?"

She hurried over. "Shh. He'll hear you. Yes, it's me." She hugged him. "Are you all right?"

His hopes rose. "I'm fine. Can you release me?"

She lifted her lips to his. "If you kiss me first."

Lilith.

He jerked away from her. "I don't think so." He should have

known—she didn't feel like Gwen.

"Sucker," she taunted as Princess scrambled for the corner. Lilith laughed and said, "You really believed I'd give up this body after making it back to this world? Not a chance in hell." She ran her hands down Gwen's sides. "You like?"

"What do you want?" he asked tightly.

"Oh, not much," she said, giving him a seductive look. "You know, in my previous life, I was a real grind. For what? It got me nowhere. This time around, I plan to have fun. Lots and lots of fun." She shook her head. "Asmodeus is a drag. But I bet you know how to have a good time."

"I'm not in the mood."

"And after I left you that aspirin so you'd feel all better?" she cooed.

He wanted to choke her. He made an abortive move in that direction.

Lilith backed away and shook her finger at him playfully. "No, no, no. You wouldn't want to hurt your friend's body, would you?"

"Why not?" he snapped. "You said you weren't going to give it back."

She pouted. "You wouldn't hurt me, would you?" She pretended to think. "I know. I'll make sure you can't." Her smile turned hard and brittle. She moved toward the doorway and cast a glance over her shoulder. "Guess. What's fast, heals quickly, and is immortal?"

"You wouldn't," Micah said, desperately hoping she was joking.

"Oh, I would," Lilith said. "In fact, I'm leaving now to find myself a willing sire."

"No." Micah rushed toward her.

But Lilith had anticipated him and ran just out of his reach. "So sorry," she said and blew him a kiss. "The next time you see me, I'll be good and undead."

With that, she slammed the door in his face.

Micah sagged to the floor, desperately hoping she was lying. She wouldn't do that to herself. Would she?

Chapter Eighteen

The demon exorcism spell in my gut made me uneasy, but I tamped it down and looked speculatively at the books. They'd given me a way to help defeat the demon, but I still needed to locate him and my friends first.

I closed the second volume and laid all three books in front of me and stared down at them. "Okay, now show me a way to find my friends."

Nothing. Maybe politeness was in order. "Please?"

No glow, not even a tiny wink of light.

"Is there a limit on how many spells you can take on in one day?" Austin asked.

"Maybe. Jack would know—" But I could no longer ask him. "I don't know."

David's phone chirped and he glanced at it. "Pia's waiting for me downstairs. We'll go to San Antonio for you." Pocketing his phone, he added, "I'll ask Tessa to arrange Jack's funeral."

I winced. I hadn't thought of that. "Thanks." Tessa would know how to do right by him.

David left and I stood there, indecisive, trying to figure out what to do next. My options seemed nonexistent at this point. "Help me think of something," I begged Austin and Fang.

"Maybe you could—" Austin started to say, but stopped when *Thriller* went off on my phone.

I checked it quickly—a number I didn't know. "I don't know who this is," I told Austin and answered quickly, hoping it was the kidnapper getting back to me.

"Hello?" The female voice sounded familiar.

Ohmigod. "Gwen?"

"Yes, it's me." Her voice was harsh with fear or uncertainty. I couldn't tell which.

ASK ABOUT PRINCESS, Fang said, jumping to his feet.

"Where are you?"

"I don't know, but he hasn't hurt us yet."

Yet? That sounded ominous, but at least it meant Micah and Princess were okay, too. Gwen sounded a little odd, like she wasn't sure how much she could say. "Is he standing next to you?" I asked her.

"Yes."

"Do you remember anything about where you are now, how you got there? Give me a hint."

"I don't know," she said, sounding impatient. "Why didn't you show up to the meeting?"

Gwen sounded angry, and she had a right to be. "I'm so sorry. I didn't get the message until the meeting time had come and gone. I called back and left a message. Didn't he get it?"

"I guess not."

"Why did he kidnap you?"

"He thought I was you, and that I had the books. The other two were just there, so he took them, too. Val, he wants to trade us for the books. Can you do that?"

"Don't worry. I'll do everything in my power to free you," I promised her.

"*No*," she ordered, then added, "Don't attempt a rescue. Please, just bring the encyclopedia."

She had to say that, with him standing next to her. "Just tell me this. Is he a mage demon?" Mage demon and encyclopedia . . . an explosive combination.

"No. Please, come soon. I'm afraid he'll burn us if you don't."

Smart girl, she was able to tell us he was a fire demon like Andrew. Probably some idiot who'd heard how strong the books had made Andrew, but thought he could remain free of the books' control. "Okay, but tell him it'll take me some time to get the books."

"Is that true?"

Just in case he was listening, I lied. "Yes. When and where does he want to exchange them?"

"Just a minute. I'll ask." All I could hear were muffled voices until she came back on the line a couple of minutes later. "He'll call you later with the details. How long will it take you to get them?"

It was at least an hour to San Antonio, and I wanted him to assume I'd left them somewhere near there. Give me more time to think and plan. "About three hours."

"All right, I'll tell him. Don't turn off the phone this time, okay?"

"Okay. I—"

But she had hung up. Or, more likely, the fire demon had hung up for her. "He'll call back later to arrange the time and place," I told Fang and Austin.

WE'RE NOT JUST GONNA SIT ON OUR BUTTS AND WAIT, ARE WE? Fang asked belligerently.

"What do you want me to do?"

FIND THEM. TAKE THEM AWAY FROM THAT DEMON BEFORE HE CAN HURT THEM OR GET HIS HANDS ON THE BOOKS.

Exasperated and frustrated, I shot back, "How? You got any bright ideas on how to find them? 'Cause I'm fresh out."

Austin settled back in his chair, one booted leg resting on top of his knee. "Think, Val. What did you hear in the background on the call? Was it silent like they were inside a house, or did it sound like they were on a road in a car?"

Good question. I thought for a moment. Neither one. "I heard voices in the background," I said. "And music." I thought harder. "Christmas music. I know—it was *Feliz Navidad.*"

"Maybe it's a Mexican restaurant," Austin said, musing.

THAT NARROWS IT DOWN TO ABOUT A THOUSAND BETWEEN HERE AND SAN ANTONIO, Fang said, sounding disgusted. OR NOT. IT'S PLAYED EVERYWHERE THIS TIME OF YEAR.

"What's your phone show?" Austin asked. "Does it say who it's from?"

"No. It just gave the number—the area code is five-one-two, in Austin."

"Maybe we can do a reverse lookup," Austin said, rising to head toward the computer. "What's the rest of the number?"

I glanced at my phone. "Wait. While I was talking to Gwen, her brother called and left a voice mail."

I listened to the voice mail. Short and sweet. "Call me immediately," Dan growled and hung up.

Dang. I'd hoped we could rescue Gwen and get her home safe and sound before Dan realized she was missing. But his cop skills could come in handy right now.

I called him and he didn't even say hello. He just bulldozed right over me. "Do you know where Gwen is? She didn't show up for work, she's not home, there's a scorched spot on her rug and she doesn't answer her cell. Is she with you?"

"No. Dan, I'm sorry, but Gwen's been kidnapped."

"What?" he bellowed, nearly bursting my eardrum. "By who?"

"Some fire demon we don't know. He has Micah and Princess, too."

"Lay it out for me. Where are they? What does he want with them? Is there a ransom demand? What are you doing about it?" The questions came rapid-fire.

When he finally paused for a moment, I said, "Yes, we have a ransom demand. He wants the books."

"You're going to give them up, aren't you?"

"As soon as he gives us the time and place. Unless we can find Gwen and Micah before then. Can you help?" San Antonio wasn't that far away.

"I'll do my damnedest." Dan paused, then asked more hesitantly, "Did he—Did he give you proof of life?"

Such a cop thing to say. "Yes, he made Gwen call me. I just hung up from talking to her."

He sighed, and I heard a lot of relief in that sound. "What's the number?"

I gave him the number, told him what I knew, and explained he'd used Micah's phone to call me earlier. "I bought us three hours—he thinks it'll take me that long to get the books."

"Good. I'll track the numbers down. Get with the Underground," Dan ordered. "Find out who the fire demons are in San Antonio and Austin. And send me the picture he took of Gwen and Micah, too."

"Of course." I wanted to find them just as much as he did.

"Let me know immediately what you find out."

"I will, but you have to do the same."

"You got it."

He hung up on me, but I didn't mind. He was good at his job and now I had a little sliver of hope that we'd be able to find Micah and Gwen without having to give up the books.

"Dan's on it," I told the other two. "And he wants me to find out what fire demons live near here." I should have thought of that, but I was too emotionally involved. It clouded my thinking. So did Lola. She hadn't fed in a while and was getting a little edgy and a lot hungry.

GOOD, CALL TESSA, Fang said. SHE'LL KNOW.

Austin typed something on the computer. "What if it isn't a local fire demon? What if it's someone from out of state?"

"Don't think that way," I said, annoyed, then shook my head at my own foolishness. What did I think? That he'd jinx it? "This is the first lead we've had. It has to help." I wouldn't accept anything else.

I paused for a moment. Something in what he said niggled at me, but I couldn't get a grip on it. Something important. No time for that now. I called Tessa, and told her what I needed to know.

"Andrew and his mother are the only fire demons recorded in San Antonio," she said.

"I know Andrew's voice, and that definitely wasn't him."

"Okay," she said. "Let me check the Austin files, as well as the rest of Texas, and I'll get back to you as soon as I can."

"Thanks. Oh, and David's on his way there. Can you send Ludwig back with him?" The water demon ought to come in handy.

Tessa agreed, so I hung up and checked the voice mail and the charge level. No calls had come in while I was on the phone this time, but I was using it more than normal and the charge was going down fast. I pulled the charger off the table from where it had been dumped from the backpack and plugged it in.

"Have you heard from Alejandro?" I asked Austin. "Are they any closer to finding the missing vamp?"

Austin shook his head. "Not yet. But they have found more evidence of . . ." He paused, then added, "More ash."

More dead vamps. What the heck? Was there a whole vein of wild vamps hiding out in the park somewhere?

I nodded, and while we waited, I asked, "How's your—" What should I call the vampire Austin had sired? His child? That didn't sound right, so I changed my wording. "How's Wes doing? And the other guy—Ronald."

"Their minds aren't whole yet, but Alejandro is confident they'll regain their sanity. It just takes time."

"What is he doing to treat them?" I didn't really care, but the conversation helped pass the time and I listened with half an ear until Tessa called back.

"What did you find out?" I asked her.

"There are two fire demons in Austin, three in Houston, and several more in West Texas."

"Give me the names of the Austin ones."

"Beth and Blaine Williamson—a brother and sister. You want the address? Apparently, they live together."

"Hold on, let me get something to write on." Austin handed me a notepad and a pen so I took down the address. "Thanks, Tessa. You may have just helped us find Micah and Gwen." I hung up.

WHERE? Fang demanded.

"I have an address here in Austin, but I'm not familiar with the town." I checked the time. Good, it was nearing midnight, but this time of year, lots of people were still celebrating. It wasn't too late to knock on someone's door, was it?

"Here," Austin said, "let me look it up."

He brought up some map app on his phone and typed in the address. It was somewhere in the southwest part of town.

LET'S GO, Fang said, standing at the door.

"Wait. I need to tell Dan first."

I called him and put him on speaker, but Dan started talking first. "We found where they were held in San Antonio, but they're not here anymore."

Surprised, I asked, "How'd you do it that fast?"

"The photo you sent was geotagged with the location where the picture was taken. We checked it out. It's an empty house, but Gwen's badge and Micah's phone, wallet and keys were inside. No sign of where they were going, though. The second number was a public phone outside a Mexican restaurant on the west side of Austin. I doubt they're still there, but I'm headed your way to check it out. You have anything?"

"Maybe. We have the address of the only two fire demons in Austin. I was just going out to talk to them."

"What's the address?" I gave it to him, and he added, "I'm on my way. Don't go in without me."

That would take too long. "Not sure I can do that," I said. If there was any way to save my friends, I was gonna do it with or without him.

"Wait, Val. Just wait."

"See you there," I said without promising anything, then hung up.

A knock came at the door. I whirled, startled. "Are you expecting someone?" I asked Austin.

"Relax. I asked Lisette to get something for you." He opened the door, accepting a couple of bags from a female vamp, then closed it and handed them to me. "I think you can use these."

Surprised, I opened the bigger bag and found a new backpack. But the color . . . "Pink?" I asked incredulously. "Not exactly subtle." And it wasn't even a hot pink. More like a baby color.

He shrugged. "Sorry. I told you I'd get you another one, but I didn't tell her what color. Look at it this way. Who would suspect such destruction potential would be hiding in that?"

He had a point, but pink? So not me.

"There should be some other things in there." He peered inside the bag, then handed me a couple of wooden garden stakes, presumably to replace the ones he'd used, and some kind of electronic gizmo bound up in that hard plastic clamshell retail packaging. I hated these things. They were so difficult to open, they put Fort Knox to shame.

"Got a sharp knife?" I asked. Then, "What is this anyway?"

Austin ripped it open like it was tissue paper. Maybe Fort Knox should hire vampires. "It's a car phone charger," he said. "So you won't lose touch while we're driving. And the other bag should hold some food. I figured you and Fang were getting hungry."

"Good thinking."

YEAH, YEAH, Fang complained. DUMP THE MUTUAL ADMIRATION SOCIETY AND LET'S GET GOING. I HAVE A PRINCESS TO SAVE.

"Okay, let's go. Are you coming, too?" I asked Austin.

"Wouldn't miss it."

Good. I could use his help, and his car. I stuffed everything into the pink backpack, grabbed the food and headed out the door.

I navigated while Austin drove. Fang and I also chowed down on chicken sandwiches and fries. Now, if only I could feed Lola as easily . . .

CAN'T HE GO ANY FASTER? Fang snapped.

I rubbed his ears. *Sorry. This has to be difficult for you.*

He licked my hand. I'M SORRY, TOO. JUST EDGY. I WANNA TAKE A BITE OUT OF SOMETHING.

Well, don't look at me.

He gave me the equivalent of a mental chuckle. But now we were going through a residential neighborhood and I needed to give Austin directions. We pulled up outside a small house and parked across the street from it. Austin cut the lights.

"What do we do now?" I asked softly. The house looked dark, with no lights on inside. Either they were asleep or no one was home.

Fang put his front paws against the door and peered at the house. PRINCESS AND THE OTHERS MIGHT STILL BE INSIDE, EVEN IF IT'S DARK. LET'S CHECK IT OUT.

"Let's do some recon," Austin said at the same time.

"If they're in there, Fang should be able to hear Micah and Princess's thoughts from here," I said and glanced at the hellhound.

NADA, he said, sounding worried. BUT THEY MIGHT BE UNDER THE INFLUENCE OF PERDO.

I relayed it to Austin, feeling just as worried and imagining all sorts of horrible things.

He shrugged and voiced the one thing I feared most. "Even if it's not Perdo, it doesn't mean they're dead. It just means they're not here right now. Maybe they're on their way back or they're unconscious. We won't know for sure until we look."

I was glad someone was thinking straight here. "What do you suggest?"

"You knock on the door and I'll hide in the shadows in case someone answers." He glanced at Fang. "You said he has a good nose. Maybe he can smell some sign of them on or around the property."

It sounded good to me, so I left everything in the car. I had the two secret weapons I needed to subdue the kidnapper—Lola and the spell.

I strolled casually up to the door and rang the doorbell as Austin and Fang faded into the shadows on the sides of the house. No answer, so I tried again, banging on the door. Still, no one came to the door. "I don't think anyone's at home," I whispered, knowing both Austin and Fang would be able to hear me. I tried the doorknob. Locked. I should have known it wouldn't be that easy.

Austin got my attention, then signaled he was going around back. Good. Maybe he'd find a window or door open back there.

Smell anything familiar? I asked Fang.

NOT YET. BUT I MIGHT NOT IF THERE'S BEEN A LOT OF TRAFFIC. OR THEY WERE CARRIED IN. I'LL CHECK IN BACK.

Dang. I was hoping for some solid evidence that they were here. I didn't want to do any breaking and entering without some assurance I was in the right. Noting some windows in the front, I went to check if they were unlocked. Maybe I wouldn't have to break, just enter.

I was tugging upward on a window when I heard a voice behind me.

"What the hell are you doing?"

Chapter Nineteen

I whirled and readied Lola before I realized the voice belonged to a woman who was pointing what looked like a can of Mace at me. "Beth Williamson?" I ventured, hoping she wouldn't spray it or unleash a fireball at me.

"What were you doing at my window?"

I held my hands out to the side and tried to look nonthreatening. "I was looking for you. We're here about your brother. From the DU."

Her tension didn't seem to ease. "You can tell Dina to go to hell, and leave my brother alone."

My eyebrows rose. So not everyone was enamored of the Demon Underground leader. "Not from here. From San Antonio, where Micah Blackburn is the leader. I'm Val Shapiro."

Her arm lowered. "The Slayer?"

Sheesh. Was there anyone who didn't know me by that stupid nickname? I nodded. "I'm also a member of the Special Crimes Unit in San Antonio." Well, not currently, but she didn't have to know that.

"What do you want with my brother?"

"There's something strange going on in this city and we think Blaine has something to do with it."

"Have you found him?"

This conversation wasn't going at all as I expected. I didn't know how to answer that, so I asked, "Can we talk inside? My partner and hellhound are here, too, and we'd like to ask you some questions."

She hesitated for a moment, then Fang said, IT'S OKAY. WE'RE NOT GONNA HURT YOU.

She jumped and looked around.

DOWN HERE, Fang said.

Fang sat with his tail wagging and his jaw dropped open in a doggie smile. He looked adorable.

Beth seemed to melt. She pocketed the Mace and knelt to pet him. "I've never met a hellhound before. And he can talk? That's great."

"Yeah, great," I lied. "That's Fang. And Austin is around here

136

somewhere."

I assumed the vamp was nearby, and sure enough, he emerged from the shadows and tipped his hat to Beth.

"Can we talk?" I repeated.

She invited us into the small house which seemed to have been decorated years ago and never updated. Avocado and gold, shag carpet, old people furniture—they must have inherited the house and all its furnishings. Fairly recently, too, since her brother's license had a different address. She'd done her best to decorate it for the season, though, with an enormous, glittery tree in one corner. She waved us to a worn couch, and in the light, I could see she was in her early twenties with the red hair I'd come to expect in fire demons.

I'LL CHECK AROUND, JUST IN CASE, Fang said, and wandered off as if following a scent.

Good. Let me know what you find.

"You say your brother is missing?" I asked. "When did you last see him?"

"He went missing around Thanksgiving. Do you know something? Do you know where he is?" she asked, clearly worried.

"I'm afraid not," Austin said.

His easy drawl and good looks seemed to put her at ease, so I nodded at him, encouraging him to keep on talking. "We believe he may be connected to a crime committed in San Antonio," Austin explained.

Beth looked taken aback. "Arson?"

"No. Kidnapping."

"You have got to be kidding me," Beth said, her mouth dropping open. "He'd never do anything like that. Blaine's friends call him a wuss. He played in the band in high school, for heaven's sake."

SHE'S TELLING THE TRUTH, Fang told me privately from somewhere else in the house. DOESN'T SEEM TO BE OUR KIDNAPPER.

That still didn't rule him out. "Did he ever say anything about books?" I asked. "A magick encyclopedia?"

"No. Except maybe in role-playing games."

YEAH. HIS ROOM IS A REAL BASTION OF GEEKDOM, Fang said.

I had to agree with Fang. Probably not our kidnapper.

"What do you think happened to him?" Austin asked.

Her eyes narrowed. "I think that damned succubus happened to him."

Austin slanted an amused glance at me but I didn't take it

personally. "I assume you're talking about Dina Bellama?" I asked.

"Yes. She enthralls every guy she comes in contact with, like a reflex or something. Blaine fell for her, hard. I think she likes the power she holds over them."

"Power enough to do anything she asks?" Austin asked.

Beth looked at him, startled. "Yes, but if he did kidnap someone, it's because she forced him to."

"Probably," I agreed. The men under my control would do anything I told them to. One vamp had even killed himself at a careless word from me. Luckily, he was one of the bad guys. "But Blaine should have come to his senses when he was out of her range."

"That's what I thought," Beth confirmed. "But he didn't. Her range must be really wide. Or he was so infatuated with her that he kept going back."

Is that what had happened to Shade? Was Dina some sort of super succubus that she didn't have to control them in person?

"If she has that much control, she could be very dangerous," Austin said, glancing at me with a frown. "And, worse, would have a pool of men with demonic powers to call upon."

Yeah. Scary.

"Other guys are missing, too," Beth confided. "Do you think she's building a male harem or something?"

Very possible. This was one person we needed to stop even if she wasn't behind all our current problems. "Do you know of any other fire demons in Austin besides you and your brother?" I asked

She shook her head. "Just us."

Too bad. I'd hoped her brother wasn't our kidnapper.

Fang came trotting back in, saying, I WAS ABLE TO CHECK THE WHOLE HOUSE. NO SIGN OF MICAH, GWEN OR PRINCESS.

I thanked Beth and asked her to call me if she heard from her brother. We exchanged phone numbers and as I walked out the door, Dan drove up.

"I told you to wait for me," Dan said, and gave Austin a dirty look. He still didn't believe the bloodsuckers in the New Blood Movement were on the side of good and right.

I sometimes wondered, myself. "Yeah, well I don't always do as I'm told."

MAKE THAT NEVER.

"What did you find out?" my former boyfriend asked. Well, I thought he was my boyfriend at the time. Turned out his definition of commitment meant, "Until demon us do part." Lola had sent him running.

I stopped on the sidewalk outside and lowered my voice. "The fire demon isn't here, just his sister. But we think a local succubus is controlling him."

Dan's hands clenched into fists. He had no defenses against a lust demon and knew it. "Who? Do you know where she is?"

"Probably at her club," I said.

He looked really stressed out. "You think that's where she's holding my sister?"

"Maybe. I don't know. The kidnapper did want to meet there to do the exchange."

"Okay, let's go."

"Wait a minute," Austin said. "If she has a lot of demons in her thrall, it might be difficult to rescue them. We need backup."

"There's no time for that," Dan snapped.

"Backup is coming," I told them. "A water demon and others who can help." The Memory Eater, especially, should be a major weapon.

"How long will it take them?" Dan barked.

"Let me find out." I called Tessa and she told me they'd just left San Antonio. "They should be here in about an hour, sooner if David speeds. Let me tell him to meet us there. It'll take us half an hour to get there, anyway."

I texted Pia since David was driving, and got a note saying they'd be there.

"Okay," Dan said. "Where is this place?"

"You can follow us," Austin offered.

"Good. But Val will ride with me. I want to know everything she knows."

Austin smirked at Dan's obvious attempt to separate me from the bad vampire's influence, but didn't say anything. He tipped his hat to me then got in his car. Fang and I climbed into Dan's vampire-proof Dodge Ram. I'm sure Dan felt safer there, since the truck was coated in silver and vampires couldn't touch it without burning themselves.

I told Dan as much as I could, but left out the part about the Memory Eater. Sheesh. Now Micah even had me keeping secrets for him. But if she still freaked me out a bit, how would Dan react?

BADLY, IS MY GUESS, Fang said.

Mine, too.

We arrived at the club and found two parking spaces fairly near each other. I got out and Fang followed me.

"Where are you going?" Dan asked.

"I assume we want to plan this out, and since Austin can't touch your truck without frying, we'll need to sit in his car."

Dan grumbled but got out and slammed the door. We walked to Austin's car and Fang and I got in the back. Lola was still a bit edgy, so letting either of these guys get inside her field wasn't a good idea.

Dan got in the front and turned around to glare at me. "What if she's not here? We could be wasting our time waiting for backup."

"Well, there's one way to find out," Austin said. He got out of the car and covered the short distance to the bar in long, easy strides. He went inside, but returned fairly quickly.

"Is she there?" Dan asked.

"No. Dina isn't performing tonight, and the woman at the door said she's probably at home."

"Did you get an address?" Dan asked.

Austin tipped his hat back and grinned. "Well, the little lady didn't want to give it to me, but I managed to convince her." He handed a napkin with writing on it to Dan.

I wondered if he'd controlled her mind or if he'd won it from her with his natural charm. He could definitely be charming when it suited him.

Fang snorted. DON'T TELL ME YOU HAVE THE HOTS FOR AUSTIN.

Don't be ridiculous. He's a vampire—one of the undead. It was Lola who had the hots for him. As she did for every man.

SOME MORE THAN OTHERS.

Shut up.

Dan and Austin both plugged the address into their map apps. "Is it near that Mexican restaurant?" I asked.

Dan shook his head. "No, but that doesn't mean anything. The kidnapper could have called from anywhere, to try and throw us off."

I reached for the napkin. "Here, let me have that. I'll tell David there's a change in plans."

"Okay." Dan slapped the dashboard and glanced at Austin. "Let's go. You drive, I'll navigate."

Austin grinned, but did as Dan told him. As we drove to Dina's house, we made a plan of sorts. I warned Dan I'd have to use Lola on him before any confrontation to keep Dina from enthralling him. He didn't like it, but at least he saw the necessity.

We pulled up a couple of houses away from Dina's address in a nice neighborhood. "Do you sense anything, Fang?"

NO. BUT LIGHTS ARE ON IN SOME OF THE WINDOWS.

Yeah, I'd noticed that. "Fang doesn't sense anything," I told the men.

"Why don't you ring the doorbell and we'll hide on either side?" Dan asked.

"It wouldn't do any good," I explained. "You're men. She'll be able to sense you, and it will make her suspicious. Remember, we want her to think we don't suspect her."

Dan and I had voted not to wait on backup. Since Dina was at home, she wouldn't have the same firepower to draw on as she would at the club. With any luck, she'd be alone. "Okay, I'm going to have Lola grab onto you now," I warned Dan. Austin didn't seem to mind, but I knew Dan would hate it.

I slid Lola's tendrils into both of them slowly, more cautious than I'd ever been before. Interesting. Austin's chakras were wide open and welcoming, but Dan's were stiff and tight. I left them in control of their actions, but held on just enough so that Dina couldn't get her hooks into them.

They stood behind and slightly to the side of me as I rang the doorbell. It took a few moments, but Dina opened the door wearing a negligee I wouldn't be caught dead in—baby blue with ruffles and flowers and girly things all over it. And she was showing off that cleavage she was so proud of.

JEALOUS? Fang asked.

Hardly. Boobs that big would just get in the way.

"Oh, look," she mocked. "It's the Slayer, and she's brought along a couple of snacks. For me?"

How many men did she need, for heaven's sake? I knew power like this could be heady and addictive, but it was also a great responsibility. One she didn't seem to know how to handle.

I ignored her attempt to get my goat. And my guys. "No. We have some more questions about the kidnapping and thought you might be able to help us."

She opened the door wider and pulled someone to her side with a malicious smile. Shade, dressed in nothing but jeans, with bare feet and a defiant expression. My heart clenched.

BOY, SHE REALLY DOESN'T LIKE YOU, Fang said.

No news there. I glanced at Shade, but all he did was glare at me.

The hell of it was, I wasn't sure why. Did he think I was barging in, checking up on him, not trusting him to do his job? Or was it something more personal?

"Do come in," Dina cooed and waved us to an elegant living room that looked like something straight out of the 1920s, with lots of white, glass, curves, and other Art Deco touches. Business must be doing well. "But not him," she said, pointing at Fang with a frown. "I don't want him shedding dog hair all over my house."

I CAN'T HELP IT, Fang said, sounding embarrassed.

She was just trying to get his goat now, and so I told him. *Ignore her. Maybe you can sort of check the place out while we talk. Let me know what she's thinking while you're at it.*

YEAH, AND I'M GONNA SHED ALL OVER EVERYTHING. MAYBE EVEN DO SOMETHING MORE RUDE.

I bit back a laugh and followed Dina into the living room. She plopped down in the love seat and petted Shade like he was a toy dog. The contact ensured that I could look straight into his eyes. Austin and Dan both gave me warning looks, but I knew better than to react. That's what she wanted.

I DON'T SENSE ANY OTHER DEMONS IN THE HOUSE, Fang reported.

Good.

"So, what do you want this time?" she asked. "I told you I don't know anything about the kidnapping." She suddenly froze. "Do you have information that someone is after me?"

I wanted to let her believe that, I really did, but it wasn't part of the plan. "No, but we have reason to believe the kidnapper is one of your demons—a man."

"Ridiculous," she said, relaxing. "My men don't do anything without my knowledge."

And that was the problem. *What is she thinking?* I asked Fang.

NOTHING USEFUL. I CAN ONLY CATCH SURFACE THOUGHTS. ASK HER SOMETHING ELSE.

"Well, in case someone slipped by you, I wondered if you'd listen to a message, see if you recognize the voice." If she did, maybe she'd think about where my friends were being held.

She shrugged. "Why not?" Dina thrust her hand out imperiously, demanding the phone.

I brought up the voice mail and played it.

She frowned. "It does sound familiar, but I'm not sure . . ." Then her eyes widened and she jumped to her feet, screaming, "You idiot!"

What the hell? Everyone else jumped to their feet, except for Shade.

Dina threw the phone at me and missed. Austin caught it, thank heavens.

Dina raved, "I should have known."

"Known what?" I asked, confused. This hadn't gone at all like I expected.

"That's the mage demon I sent to New Orleans."

Oh, crap.

Chapter Twenty

Micah sprawled on the mattress, spent. The woman in the house next door still slept, and though he tried, he couldn't get her to wake up or acknowledge him. He had to think of something he hadn't tried yet.

DON'T STOP, Princess said, pawing at him. I WANT TO LEAVE.

He stroked her fur. "I do, too, but I need to rest for a moment." He hadn't known that using his power for an extended period of time could be so exhausting.

She flopped down with a huff. MY HELLHOUND WILL RESCUE ME.

"That wouldn't hurt my pride a bit," Micah acknowledged wearily. "We can hope that Fang and Val are tracking us down this very minute."

YOU DON'T BELIEVE THEY ARE.

No, he didn't. If Val had a clue where they were, she would've been here by now. But, knowing Val, she'd never settle for a partial victory. She'd go for the whole enchilada—try to keep the books and rescue them. If she didn't get them killed in the process.

I DON'T WANT TO DIE, Princess whined.

Micah felt strangely protective toward the selfish spaniel. "I don't either, so let me see what I can do about that." He hoped he wouldn't be too late to stop Lilith from doing the unthinkable with Gwen's body.

How long had it been since she left? Asmodeus had taken his phone, so he had no way to tell the time. It felt like hours had passed, but he didn't trust his sense of time in this situation. How long would it take to find a vampire willing to turn her? It wasn't something he'd ever needed to know, so he had no clue. Days, hours . . . minutes? She seemed very confident she'd be able to find a sire right away.

Micah shook his head. He couldn't give up hope. He had to get out of here and stop her.

He gave up on the sleeping woman and concentrated. Maybe there'd be another woman nearby who was awake and susceptible.

This time he shut out the world, shut out all concerns, and went deep inside himself as he closed his eyes, dredging up every particle of incubus power he could scrounge. He paused for a moment, then thrust the tendrils out into the world, seeking a woman . . . one who was awake and willing.

He went farther than he ever had before, farther than he ever believed possible. He brushed across several other sleeping, unresponsive targets before he finally found one that seemed to yield a bit. Maybe she was only partially asleep.

Micah thrust his energy into her pleasure centers, urging her to wake, to help him. The response was tentative at first, then became more focused, more pliable.

Finally.

Val had been able to send messages to her subjects along the energy path, so he should be able to do the same. *Get up,* he urged. *Rise and shine. For me.*

He felt her acquiescence, and assumed she'd risen. Excellent. *Now go to the phone.*

She hesitated, and he concentrated everything he had on her. This had better work. He was at his very limit. *Go to the phone,* he repeated, gritting his teeth and gripping the edges of the mattress.

He felt her obey his command. When she stopped moving, he said, *Now dial this number . . .*

"That looks painful."

The unexpected voice startled him into letting go of the strands. No, no! He reached for them again, but they felt limp and drained. Useless.

He opened his eyes to see Lilith standing in the doorway again, wearing Gwen's body.

"Well, well. What were you doing?" she asked, cocking her head in curiosity. Her smile suggested she knew exactly what an incubus on a bed might be doing.

He wasn't about to explain. "Lifting weights," he snapped.

"Fine, don't tell me," Lilith shot back.

"What do you want?" Micah asked, closing his eyes against the exhaustion. Was she here to taunt him again?

"I thought you might like to see what I've done with this body, see the new me."

His eyes flew open and he searched her body with his gaze. She didn't look any different. Then again, vampires usually didn't. "You didn't have time to find a vampire," he said, hoping he was right.

Parker Blue

She shrugged. "Like it was hard. Ever hear about the colony of bats under the Congress Avenue Bridge?"

"Vampires don't turn into bats," Micah said, managing to sit up. "That's a myth. Besides, the bats aren't there this time of year."

"Yes, it is a myth, sadly. But that doesn't mean vampires don't hang out there to, you know, encourage the rubes to believe it."

"I don't believe you."

"Why not?"

"You don't look like you've been drained of blood."

She laughed. "How quaint. You believe what you see in the movies."

Feeling a little uncertain now, he asked, "Isn't that how it works?" He didn't know of anyone who had actually witnessed a vampire being sired.

"Well, there is an exchange of blood, but it doesn't require buckets of the stuff."

"How much?"

"Oh, he didn't charge much, just the use of my body for a roll in the hay. It was kind of fun."

He closed his eyes in pain. She was obviously trying to get to him. Unfortunately, it was working. In fact, she was trying so hard, maybe she was lying. "If you were really turned tonight, wouldn't you be lethargic, unable to move yet?" Maybe mindless?

"No, quite the contrary. It takes very little time for the conversion to happen. My blood mingled with his, creating a chain reaction. A few sips of that heady wine is all it took to let the change sweep over me. The vampire virus, if you'd like to call it that, kills all life in the cells in a matter of moments, replacing them with vampire vitality." She fanned herself with one hand. "It's a hell of a rush."

It certainly sounded plausible, but he couldn't believe it. "Why would you do that?"

"Hello? Immortality? I've been dead and I didn't like it. This time around, I plan to be here a looong time." She ran her hands down Gwen's sides. "It'll take a little bit to get this body in shape, but I have lots of time. Forever, in fact."

Micah bristled at the aspersions on Gwen's appearance. He liked her just the way she was. He still couldn't believe it, still couldn't imagine someone choosing an undead existence. "Prove it."

She sauntered a little closer. "You want proof? Here's proof." She pulled aside her collar and there, on her carotid artery, were two

146

punctures.

No.

She flew at him inhumanly fast, grabbed the front of his shirt and hauled him to his feet, then slammed him against the wall with the strength of five men. "How's this?" she asked and bared her fangs. "Proof enough?"

Chapter Twenty-One

I stood there, staring at Dina, feeling stunned. No wonder the demon kidnapper wanted the books. He was a *mage* demon. So why had Gwen told me he was a fire demon?

MAYBE YOU MISUNDERSTOOD HER, Fang said. OR MAYBE THAT'S THE ONE ABILITY THE MAGE DEMON CHOSE TO KEEP.

Maybe. "That changes things."

I didn't realize I'd spoken aloud until Dan said, "No, it doesn't. Gwen is still in danger. You hand over the books, she goes free. Simple as that."

"No," Dina said. "You have no idea what a mage demon could do with those books. The word *apocalypse* mean anything to you?"

"She's right," Austin agreed. "We can't turn over the books to him. We have to find a different way."

They started arguing, all but Shade, and didn't stop until I put two fingers to my lips and let out a piercing whistle. When they quieted, I said, "I have a better idea."

Dina's gaze narrowed. "What is it?"

Ignoring her, I said, "I'll need Shade. He helped capture the last mage demon and sent him to another dimension."

Dina shook her head. "No way. I heard what happened when Shade grew angry. He lost control and almost let more full demons into this world. Why do you think I've been keeping him so happy?"

Huh? *That's* why she was so chummy with Shade? "He'd never intentionally do that. In fact, he tried to kill himself to keep that very thing from happening." I reached for him with Lola, to pry him from Dina's clutches, but it was no use. She had him first, so I couldn't get even a tiny hold on him.

"You don't need me," Shade said, his voice calm and even. Dina's influence, I'm sure. "You've never needed me. You have all the resources of the two Demon Undergrounds, the New Blood Movement, and the Special Crimes Unit to fall back on. I think you can handle one mage demon."

I hoped he was right, but I wasn't sure we could pull it off without getting Micah, Gwen and Princess killed. But convincing him would take too long. "Who is he?" I asked Dina. "The mage demon. What's his name?" Maybe Dan could do a search on credit cards or something.

She made an impatient gesture. "He called himself Asmodeus. That can't be a real name."

"King of the demons," Shade murmured.

No way. He wasn't going to rule any kingdom I was a part of. "Come on," I told my guys. "Let's go."

Fang met us at the door. Dina followed. "Aren't you going to help me find the kidnapper?"

I noticed she didn't offer to help us. Not that I'd accept it. I still didn't trust her.

WE DON'T NEED YOUR HELP, Fang said. BACK OFF, BITCH. WE HAVE FRIENDS TO SAVE.

I couldn't have said it better myself. We hurried back out to Austin's car.

"What's your plan?" Dan asked.

"The books, I presume?" Austin asked as he opened the trunk where I'd stashed the girly backpack.

"Right." I grabbed the backpack and closed the trunk. "Let's get out of here."

We all piled back into the car as another vehicle pulled up in front of Dina's house. David, Pia, the large Ludwig, and the Memory Eater had arrived.

I rolled down the window and waved at them. "Follow us!"

Pia waved back in acknowledgment and Austin got the hell out of Dodge. I pulled the books out, cursing myself for not understanding what they were trying to tell me in the first place. Why hadn't I realized it was a mage demon who wanted the books? It should have been obvious. Mage demons were the only ones who could use their whole potential, besides keepers like me. The fire demon angle had thrown me off.

DON'T BEAT YOURSELF UP, Fang said. WE ALL MADE THAT MISTAKE. LOTS OF DEMONS WANT THE BOOKS AND THE POWER THEY REPRESENT. LOOK AT DINA.

"You look at Dina," I muttered. "I don't want to."

Dan twisted around in the seat to glare at me. "What are you doing? Do you actually have a plan?"

One of the books was glowing softly. "Yes, I—" My phone rang and I held up one finger as I looked at it. "I don't know the number. This might be Asmodeus." I answered it.

"Do you have the books?" the kidnapper asked.

"Yes, and I'm almost to Austin," I said, trying to buy us a little more time.

"Ask for proof of life," Dan said in a fierce whisper.

I nodded back at him. "Are my friends okay? Can I talk to them?"

"They're fine. Here, I'll prove it."

"Val, it's me," Gwen said. "We're all alive. But please, do everything he says." With a relieved smile, I nodded at Dan and gave him a thumbs-up.

The mage demon came back on. "Okay, here's how it's gonna work. You come alone and bring me the books at a place I specify, then I'll tell you where you can find your friends."

"How do I know you'll keep your part of the bargain?"

"You don't," he said, sounding arrogant. "You're just gonna have to trust me."

Yeah, right. But I let him think he'd won. "You promise you won't hurt them?" I asked.

Dan looked like he was about to say something, but Fang jumped up to place his paws on the back of Dan's seat and growled at him. The hellhound could read my mind, so he knew my plan.

"Wait," Austin said quietly to Dan.

Dan's mouth formed in a grim line but he kept his mouth shut. He had to know he could trust me to do what was best for Micah and his sister.

"I don't have any reason to hurt them," the demon assured me. "I don't care about them or you. All I want is the books. But I *will* hurt them if I don't get what I want."

I sighed heavily so he'd think I was resigned to the situation. "Okay. Where and when?"

I listened to his instructions but didn't plan on following them. "I'll be there," I said finally and hung up.

"Give me the number," Dan said. I handed him the phone and he punched some information in on his, asking, "Where does he want to meet?"

"It doesn't matter. We're not going there." I opened the glowing book and it flipped open to the spell for finding mage demons. "The spell will tell me where Asmodeus is at this moment, but if he moves, it won't follow him. So, we're going to where he is right now. That's where Gwen is." And Micah and Princess.

"Good thinking," Dan said.

A COMPLIMENT FROM DAN? Fang said. YOU'VE COME UP IN THE WORLD.

Ignoring him, I read the spell silently first. The words burned in a glowing script across the page, visible even in the dark interior of the car.

Austin glanced in the rearview mirror. "What's the limit on this one?"

I hadn't really paid attention before. "The spell will only work once every twenty-four hours, and only within a hundred miles."

"That doesn't sound real useful," Austin said.

"Well, it'll work now to find Gwen," Dan said. "The phone number is a dead end. It's a disposable cell."

"You should also realize that if I use this spell, the mage demon will be able to sense it and know approximately where I am," I explained.

Dan made an impatient gesture. "No problem. He'll think you're on the way to meet him."

Right. A small part of me yelled that I should wait, hold back on using the spell until I knew exactly what this would do to my succubus powers. But that was probably Lola, afraid to lose some of her *oomph*. I had to ignore it. Saving my friends was more important. I took a deep breath and read the spell out loud.

As I read each word, it vanished. When I was done, the spell settled uneasily in my gut alongside the other one. I said the activating words. "Beacon, show me the way."

My stomach lurched and a wave of dizziness rolled over me, making me nauseous. "Pull over," I gasped, not sure if my stomach contents would stay where they were. Worse, Lola's cork had popped and she was like a genie let out of the bottle. My control was disintegrating and she was thirsty for the kind of male energy served up like a free buffet in the front seat.

"Why?" Dan asked.

Fang barked commandingly at Austin, so the vampire did as I asked. He pulled into the parking lot of a convenience store and I stumbled out of the back seat. I ran as far away as I could from them, desperately trying to hold what little shred of control I had over Lola.

They tried to follow me, but Fang jumped in front of them and bared his teeth. As I closed my eyes and doubled over against the side of the building to concentrate on holding it together, I heard Fang say, DAVID, LUDWIG, TELL THEM TO STAY BACK. SHE'S ABOUT TO LOSE IT.

There was a lot of talking, but I ignored it. Damn it, Jack had said I'd lose some of my succubus abilities. I thought he meant I'd lose some power and strength, not lose control as well.

Someone rushed over to me. "You mussst feeed," a voice said. The Memory Eater.

"No time," I gasped out. I wasn't sure which was worse. Her concern for me or the all-consuming lust. She didn't sound entirely sane right now.

"Make the time," David snapped. "You've waited too long."

But Shade wasn't here. "On who?" I snapped. David was an incubus so that wouldn't work. My ex-boyfriend? No—Dan would never forgive me. Ludwig or some random stranger? I couldn't do that. That left Austin. He didn't have a problem with Lola. It wasn't only Lola who liked that about Austin, which somehow made considering the sexy cowboy as a feeding source infuriating. Not that I had a choice anymore.

AUSTIN, Fang barked at David.

David must have gestured him to come over because he was suddenly there, overwhelming my senses with his powerful male energy, making Lola crave what he had to give.

Still, I fought it. It felt like a betrayal of Shade.

"Do it," Austin said and wrapped his arms around me.

He was inside my personal energy field and there was nothing I could do to fend him off. Suddenly, I no longer wanted to. Lola took over, enveloping Austin in need and want. My arms crept around his neck and my lips lifted to his as her energy tendrils sank into him, permeating his entire body, making him quiver with longing for everything Lola had to give.

I wasn't able to maintain any sort of detachment at all, and I jumped up to wrap my legs around his waist. We merged into one being . . . one big roiling messy . . . something. Something I didn't want to name. Not with Austin.

Finally, when Lola was satisfied, our chakras filled, I was able to regain control. I gasped. Good grief, I was wrapped about him like a clinging ivy. I disentangled myself rapidly and pushed away from him. Austin stumbled backward, looking stunned. I wanted to tell him that made two of us, but I didn't.

The small crowd staring at the two of us looked equally stunned. I closed my eyes briefly. *Please tell me I didn't practically just do the dirty in public with my friends watching.*

SORRY, BABE. NO CAN DO.

Crap. Mortified much?

I opened my eyes and saw Austin running his fingers through his hair. He resettled his hat low on his forehead, hiding his eyes. "Well, darlin'," he drawled. "I think I need a cigarette."

"I think we all do," Ludwig said in awe.

I glared at the man mountain, but since he made everyone laugh, I couldn't be too angry at him.

But Dan could. He glared and stepped forward. "If you're done enjoying yourself, maybe we can find Gwen now?"

Austin tucked his thumbs in his belt loops and glared down at Dan. "She had no choice. You know that."

It looked like they were about to take a swing at each other, but the Memory Eater spoke up. "We gooo nooow," she said in a tone that brooked no argument.

Dan and Austin glanced at her, and she threw back her hood so they could get the full effect of her skeletal appearance. They both recoiled and it seemed to take the fight out of them.

"Yes, we go," I said firmly and looked for the beacon, but didn't see it until I turned around. Behind me, a rippling column of green fire appeared against the night sky, reaching about a mile above the city. "Oh, crap. He'll be able to see that."

"See what?" Austin asked.

I pointed. "The beacon—that column of green fire."

"I don't see anything," Dan said.

Fang looked in the direction I was pointing. ME EITHER.

Everyone else shook their heads, too. I relaxed. "Good. Maybe only I can see it. Let's go. I'll guide you."

I pointed the way, Dan drove since Austin was feeling a little drained, and Austin used the map on his phone to find where roads intersected and ended. We made our way in fits and starts toward the coruscating beacon of light.

Finally, we arrived at a house where the light was strongest and it vanished. "Stop. This is the place." Opening the door as Dan abruptly braked, I asked, "Fang, do you hear anyone inside?" Windows were boarded up and it looked dark inside.

I HEAR PRINCESS, he said and pushed the car door the rest of the way open, charging toward the front door.

"Wait," I called out. "Anyone else?" I wanted to make sure the mage demon hadn't doubled back.

Fang didn't answer. His eyes flashed purple and he threw his small body at the front door with all his might. It held, but he managed to put a big dent in it.

"Let me," Austin said. He kicked the door open with inhuman strength, and Fang charged through it, vanishing in an instant.

"Wait," Dan said, pulling his gun. "The mage demon might not be acting alone."

Fang was too intent on finding Princess to think coherently. And though he was part hellhound and had a huge heart and enormous will, his body was small. No match for a powerful demon. I couldn't leave him to face that danger alone, so I plunged after him. Dan cursed, but as I ran through the house, they followed me anyway.

DOWN HERE, Fang yelled.

I located the basement and thundered down the steps, holding Lola at the ready in case I needed her. Fang threw himself at another door, so I hurried forward to try the knob. It was unlocked so I opened it for him.

Princess met him there, and in the harsh glare of the single lightbulb, Princess and Fang rubbed up against each other in the doorway, their necks entwined, looking like a scruffier version of Lady and the Tramp. Cute.

YOU SAVED ME, YOU SAVED ME, Princess repeated over and over.

Fang was occupied with checking out her well-being and that of his unborn puppies, so I stepped over them to check out the rest of the room. Micah lay sprawled on his back on a dirty bare mattress, his wrists chained and bloody, his face bruised and swollen, and his eyes closed.

My heart skipped a beat and I came to an abrupt halt. "Ohmigod. Is he dead?" Had our gamble failed?

"No," Austin said behind me. "He's alive but unconscious."

"Where's Gwen?" Dan demanded, looking around.

As Ludwig and the others rushed to Micah's aid, I darted around the room looking for any sign of Gwen. Nothing. Suddenly fearing for my roommate, I glanced at Dan, appalled.

"Maybe she's upstairs," he said.

I nodded and we both ran back up the stairs. We split up, each taking half the house. In no time, we were back at the center.

"Find anything?" Dan asked, looking frantic.

"Nothing. You?"

He held out the fabric he had clutched in his hand. "I found her scrubs. And more women's clothing." His expression was tortured, as if he were imagining all sorts of horrible reasons why Asmodeus would buy her clothes.

"Don't think about it," I told him. "Princess might know where she is."

We rushed back downstairs. Everyone was hovering around Micah, who looked like he was starting to come around. Pia unlocked his cuffs and chains.

"She found the keys on a hook upstairs," David explained. "Did you find your roommate?"

"No." I knelt down next to where Fang and Princess looked like they were stuck together with superglue. "Princess, do you know where Gwen is?"

The spaniel turned sad eyes to me. SHE IS NOT GWEN.

"Huh? Who isn't Gwen?" I asked.

GWEN ISN'T GWEN.

What did that mean? I turned to Fang to ask if he understood, when I saw the Memory Eater kneel next to Micah. "Stop her," I yelled. I didn't know what she planned to do to him, but it couldn't be good.

"It's okay," David said soothingly. "Micah's coming around. She can read his memories to see what happened."

The woman leaned over Micah and held her bony hands about a foot from Micah's head, as if cupping an invisible sphere about his head. Everyone else backed away.

"Tell us what Princess means," David urged.

The rest of us watched the Memory Eater intently, but no one seemed willing to go any closer to the creep show.

"She . . . isss . . . Liiilith," the Memory Eater gasped out.

"Please, concentrate," I begged her. "Tell us what that means. Our friend's life is at stake."

She took a deep breath and seemed to settle down into herself. Bowing her head, she spoke, and her voice came out sounding less crazy. "Asmodeus has the power . . . to bring spirits . . . from the other side."

"You mean he brought one over?" I asked, confused.

"Yesss."

"Did he put that spirit inside Gwen?" Ludwig asked, his lips compressed in a line as if he suspected something but didn't want to say it aloud.

"Yesss."

"Gwen is possessed," Ludwig explained. "And the mage demon controls the spirit inside. Whose name, apparently, is Lilith."

Ludwig had to be wrong. Gwen couldn't be possessed, could she?

"But you can get her out again," Dan said, grabbing my arm. "Right?"

The Memory Eater took a deep breath. "There is mooore."

"What?" I demanded. It couldn't get any worse, could it?

"She isss . . . vampiiire."

Everyone gasped this time.

"No," I said, backing away. "That can't be true. That's not true, is it?" I asked Micah, pleading with him to deny this horrible thing.

"Yes," Micah said weakly from the mattress. "Gwen is possessed by an evil spirit who turned her into a vampire."

My knees gave way and I collapsed onto the floor. "No."

Chapter Twenty-Two

Ohmigod. How could this happen to Gwen? She was the nicest, most generous person I knew. And the most innocent. She didn't deserve this. Nausea churned through me, along with searing guilt. This was my fault. If she hadn't been associated with me, none of this would have happened. I turned my face toward Dan, looking for . . . something. Forgiveness, understanding?

His face was pale with shock and his mouth opened and closed several times before he finally came out with, "Can she be changed back?"

"I'm afraid not," Austin said. "We've been looking for a way to reverse the effects of vampirism for a very long time, but our efforts have only led to the person becoming permanently dead. Or worse."

"What's worse?" Dan asked, looking incredulous.

Austin grimaced. "Half-dead, half-alive. Mindless. Zombielike."

I gulped, swallowing hard. Being a vampire suddenly sounded like it wasn't so bad.

"Are you sure—" Dan began.

Ludwig cut him off. "Even if we could, don't forget she's possessed by an evil spirit. She's no longer the Gwen you knew."

Dan turned to me. "But you talked to her on the phone."

"That was Lilith," Micah said, rising from the mattress, looking a little shaky. "Asmodeus wanted you to believe it was Gwen so you'd rush in to exchange the books without thinking."

The Memory Eater pointed at Austin. "Dawn . . . comes."

Austin looked a little creeped out, but nodded. "I need to find a safe place soon."

With fists clenched and mouth set in a grim line, Dan said, "I don't give a damn about your needs. I'm going to wait right here for her to come back. I'll take Gwen home and figure something out."

Micah shook his head. "You won't be able to. Lilith will fight you."

Austin added, "They won't come back here. This place is

obviously either rented or abandoned. Once Val doesn't show up to the rendezvous, he'll figure out what happened."

Dan's face scrunched in a kind of agony and he grabbed the discarded chains, hauled the heavy things up and swung them at the wall. The crashing, clanking sound of metal against wood was horrendous and the chain left huge dents in the studs.

WELL, THAT'S ONE WAY TO LET YOUR AGGRESSIONS OUT, Fang said. It wasn't so much snarky as sad. Fang liked Gwen, too.

Dan reared back to swing them again, but Austin stopped him with a hand on his. "Why don't you all come to my rooms at the blood bank?"

I nodded. "Yes, let's go. Asmodeus will be able to sense the books if he gets within five hundred feet of them. Your building isn't that tall, but your room is almost on the top floor and it'll make it harder to sense them there. Besides, the security is excellent."

Austin didn't take his eyes off Dan. "We'll be able to see anyone coming up the stairs or elevator and we can plan how to get your sister back to you."

Dan stood for a moment, his head bowed, then nodded. He dropped the chains and ran a hand over his face, looking resigned and defeated. "I'm out of my depth here," he admitted. "I don't understand your world."

"It's okay. We'll find a way to bring her back," I told him. I hoped. "Come on."

He gave one decisive nod of his head, and we all headed for the cars, David promising to follow us back to the blood bank.

Micah and Princess rode in the backseat with Fang and me. As the two hellhounds snuggled together, I said to Micah, "Can you tell us what happened? What made him kidnap the two of you?" Hearing the story would help us focus and we might learn something useful.

Micah told us the story, obviously blaming himself for everything that had happened to Gwen. Dan didn't disagree, just remained stoic and silent. Maybe he needed someone to blame.

DON'T WORRY, Fang said. KNOWING DAN, HE'S FOUND REASONS TO LAY THIS ON EVERYONE.

In my case, it was true. Why hadn't I anticipated something like this? Why hadn't I taken the mage demon–locator spell the first time the books offered it? Why hadn't I warned Dan that Gwen might need more protection?

STOP IT, Fang said. YOU DID WHAT YOU COULD. IT'S NOT YOUR

FAULT SOME IDIOT MAGE DEMON IS LUSTING FOR POWER. DON'T USE YOUR ENERGY TO BEAT YOURSELF UP. FUNNEL IT INTO FINDING GWEN.

Good advice, though not all that easy to put into practice.

When Micah finished his story, Dan said, "Tell us everything you know about this guy who calls himself Asmodeus."

Micah did so, thoroughly, finishing as we arrived back at the blood bank.

Dan twisted around in the front seat to give Micah a piercing glare. "Tell me the truth. Will he hurt her?"

Micah shook his head. "I don't know for sure, but I can't think of any reason why he would. She's his slave and will do his bidding. She's more valuable to him unharmed."

Dan nodded and returned to his thoughts, that grim look on his face.

Austin had called ahead to let the vampires know they were about to be invaded by a horde of demons. Lisette agreed to host the San Antonio Demon Underground leader and his entourage, so we had no problems going up in the elevator.

Once we were all assembled in the living room of Austin's suite, and the metal shades clanged shut against the coming rising sun, Micah took charge. "What we need is a way to bring him to us, at a place and time of *our* choosing."

I explained to Micah that we'd already ruled out using the finder or a prophecy. I hated to suggest it, but . . . "Maybe we could use Jack's funeral?" I suppressed a twinge of guilt. "He wouldn't mind. His entire life was spent protecting the books." Now, he could do that even in death. "Asmodeus will expect us to be there, and he won't question the presence of additional demons."

"Funeral?" Micah repeated, looking concerned.

Oh, crap. He didn't know about Jack. I explained it quickly.

Looking pained, Micah said, "It isn't necessary to use the funeral. I know you want to honor Jack in the right way, so we'll do that later. Instead, we'll lure Asmodeus to the Naming Ritual David requested."

"Are you sure?" I asked. There was no guarantee Micah would still be leader after that.

"I'm sure," Micah said with finality. "And if he doesn't show for the Naming Ritual, we can set a trap at the funeral."

Dan perked up. "That could work. We could deliberately leave Val alone so he'll think she's unguarded and vulnerable. I think he'll take the bait."

"How do we get the word to Asmodeus so he'll show up?" David asked doubtfully.

I shrugged. "He obviously knows where the demon hangouts are. We'll put out the word to all the demons we know and he's bound to hear about it."

I checked my phone, surprised by the date. "Today is Christmas Eve. Can we get enough people to attend a Naming Ritual today?"

WE HAVE TO, Princess suddenly said. THE BAD MAN WANTS TO BE LIKE GWEN.

Fang translated. PRINCESS HEARD ASMODEUS THINK THAT HE WANTS TO TURN HIMSELF INTO A VAMPIRE, LIKE LILITH DID. TO BE EVEN MORE STRONG AND POWERFUL.

Austin looked puzzled. "If vampires go crazy when they drink demon blood, what happens to demons who are turned into vampires?"

Whatever happened, it couldn't be good. Luckily, Gwen was fully human, so we didn't have to worry about the mixing of the blood.

"The process of combining the two does one of two things," Micah said, looking sick. "It usually drives the demons crazy as well as the vampires, and they turn into raving beasts. Most of the time, they accidentally kill themselves by wandering into the sunlight."

"What's the other thing?" I asked impatiently.

Micah seemed reluctant to respond, and wouldn't meet my eyes.

"Telll theeem," came the creepy voice from the bundle of bones huddled in the corner.

YES, TELL THEM, Fang said, sounding grim.

Micah rubbed his hand across his face and sighed. "It's rare, but sometimes, you get something else."

Impatient with his reluctance, I said, "Come on, spit it out. What do you get?"

"A . . . Memory Eater," he said reluctantly. "They're able to read minds and memories with the vampire part, while having the added ability of being able to remove those memories. But the two sides are constantly at war within."

We all turned to stare at the one in the corner. Ohmigod. No wonder she never seemed quite sane. "You mean the Memory Eater isn't a type of demon?"

"Yes and no. She had demon powers once, but I don't know what they were. She rides on the edge all the time, balancing the demon and vampire sides of her nature. If she lets one have too much control over the other, she slips further into madness."

"Is the reverse true?" Austin asked, his eyes narrowed. "Can some vampires become Memory Eaters by drinking blood from a demon?"

Micah shook his head. "I don't know, but our history doesn't mention the possibility."

Austin's jaw looked like a block of granite. "We never knew."

I could see why they wouldn't tell the vampires. Any vampire who turned a demon into a Memory Eater wouldn't have survived with his sanity intact. I hadn't realized how much Micah had to worry about as leader. Maybe there was a good reason for keeping some secrets.

Tension rose as Micah and Austin stared at each other.

Ludwig broke it when he stood. "So, the overwhelming odds are good that Asmodeus will be driven crazy, right? Problem solved. Why disrupt his plans?"

"You don't understand," Micah said, seeming grateful for the change in subject. "Asmodeus brought Lilith's spirit into this world, and he's the only one who can let her go. So, if he's killed or goes mad before he does that, we won't be able to get Lilith out of Gwen."

NOT GOOD, Fang said. I WANT GWEN BACK.

ME, TOO, Princess said in a small voice.

We all did.

"What about that demon-exorcising spell?" Austin asked. "Would that allow you to free Gwen?"

"I don't know," I admitted. "Maybe. Will the spell treat Lilith's spirit as a demon and exorcise it? I have no way of knowing."

Austin nodded slowly. "And if you exorcised Asmodeus's demon, it would leave him incapable of freeing her."

"We can't chance it," Dan said. "We have to capture him, not kill him, and force him to free Gwen." He turned to Micah. "Are you sure he hasn't tried to become a vampire yet?"

"Not when I saw him last. He had Lilith knock me out, then he was on his way to meet Val to get the books."

Oh, crap. "He knows by now that we rescued you, and that we know Lilith has control of Gwen. Nothing is stopping him from getting turned right now."

Dan whipped his head around to stare at Austin. "Is that true?"

"Possibly," Austin said. He asked Micah, "Who turned Lilith?"

"She found some random vamp under Congress Avenue Bridge."

Austin relaxed a little. "Some hang out there at night, but they won't be there during the day. And none of us will let others know the locations of our daytime resting places."

"What about here, at the blood bank?" David asked. "There are obviously vampires here."

"They don't see clients during the day here," Austin explained. "And none of them would turn a stranger simply because they ask it."

Not good enough. "But what's to keep *Lilith* from turning him?" I asked.

Austin looked surprised. "I thought you knew. She can't. She's too newly turned to be able to turn someone else, especially during daylight hours."

I'd never learned the details of how someone got turned into a bloodsucker. Mostly, I just made the undead very *dead* dead. But I was *really* glad to hear that.

"So the odds are good that he won't be turned anytime during the day today?" Dan asked, looking intense.

"Right," Austin confirmed. "But once the sun goes down . . ."

THE POOP HITS THE ROTARY BLADES, Fang said.

An understatement.

"Okay," Dan said decisively. "We plan the ritual for today. Right after sunset so he won't have time to get turned and can bring Gwen with him. Can you make arrangements that fast?"

"Tessa can," I said. I had faith in Tessa's ability to make just about anything happen. "She's the ultimate organizer."

"Even making a ritual happen today?" David asked doubtfully.

"You don't know Tessa," Micah said. "I'll call her. If I can borrow your phone?"

I handed it to him and he went into the corner to make a low-voiced call to his assistant.

Pia talked at David with her hands, and he nodded. "We'll work on getting the word out to the Demon Underground in both cities. And let a few we trust know that we'd like a good turnout . . . and why. They'll come."

"Asmodeus better damned well come," Dan said. "And when he does, what's the plan to take him alive?"

I raised my hand. "That's my department. Micah said he doesn't have a shield like Trevor's, so I should be able to use Lola on him." So long as I still had control of her, that was. "Then I can force him to get rid of Lilith."

"What if Lilith tries to control your mind?" Dan asked.

I grinned. "It won't work. If she tries to control me, it will allow me to read her mind, know what they're planning."

"What if he tries for you first?" Micah asked, rejoining us. "He's awfully handy with that dart gun and the Perdo."

"I'll take care of that with a vest that will stop any darts," Dan said. "But Lilith is in control of Gwen's body. How do we take her without hurting Gwen?" He looked at Micah. "Can you do that?"

"Not while Asmodeus is still in control of Lilith as the demon who brought her here. No incubus can."

That left David out, too.

"I can help with that," Austin said.

"How?" Dan asked doubtfully.

"Superior strength. She won't be used to her new abilities yet, and I still outweigh her, even if she has figured out how to use them. I'll hold onto her until Val forces Asmodeus to change Gwen back."

I nodded slowly. "Thanks for offering to help, Austin. This could actually work."

He tipped his hat at me. "Consider this a favor returned. Besides, once we deal with the mage demon, you can finish helping the Movement find the person creating chupacabras."

"What?" Dan asked. "How is that pertinent?"

We explained to everyone what we'd learned about the chupacabra menace. I finished with, "The only problem is, we don't know where they're coming from or how they're being made."

"I think we just learned the second part tonight," Austin drawled. When we all looked at him questioningly, he added, "Someone is forcing vampires to turn demons. Mixing their blood makes victims of them both."

Now that he said it, it was obvious. "They're crazed so they're attacking anything that moves." And it explained the random piles of ash we'd found—a demon-turned-vampire would be too crazed to realize sunlight was dangerous.

"Everyone in the New Blood Movement was warned," Austin added. "Lisette's people wouldn't deliberately drink blood from a demon or turn one. They knew what would happen."

"And a demon wouldn't willingly be turned into a vampire," Micah added.

The light dawned. "They'd do it if they were forced to."

"Yes, but who could force—" Austin broke off and stared at me.

"I could," I confirmed. "The missing vamps were all male, right?

And if I could—"

"—Dina could," everyone else finished in unison.

And Dina's house was very near the park. *Didn't you read that in her mind?* I asked Fang.

NOPE. I CAN ONLY READ SURFACE THOUGHTS. AND WHEN I WAS WITH YOU, SHE WAS ONLY THINKING ABOUT KIDNAPPING, SHADE AND THE BOOKS.

That's right. Fang wasn't with us when I asked her about the chupacabras. So it probably was her. But she could only control men. Why would she toss away her own people like used tissues?" Then again, it would explain why I'd found Adam Bukowski's wallet under that rock, and maybe what had happened to Blaine Williamson. Not to mention the ash piles.

"But why?" Ludwig asked.

"To cement her power base," Micah said with a grim look. "She's power hungry. She wants to control the women too, so she's trying to make her *own* Memory Eater from a man she can control. If she can, she'll be able to rule with an iron fist."

"Yesss," came confirmation from the nightmare in the corner.

Micah looked pained. "There is a ritual to identify demons who have the potential to become Memory Eaters. The demon then has the choice whether to accept the role or not. But most soothsayers, who have all control over the rituals, refuse to subject anyone to that." He nodded toward the skeletal woman. "This one has been on the job for hundreds of years."

The poor woman.

Suddenly, the Memory Eater was standing before me, grabbing my shoulders, staring into my eyes. "You seee nooow. Releassse meee," she insisted.

Obviously, she wanted me to end her torment, kill her. "No. I—I can't." I didn't kill the good guys. And no matter how monstrous she appeared, she was on our side.

She seemed to make an effort to bring her mind into focus. In a barely audible whisper, she said, "I can offer . . . much. Remove . . . your memories of . . . what your family . . . did to you, remove their memories . . . of you. Just . . . release me from . . . this nightmare."

Shocked, I backed away from her. This woman was powerful. And very, very scary.

Micah stood and laid a hand on her shoulder. "Come," he said gently, and I felt him use his incubus powers. "Rest in the corner until we're done."

Sudden realization made sheer panic stab through me. Ohmigod. Was Dina planning to turn *Shade* into a Memory Eater?

Chapter Twenty-Three

I didn't realize I'd said that aloud until everyone stared at me.

"You can't think that way, Val," Micah said.

I not only could, I did. "He's in danger. Right now." He might even already be insane and a vampire.

"No," Micah said in a soothing tone. "You heard Austin. She won't be able to find any vampires until it turns dark again."

I glared at him. "What about the ones she's *already* used? There's still at least one out there unaccounted for."

"The ash . . ." Austin protested.

"Weren't necessarily all Lisette's vampires," I reminded him. "They could have been demons-turned-vampire." I stopped to think for a moment. "And Dina might come to the blood bank to try and force one of them to help her. That's probably where she's been getting Lisette's vamps, anyway." And they'd made it incredibly easy for the succubus to find them, enthrall them, and use them.

Austin nodded grimly. "But she won't be able to do that until nightfall."

"I'll take care of it," Micah said. "I'll let her know I'm in town, and that she risks my wrath and the touch of the Memory Eater if she does *anything* to harm him. Dina fears her."

"That's fine," I said. "But why the hell should we leave him there any longer? We know what she is. We know what she could do to him. We have to get him out of there." Whether he wanted to come or not.

"No, darlin'," Austin said. "You can't let her know we've figured out what she's doing. Wait until dark, and the entire New Blood Movement will help you take her down and rescue Shade."

"But it might be too late," I protested. Shade was in danger. Couldn't they see that? "Once it turns dark, what will stop her from forcing a vampire to turn him?"

Dan looked up sharply. "Gwen is in more danger. She's the priority here, and you're the only one who can stop Asmodeus and force him to free her. You need to work on that."

166

"I'll tell Alejandro and Lisette what we've learned," Austin said. "And they'll round up some folks to send to Dina's house as soon as it turns dark."

But I wanted to *be* there, to ensure Shade stayed safe.

You can't be in two places at once, Fang said, sounding regretful.

"I know that," I snapped at him. But how could I possibly choose between them? Save my roommate and my only real nondemon friend? Or Shade, my first and only lover, my very good friend?

My gut roiled with indecision.

You know what the choice has to be, Fang said, looking up at me with sad eyes.

I buried my fingers in his fur. Yes, I did, unfortunately. Gwen was an innocent in all this, and Dan was right when he said I was the best one, the only one, to stop Asmodeus. I blinked back tears and glared fiercely at Austin. "You swear they'll be at her house at sundown?"

"As soon as they can make it," he promised. "I'll arrange it now."

That would have to do. "Okay," I said. But if anything happened to Shade, I'd never forgive myself.

As Austin and Micah excused themselves to make phone calls, Dan's phone rang. He glanced at it. "It's that same disposable cell number," he said. "Why would Asmodeus call me?"

I was baffled for a moment, then realized. "It's not him. It's Gwen. I mean Lilith. She doesn't know that you're with us."

"What would she want of me?" Dan asked.

"I don't know," I said impatiently. "Answer it."

He frowned but went out into the hall to answer the phone. We all waited impatiently for him to come back. When he did, the expression on his face was grim, but satisfied.

"What did she want?" I asked.

"Lilith pretended to be Gwen and asked if I knew where you were. I didn't let her know I was on to her. I told her you were in Austin and that I didn't know where you were right now, but that you'd be at the ritual tonight."

"Good," Micah said. "So the trap is set."

We finalized the plans as much as we could, made arrangements to meet back at Austin's room later, then split up to eat, sleep and get whatever we needed for tonight. The ones who'd driven up from San Antonio went to the floor Jack and I had stayed on earlier. I didn't care to go back there, and since I couldn't get much higher in the city and away from the mage demon than Austin's suite, I chose to stay with him. In one of the *other* bedrooms.

My sleep was restless, haunted by dreams of everything that could possibly go wrong. And in every one of them, I screwed up, ensuring Gwen and Shade both died horribly.

I woke in a cold sweat in midafternoon and decided that going back to sleep wasn't an option. The vampires had excellent time-controlled black-out shades on the windows, so no light penetrated into the room. I turned the bedside lamp on low and saw that Fang and Princess were curled up together at the foot of the bed, snoring softly. Well, at least if nothing else had turned out right, this had. I was happy for them.

I used the time and the quiet to stare at the ceiling and think. I hadn't had the luxury to do much of that lately and it felt strange, and good.

Heck, who was I kidding? I was more of a doer than a thinker. The problem was that lately it seemed like I was in constant react mode, always responding to other people's agendas, other people's wants and needs. When had that started? Oh yeah, when my parents kicked me out of the house a couple of months ago.

And *that* was why I didn't like to do much thinking. That memory still hurt. No matter that I finally understood why they had done it, no matter that our relationship was getting back on an even keel. I still craved my old life. It seemed so simple, so uncomplicated compared to this existence. No responsibilities, no contracts with bloodsuckers, no touchy ex-boyfriends, no—

NO FAITHFUL HELLHOUNDS, Fang put in sleepily.

I chuckled. "You're the best part of my new life," I whispered. Fang and Shade. At least, Shade used to be. Plus having found the Demon Underground and learning there were other freaks like me didn't suck either.

Fang moved over to snuggle against my side. YOU CAN'T GO BACK.

"I know," I said regretfully, stroking his wispy ears. But I wished I could. Back to before Shade met Dina, before he had turned so cold. What had happened there? It seemed out of character, but I had to admit I really didn't understand men. "I wish I could combine the best of the past and the present."

Then again, maybe I could. The Memory Eater's offer came back to me. She could make my parents forget they'd ever kicked me out, make my half sister forget she was ever stupid enough to want to be just like me, make me forget the pain of their rejection. Everything would be like it was. Almost.

IS THAT WHAT YOU REALLY WANT? Fang asked.

"It's tempting." Very, very tempting.

AND ALL YOU HAVE TO DO TO GET IT IS AGREE TO KILL THE WOMAN.

I sighed. Yeah, that was the problem. "After hundreds of years of being half-sane, wouldn't you want to end your life?"

I DO JUST FINE.

I stared at him. "You couldn't be hundreds of years old. Though the half-sane part I'll grant you."

GEE, THANKS.

I noticed he hadn't answered my unspoken question. "You're not that old, are you?" How long did hellhounds live, anyway? The encyclopedia didn't say.

NOPE, he said lazily. JUST TRYING TO DISTRACT YOU.

It worked, too. I checked the clock. About three hours until sundown. Maybe I could make good use of it. I rolled over and got out of bed.

Fang raised his head to look at me. WHERE ARE YOU GOING?

"To take a shower. After that, I'm not sure," I hedged.

He laid his head back down. LET ME KNOW IF YOU NEED BACKUP TO RESCUE SHADE.

"I wasn't thinking that," I protested.

WELL, YOU WERE GOING TO, REAL SOON. AND EVEN THOUGH WE BOTH KNOW IT WOULD BE A STUPID MISTAKE, YOU'RE PROBABLY GOING TO TRY IT ANYWAY.

Okay, maybe I *was* thinking about sneaking out and rescuing Shade before I had to meet everyone back here. But how could that be a mistake? Just because I rescued him didn't mean Dina would know we were on to her. And maybe Shade would even be grateful.

Fang snorted. SELF-DELUSION IS THE WORST KIND.

"Oh, shut up," I said. I didn't need a puny hellhound acting as my conscience.

PUNY? Fang said. *PUNY?* ARE YOU SURE YOU WANT TO GO THERE?

I ignored him and took a long, hot shower in the adjoining bath, enjoying the hell out of it. When I was done, I dressed and returned to the darkened bedroom.

HAVE YOU COME TO YOUR SENSES YET? Fang asked. When I didn't answer, he said, GUESS NOT. WELL, IN THAT CASE, I'M COMING WITH YOU.

"You don't have to," I protested. I didn't want to hear his complaining all the way there and back.

SOMEONE HAS TO SAVE YOU FROM YOURSELF, he said and jumped down off the bed.

Well, he was great backup. Not that I'd need a whole lot against a lightweight like Dina. I opened the bedroom door, intending to tiptoe out of the suite. I didn't want to wake Austin and answer more pointed questions.

Too late. A light came on, blinding me, and Austin's voice stopped me in my tracks. "Where do you think you're going?" he drawled.

I held a hand up to block out the glare of the lamp. "Just going to . . . you know, get something to eat." Noticing the bedclothes and Austin's bare chest, I asked, "What are *you* doing sleeping on the couch?"

"Keepin' an eye on you." He stretched lazily. "I thought you might try to sneak out and play hero to Shade's damsel in distress."

Annoyed by his attempt to make Shade appear a wuss, I snapped, "It's none of your business."

"Actually, it is." He stood up, and I was glad to see he was still wearing his jeans. "It's just as much my business as yours. And I promised Micah I'd call him if you tried anything stupid."

Fang chuckled in my mind. EVERYONE HAS YOUR NUMBER.

Crap. I hated being that transparent. "Okay, fine," I spat out. "I won't go to Dina's. But I can't just sit around here and wait for something to happen. I need to do something." I flopped down in a side chair, feeling sulky.

Austin sighed and sat down again. "Darlin', I know you're chafing at the bit, but the plan we came up with is a good one. You need to have patience, let it play out."

"Do Lisette's vampires know Dina's a succubus?"

"They do," he confirmed. "And Lisette is bringing only women to confront her."

"They know not to hurt Shade, don't they?"

"Of course," he said soothingly. "Don't worry so much. Everything will be fine."

I shook my head then rose to pace. "I don't know. There's

something wrong. Something else that's bugging me, about how her men act. If I go there, confront her, maybe I'll be able to figure it out." I turned to Fang. "You said it yourself at the club, there's something odd with Dina."

I SAID SHE WAS HIDING SOMETHING. NOW WE KNOW WHAT THAT WAS.

"Not necessarily. There's something else. How can she keep so many men on a string?" I guess I could if I wanted, but it seemed like a heck of a lot of work.

Austin grinned. "Well, obviously, she keeps them all very happy. I reckon I understand why."

"Wait. That's it."

IT IS? Fang said. WHAT'D HE SAY?

I pointed at Austin. "You just said she keeps them all very happy. But, what about when she sleeps? When they're not in her vicinity? How is she keeping the men all silent about this? Surely some of them object to her control and would complain or get the hell out of there when she sleeps. Wouldn't you?" Wouldn't Shade?

He nodded slowly. "I would. What do you think is happening? Do you think she's threatening them?"

"I don't know. But she shouldn't be able to do what she's doing. The question is, *how* is she doing it?" I continued pacing, hoping it would help me think. "I need more information."

"If this is an excuse to show up on Dina's doorstep—"

"It's not. I think I need to talk to someone else. Someone who knows Dina but has no reason to love her."

"A female demon?" Austin ventured.

"Got it in one. Remember, Beth didn't like Dina at all. Maybe I can probe a little, ask more questions, see if she can tell me what's different." I glanced at the clock. "I still have time to get there and back before we head out to the ritual."

"Are you sure that's the only place you're going?" Austin asked.

Damn it, why was he bugging me about this? "That's what I said," I snapped, more harshly than I intended.

WHOA, BABE, DIAL IT BACK A BIT.

I stopped and ran a hand over my face. "Sorry, I'm just antsy. I need to do something, not sit and wait for something else horrible to happen to my friends. Look, if you don't believe me, you can come with me."

Fang chuckled in my mind. NOW THERE'S A SAFE OFFER.

Austin raised an eyebrow. "A little matter of some sunshine."

"Okay, then I'll take Micah along."

"Good enough. And good luck." Austin tossed me the keys to one of the cars.

"Thanks. I'll be back in time. Don't worry."

He crossed to open the door for me. He leaned one arm up against the jamb and grinned down at me. "I never worry about you, darlin'. Whenever you fall in manure, you always manage to come out smelling fresh as a daisy."

I didn't know how to take that, but Lola kind of wanted to get a little closer, question him some more, fall into that seductive cowboy charm.

Nope. Didn't want to fall into *that* manure pile. I backed off hastily and, feeling foolish, made some kind of lame wave and got the heck out of there.

Fang poked me in the calf. HE'S FLIRTING WITH YOU.

So? That didn't mean I planned to flirt back. Talk about an age difference. Couple hundred years, at least. Shade was the guy for me . . . if he still wanted me.

Chapter Twenty-Four

This time, Fang and I took the elevator. I glanced down at him. "Aren't you worried about Princess waking and finding you gone?"

NOPE. SHE ALREADY WOKE AND I TOLD HER WHAT WAS GOING ON AND TO STAY IN BED.

I grinned. Fang was going to be an overprotective father, too, I bet.

He snorted. OVERPROTECTIVE? LOOK AT WHAT HAPPENED TO PRINCESS ALREADY. I CAN'T BE TOO PROTECTIVE.

"Point taken."

As promised, I stopped by Micah's room, but tapped quietly on the door so I wouldn't wake him if he was still asleep.

YEAH, KEEP TELLING YOURSELF THAT, Fang said with a snort. BUT WE BOTH KNOW YOU HOPE HE DOESN'T ANSWER THE DOOR.

Sheesh. Sometimes hellhounds were a pain in the butt.

BESIDES, I CAN HEAR WHAT HE'S THINKING. AUSTIN CALLED HIM. MICAH IS ALREADY UP AND DRESSED, AND HE'S COMING OUT TO MEET YOU NOW.

Make that *always* a pain in the butt.

Micah opened the door and had evidently borrowed some clothes because he wore black jeans and a long-sleeved black shirt. Very vampish. I totally understood why he wouldn't want to wear the clothes he'd been kidnapped in for a second longer than necessary. His face still looked battered, but freedom made him look a hundred times better.

"Where are we going?" he asked.

"To the house of a fire demon I met the other day, Beth Williamson. She doesn't like Dina much so she might be able to tell us a few things."

Micah nodded. "I've met Beth. I'll call her, make sure she's there and let her know that we're coming to see her."

"Why wouldn't she be there? It's Christmas Eve. Most people aren't working."

"Some people spend time with family and friends this time of year," he said drily. "Besides, it's polite."

I just shook my head as Micah made the call. When he finished, he said, "She's there, but she's having a tea at her house in about half an hour. When I explained the importance of it, she agreed to see us."

Good, 'cause I was going to see her whether she liked it or not.

We arrived at the same time as a guest did. Beth welcomed us and showed us into the living room where two ladies were already seated. This time, the seventies-decorated room was crowded with chairs, and a coffee table sat in the center loaded with lace, fussy ribbons and bows, as well as a pink floral-patterned china tea set. All four tea ladies looked so elegant and feminine, they made me feel kinda grungy in my T-shirt, jeans and vest.

"Can we speak to you privately?" I asked as Beth gestured Micah and me to join them.

"No need. We're all members of the Underground," she said with a tight smile.

The other three ladies nodded. But they all looked as stressed out as Beth sounded. What was going on here?

RELAX, Fang said. THEY'LL EXPLAIN WHEN THE REST ARRIVE.

Well, if Fang said it was okay, I'd wait for an explanation.

Beth introduced us, and the women were coolly polite to Micah and me, but friendly with Fang. At least he kept the silence from being too awkward while Beth welcomed two other women.

"You wanted to talk to me about something important?" Beth prompted after everyone was seated and all six women sat staring at us.

"Yes," Micah said, taking charge. "We're sorry to interrupt your celebration, but we have some questions we'd like to ask you."

They said nothing. Weird. Some even had hostility and distrust in their expressions as they stared at Micah. Was it his battered face? He did kind of look like a hoodlum.

IT'S OKAY, Fang broadcast to everyone. HE'S AN INCUBUS. A SUCCUBUS CAN'T CONTROL HIM.

Oh, they were worried about him being under Dina's control. A sigh of relief went through the group, though a couple of them looked startled at Fang's voice in their heads.

Beth gave a wry smile. "This isn't really a celebration. It's the only way we can get together without the men of the Underground wanting to come. The few who are left, anyway." She cut her eyes toward the explosion of femininity on the table. "The tea party theme wards them off."

Yeah, I could see how that would work. "I take it Dina wasn't invited," I said carefully.

"That bitch," one dark-haired woman said, twisting a tissue in her hands. "She has hold of our men and won't let them go. That's why we're meeting here today. We can't take it anymore, and we want to find a way to stop her."

I smiled. "Then we have the same goal. She has my boyfriend in her clutches, too."

Beth nodded. "We all have husbands, brothers, sons who have either turned against us or gone missing. Micah said you know something about that?"

"I'm afraid we have bad news," I said and glanced at Micah.

He told them what we'd figured out about Dina trying to make male demons into Memory Eaters, and the horrible consequences.

All the color drained from Beth's face. "You mean my brother—" She stopped herself, then said, "The missing men . . . they're all . . . dead?"

The rest looked as shocked as she, if not more so. "That's one possibility," I said gently.

An older woman glared at me through tear-filled eyes. "The only other possibility is madness. How is that better?"

I hadn't said it was better or worse, but the poor woman needed to vent, and I was a convenient target, so I let it slide.

"Will they be able to recover?" another woman asked.

Micah shook his head. "I don't know. But, to be completely honest, I doubt it."

Blunt, but I had to admit that if I were in their place right now, I'd want to know the truth, too. Not listen to namby-pamby platitudes.

THEY NEEDED TO KNOW, Fang confirmed. AND THEY TRUST MICAH EVEN MORE NOW FOR TELLING THEM THE TRUTH.

That was good, at least.

"I knew it," one woman said—Annie, I think her name was. Petite and fragile looking, she didn't look old enough to have come into any powers. But I knew all too well that appearances could be deceiving. "When Dina wouldn't let any women but her and me into the Naming Ritual which produced her name as leader, I knew something hinky was going on."

"You're a soothsayer?" I asked. At her nod, I added, "Of course. You wouldn't remember what you said while in a prophetic trance. She could have lied about whatever you said."

"Right. And the men present all swear I chose Dina." Annie shook her head. "It just doesn't feel right."

Which led to my next question. "That's true," I said. "But a succubus or incubus can control the opposite sex only while in their proximity, not while they're unconscious or sleeping. Dina should have lost control of them then, and they'd have regained their senses."

"Wrong," the older woman said. "Once she got her hooks into the men who were at the ritual, she had them twenty-four/seven."

"That's not possible," I protested. I mean, I wasn't Super Succubus or anything, but if I couldn't do it, I didn't know how she could.

"It's true," she insisted. The rest nodded to confirm she was telling the truth.

Were they all deliberately deluding themselves? I glanced at Micah for help.

He frowned. "Has she always had this ability?"

Annie shook her head. "Just for a few months. After our former leader died—under suspicious circumstances, I might add—Dina arranged for the secret Naming Ritual. It's just too convenient that she was named leader."

"I've heard of a way an incubus or succubus could extend their power," Micah said thoughtfully. "But I always thought it was a myth."

"What?" we asked in unison.

"My father used to tell me stories about an amulet, a stone, that would extend our powers. He said all you had to do was concentrate on the person you wanted to control and you could implant commands they would obey even beyond your normal range. Kind of like hypnosis, and it would work for a very long time." He grimaced. "Of course, in the bedtime stories he told me, the succubi and incubi only used it for good."

DINA PROBABLY HEARD IT AS A BEDTIME STORY, TOO, Fang said to everyone.

"But how would she have found such a thing?" I asked, bewildered. I wouldn't know where to start to look.

"I think I know," the older woman said. "Dina and her father were estranged. He was in another state—Montana, I think. She didn't even attend the funeral when he died. But a couple of weeks after that, she got something in the mail from him. I remember hearing her say it was the only good thing he ever gave her."

I leaned forward, intent. If Dina had this thing, I had to get it away from her. "Do you know what it was?"

"She didn't say."

"What else do you remember?" I asked Micah. "Did the story say what it looked like?"

He shrugged. "No, but an amulet is usually worn as a piece of jewelry, something held close to the body. She'd probably wear it all the time."

"The crystal," I exclaimed. "Every time I saw her, she was fondling that crystal teardrop." I thought she'd been trying to draw attention to her boobs, but instead, she was controlling male boobs. "How long has she been wearing it?"

"A few months," one of the women said, and the rest agreed. Coincidence? Not.

The dark-haired woman with the shredded tissue stood up, looking determined. "We've got to get it away from her. Smash that thing to smithereens."

"We'll take care of that," I said firmly.

"When?" Beth asked, and the others looked hopeful.

"Tonight, right after sundown," I told them. "We have the help of some female vampires to take her then. They won't be swayed by her, and we'll make sure they get her crystal."

They appeared doubtful, and Micah added, "Val's right. The local vein of vampires has just as much incentive to want her stopped as we do."

Yeah. No more Dina, no more chupacabras. And they could move on with their legislation.

"Will they kill her?" one hard-faced woman asked.

That idea even took me aback. "Uh, I don't know. Depends on whether she resists or not, I guess." Though it would solve some problems if they did ensure she never saw the light of day again. Wonder if I could plant a tiny suggestion in their ears.

THAT WOULD TEACH HER FOR STEALING YOUR BOYFRIEND, Fang said with amusement.

Oh, shut up. I wasn't going to do that, and he knew it.

"What about the men under her control?" Annie asked. "The vampires won't hurt them, will they?"

"I'll ask them not to," I promised. Though I couldn't swear it wouldn't happen, not if Dina forced them to attack the vampires on her behalf. I turned to Micah. "What happens to the men if Dina dies?

Will the stone still control them?"

"I'm not sure, but let's hope her control would end with her death."

Yes. Then Shade could return to his senses. I hoped.

"Why aren't *you* helping the vampires with Dina?" Beth asked.

"There's a rogue mage demon in town who has kidnapped one of our people. We set up a Naming Ritual tonight to lure him in." I explained the situation to them. "You're welcome to come, but if you do, be aware there may be danger."

"I'll help," Beth said instantly. "It's the least I can do after what you've promised to do for us."

"Thank you." A fire demon might come in handy.

"Me, too," Annie said.

"Are you sure that's wise?" I asked. The soothsayer looked like she'd break in two if someone looked at her.

"I'm sure," she said firmly. "Where is it?"

Micah glanced at me. "Tessa was going to text you and David on where we're holding it."

I pulled out my phone. She had. "She reserved a pavilion in Mountain View Park in the Spicewood Springs area. She sent a map." I opened it and showed it to them.

"Yes," Annie said. "I recognize the area. Just north of the Bull Creek greenbelt."

"Good," Micah said. "We set the time for an hour after sunset. The weather is supposed to be a little warmer than normal, with no rain. We expect the attack to come then."

"We'll be there," Beth promised.

"Thank you," Micah said. "Now, we'll leave you to your tea."

It was probably cold by now, but I'm sure they didn't care. Not when success was within their reach.

As I drove back to the blood bank, Micah asked, "Are you sure it's wise to have those women attend? They could get hurt."

"It's their choice, and I gave them the option to stay home," I reminded him. "You know, some of us frail womenfolk like to have a little more control over our destiny. We don't always want to leave it to you big, strong men to take care of us." I batted my eyes at him.

He grimaced. "That's not what I meant. You're trained and they're not. Aren't you worried about having to protect them?"

"Not really. We'll way outnumber Asmodeus and Lilith. The women will be fine."

"Ever heard that saying, 'No battle plan survives contact with the enemy'?" Micah muttered.

"Don't be such a negative nelly. Our plan will work."

It had to. I couldn't live with any other option.

Chapter Twenty-Five

Micah glanced at Val, who was concentrating on her driving. She might be completely certain everything was going to work out just the way they'd planned, but Micah wasn't so sure. Something was bound to go wrong.

"You don't have to go," Val said. "You can stay at the blood bank if you like."

What was that? Some kind of dig?

No, IT WAS A GENUINE OFFER, Fang told him. VAL KNOWS YOU'RE MORE OF A LOVER THAN A FIGHTER.

Micah firmed his jaw. Maybe that was part of the problem. Maybe that's what he needed to change. "I need to be there," he said with finality. With luck, no one would get killed.

Val shrugged. "Suit yourself."

They spent the rest of the trip back to the blood bank in silence. Micah had been given a lot of time to think in that basement, to ponder on what a good leader should be. His father had been charismatic and beloved, praised for bringing the Underground into the twenty-first century, for setting up the watcher system, and for creating positive relationships with the New Blood Movement and the Special Crimes Unit.

Micah had carried on with his father's legacy, following in his footsteps to strengthen the ties among demons and relationships with the outside world. He hadn't wanted to mess with what worked.

BUT IT DIDN'T WORK FOR EVERYONE, Fang said, obviously talking so only Micah could hear. SHARING WARM FUZZIES WITH BLOODSUCKERS IS OKAY, BUT WHAT GOOD IS IT IF YOUR PEOPLE DON'T FEEL SECURE?

Micah was beginning to believe Fang was right.

YOUR FATHER WAS A GOOD MAN, BUT HE GLOSSED OVER THAT PART OF HIS RESPONSIBILITIES.

Why didn't you tell me this before? he asked the hellhound.

I TRIED TO, BUT YOU WOULDN'T LISTEN. YOU WEREN'T READY

TO . . . UNTIL NOW.

Yeah, the past few days had brought it home to him. Micah hadn't been able to keep the club profitable, hadn't been able to prevent the mage demon from kidnapping and enslaving Gwen, hadn't even been able to keep himself safe.

Fang snorted. YOUR FATHER WAS NO BUSINESS GENIUS, AND HE WOULDN'T HAVE BEEN ABLE TO KEEP HIMSELF OR GWEN SAFE EITHER.

What do you mean? Hadn't his father done an excellent job of running things?

SOMETIMES. BUT IF YOUR FATHER WASN'T GOOD AT SOMETHING, HE IGNORED IT OR PRETENDED EVERYTHING WAS HUNKY-DORY. THE CLUB DIDN'T DO AS WELL UNDER HIS GUIDANCE AS YOU THINK. OR THE UNDERGROUND.

Well, that was a revelation. Micah had always thought his father was the perfect leader. Why had no one told him this before?

NO ONE WANTS TO SPEAK ILL OF THE DEAD . . . ESPECIALLY TO HIS SON.

Except David and Pia. They'd tried to pound some sense into Micah's thick head and Micah had ignored them. Hadn't wanted to accept that his father hadn't been a visionary, because that meant he'd wasted his life in service to an ideal that hurt the people who trusted him.

YOU ARE YOUR FATHER'S SON, BUT YOU HAVE YOUR OWN STRENGTHS. LIKE COMPASSION, HONESTY, INTEGRITY, AND COURAGE. NOT TO MENTION A WILLINGNESS TO TAKE RESPONSIBILITY FOR YOUR OWN ACTIONS AND LEARN FROM YOUR MISTAKES.

Maybe. Micah appreciated the pep talk, but he wasn't convinced. Trust wasn't easily earned after you'd lost it. The hell of it was, he hadn't been ready to be a real leader the first time he was named. And now that he was ready, now that he understood the job, the Naming Ritual would confirm his suspicions that he'd waited too long to see the future. It was time for a new vision, a new leader. He'd accept whatever the decision would be.

WE'LL HOLD YOU TO THAT, Fang said.

They arrived back at the blood bank and Austin's suite in time to make the rendezvous, meeting Dan at the elevator. David, Pia, the Memory Eater and Ludwig had already arrived, and Tessa had come up from San Antonio as well. Once everyone settled in Austin's suite, Val told them what they'd learned.

Austin nodded and dug his phone out of a pocket. "I'll let Lisette know about the crystal and ask her not to harm the men. I'll be right back."

Dan glanced at Tessa. "Where are we going?"

Tessa pulled out a map and some pictures. Laying them on the coffee table, she said, "Mountain View is a small neighborhood park, but I chose it for the ritual because it's sheltered by trees from the surrounding houses and has a covered pavilion."

"Why outside?" Dan asked. "Why not reserve a space indoors?"

"Because rituals are traditionally held outdoors," Micah explained. "If we held it indoors, Asmodeus would be suspicious."

Dan sighed. "It'll make it harder to defend. What about light?"

"I brought some torches," Tessa said. "And I've arranged for members of the Underground to bring refreshments for afterward."

"Refreshments?" Dan repeated incredulously. "We don't—"

"It's tradition," Micah said, interrupting him. One of the few his father had kept. "Again, we want to make everything look as normal as possible." And if all went well, maybe they'd be able to conduct the ritual, get it over and done with. "Did you remember to bring robes?" he asked Tessa.

She nodded. "They're in the car."

Dan rolled his eyes. "Robes? Are they necessary?"

"It's tradition, too," Micah said, "representing our need to keep our true faces hidden from the rest of the world."

Dan sighed. "How bulky are these things?"

"They tie at the neck," Micah told him. "So they come off easily."

Austin returned, letting them know Lisette had agreed to secure the crystal and not hurt the men. "They're on their way to Dina's house," he told them. "In darkened vans driven by female human volunteers. Once the sun goes down, they'll surround her house and bring her in for justice."

Uneasily, Micah wondered what sort of "justice" the vampires had in mind, but decided not to ask. He was better off not knowing.

"What about . . . her?" Dan asked, nodding at the Memory Eater still huddled in the corner. "Is she traditional, too?"

Micah shook his head. "No, but we may need her to pry some information from Asmodeus to save your sister."

They went over the plan one more time using the pictures and maps. "Remember," Val said. "Don't hurt Gwen and don't kill Asmodeus. We need him alive to free Gwen."

Everyone nodded, then headed out in twos and threes so as to not draw suspicion.

Princess insisted on coming along with Fang, so Micah rode in the car with the two dogs and Val. Austin used a cloak to cover up in the backseat until the sun went down, which should be any moment now.

"Turn left here," Micah said, checking their location on the map app. "It should be right there."

It was, and as promised, it was secluded enough from the houses surrounding it that people wouldn't be able to see exactly what was happening.

Val parked in the small lot, and Princess stayed in the car at Fang's order. So did Austin, and Micah noticed the Memory Eater was similarly cloaked against the sun in David's car. As darkness fell, the two undead slipped silently away into the night, leaving the car doors slightly ajar so the noise wouldn't attract attention. Austin went to canvas the area and left the Memory Eater under David's control until she was needed. If at all.

The rest of them headed toward the pavilion. Ten or so demons had already arrived, and Tessa was organizing things, as she always did. That was one thing Micah would miss if someone else was named in the ritual. She was a great assistant.

She set up the altar in the center of the pavilion and showed Val where to put the torches, asked Annie to get some water, and directed the others where to put the refreshments. The plan was to make it look as much like a normal ritual as possible.

They figured Asmodeus would either go after Val, or go directly for the books. After he scouted the area, Austin would keep an eye on the books, which were hidden in the trunk of his car. Val would pretend to get a phone call right before the ritual started and wander off by herself, making herself a tempting target.

The plan was simple, as Dan insisted the best plans were, but Micah could think of too many things that could go wrong. Feeling uneasy, he scanned the area, trying to look nonchalant, but in reality searching for any signs of danger. His gaze slid past the parking lot, then his brain caught up with what he'd seen and he swiftly glanced back at the parking lot.

Had someone slipped behind Austin's car? Micah caught a glimpse of a petite silhouette and realized it was the Austin soothsayer, Annie. He relaxed. She was probably getting something from her own car. But Austin's trunk opened and Micah caught a glimpse of pink as

Annie lifted out the backpack. What was she doing with the books? And where the hell was Austin?

Princess started barking and Micah took off running. "Stop her," he yelled.

Annie heard him and took off like a flash, toward the trees. He reached out with his incubus powers to snag her. Better that than risk a foot race. The reaching tendrils slid right off her and Micah faltered for a moment. What the hell? Annie was no succubus.

Fang flashed by him. SHE'S ENTHRALLED BY A VAMPIRE, he yelled to everyone.

No wonder Micah's powers wouldn't work—Lilith had already taken over her mind and will. He continued running after her, the others close on his heels, when she ran into the arms of a shadowy figure who stepped out from behind a tree. He grabbed Annie and the backpack.

Asmodeus. And he was holding a gun to Annie's head. Was it the dart gun, or a real one with a silencer?

"Everyone stop," the demon yelled. "Or I shoot the girl."

His heart suddenly in his throat, Micah stumbled to a halt, and so did almost everyone else.

But Val, stubborn as always, didn't stop. So, the creep shot her.

Val spun around, then fell to the ground in a tangle of limbs, unmoving.

Definitely a real gun, but louder than he expected of a silencer. *Please, let her only be stunned. Please don't let that bullet have found a spot not covered in Kevlar.*

"As you can see, I'm serious," Asmodeus shouted. "No one else move, or the girl is next."

Everyone stopped, including Fang, who was snarling and growling so much, he didn't hear Micah's concern or broadcast an answer about Val's condition.

The mage demon shoved his pistol up against Annie's head and didn't even have to hold onto her. Lilith, who must be somewhere close by, made sure she was nice and pliable.

Dan raised his hands above his head. "Don't worry, pal. Let's keep this civil, shall we, so no one else gets hurt?"

"Sure," Asmodeus sneered. "All you gotta do is let me leave with the books without pulling any of the tricks I know you must have planned. I'll keep the girl as a hostage until I'm sure you're not following me."

As Dan and Asmodeus negotiated, Micah seethed, his mind whirling. Val was down, and he was still leader, damn it. He had to take charge. Wait. Where the hell was Lilith? He had to find her. He might not be able to control her, but at least he could discover where she was hiding. The practice in the basement had helped, and Micah was able to thrust out his female-seeking strands of energy and quickly identify all the women in the area. There were only two he couldn't get a hook into besides Val. One was Annie, so the other must be Lilith.

She was hiding in the women's restroom. So that's how she'd been able to enthrall Annie. Lilith had probably captured the soothsayer with her gaze when Annie went to get water for Tessa. Now, how could he get word to Austin so the vampire could secure her?

Asmodeus's voice rose in anger and Micah glanced in that direction. Damn. It looked like negotiations were going south.

All of a sudden, a knife sprouted from the mage demon's shoulder—Pia!

Someone else plunged from the branch above Asmodeus, kicked the gun away, and fell on top of the mage demon. The cowboy hat gave him away.

"Lilith's in the restroom," Micah yelled at Austin and ran toward the small building on the other side of the park.

Austin was up in a flash and running as Dan and David leapt toward Asmodeus.

Lilith darted out of the restroom, intent on making a getaway. She was too fast for Micah, but Austin tackled her and they both ended up on the ground, Austin locking her arms behind her.

Micah glanced quickly toward Annie. She was free of Lilith's control and had collapsed in David's arms. Good—she'd be all right. David and Dan had managed to subdue Asmodeus and Dan locked cuffs on him.

Asmodeus started to mutter something and Micah yelled, "Don't let him speak!" Thank heaven for a cop's fast reactions. As Dan punched the guy in the mouth, Micah swerved to grab some duct tape Tessa had left on a table and ripped off a large piece to slap over the mage demon's mouth. "So he can't use his only power to possess someone else," he explained. He didn't know if the guy could control more than one person at a time, but he wasn't taking any chances.

With that taken care of, Micah ran to Val and knelt beside her, checking frantically for blood.

SHE'S ALIVE, Fang told him, running over to snuffle into her hair and lick her face. THE BULLETPROOF VEST TOOK THE BRUNT OF THE IMPACT—THE BULLET HIT HER ON THE SIDE.

Val moaned and relief filled Micah. Thank God, she was alive.

"What's that thing doing?" Dan yelled.

The urgency in his voice made Micah glance up. The Memory Eater stood in front of Asmodeus, her skeletal hands locked on both sides of his head. As his face contorted in pain, she intoned, "Guilty. Sentence, death."

Her hands flew away from his head as if thrown by an explosion and Asmodeus fell to the ground, twitching.

Micah grabbed control of her with his incubus, but it was too late. The damage was done. He stared, stunned. Why the hell hadn't David stopped her? That was the man's one job in this mess.

"What happened?" Dan asked, staring down at the mage demon in bewilderment.

Micah stood and said grimly, "I believe she ripped all the memories out of him." He glared at her, willing her to speak. "Is that right?"

"Yesss," the traitorous creature said.

Micah closed his eyes against the pain. He'd hadn't expected the plan to be perfect, but he hadn't expected things to go this wrong.

Damn it, now how were they going to get Gwen back?

Chapter Twenty-Six

I sat up, feeling like someone had whacked me in the side with a sledgehammer. But the pain faded into the background when I realized Asmodeus was lying on the ground . . . and what that meant for Gwen. Damn.

"I'm okay," I told Fang and the others who were hovering around me.

Fang licked my hand. GOOD. I'M GOING TO CHECK ON PRINCESS.

"I—I'm sorry," David sputtered as Fang dashed away. "When we grabbed him and Annie fell, I lost control of the Memory Eater."

I shook my head. There was plenty of blame to go around, starting with me and my "foolproof" plan. Why had I assumed Asmodeus would attack on our timetable? I should have listened to Micah.

"Is he dead?" I asked.

Micah grimaced. "He will be soon. He can't even remember how to breathe—the Memory Eater is that thorough when she executes." He glanced at Tessa and the crowd of demons surrounding our little drama. "Could you . . . ?"

Tessa apparently knew what he meant, because she gathered the dozen or so bystanders together and herded them back to the pavilion. She picked up the gun on the way.

Dan looked like he wanted to murder the Memory Eater. I couldn't blame him. "Didn't she know we needed him alive and aware to save Gwen?" he demanded as Austin frog-marched Lilith over toward us.

"She did," Micah confirmed.

"Then why the hell did she do that?"

"He isss aliiive."

Yeah, but brain-dead and unable to do anything but drool. Not helpful.

"Tell us why you did it," Micah said, his tone implacable.

David helped me to my feet as the Memory Eater raised one arm to point at me. "So sheee will freee meee from thisss exissstence."

Good thing for her I no longer had a problem with letting her commit suicide by Slayer. Not after what she'd done to Gwen. Just as soon as I got my breath back and got rid of this agonizing pain in my side.

"Your death won't solve anything," Micah protested.

"Not death. Liiife," the creep show said. She pointed at the backpack lying next to the mage demon's crumpled form. "Spelll."

She couldn't mean the mage demon–locator spell. "You mean the demon-exorcising spell?" I asked.

The Memory Eater nodded.

"You want to exorcise the demon from you?"

"Yesss."

"You realize I don't know what this spell will do? It might kill you, leave you mindless, or, or I don't what."

"Yesss. It isss my only hoooope."

So that's what she meant by releasing her. "Why should I do anything to help you?" I spat out.

This time, the Memory Eater raised her arm to point a bony finger at Lilith. "To help herrr."

Lilith squirmed in Austin's hold but couldn't get loose. It was hard to think of her as Lilith and a vampire when all I saw was Gwen.

"You already helped me by ridding me of that creep who was controlling me," Lilith said. "Now, if you'll let me go, we can all get on with our lives."

"Hell, no," Dan barked. "You're going to let my sister go, and you're going to do it now."

Lilith tsked at him. "Sorry, Dan, or should I say Mr. Hero? This time, you and your girlfriend don't get what you want. I hold the cards now. And it's sooo satisfying to be occupying your sister's body. Poetic justice, don't you think?"

What the hell was she talking about? Dan and I were no longer an item. And how did she know his name, anyway?

"What do you mean, poetic justice?" I asked.

"Haven't you figured it out yet?" the woman inhabiting Gwen's body taunted. "You know me by a slightly different name. Lily. Lily Armstrong."

Lilith . . . Lily. Crap, I should have known. The woman I'd beheaded to save my sister was now back in the body of Dan's sister. Not good.

THAT'S AN UNDERSTATEMENT.

Austin's expression turned grim and he tightened his hold. "Traitor," he muttered. Lily had been one of Alejandro's lieutenants alongside Austin and caused them quite a bit of pain as well. A very unpopular lady.

Dan said, "Don't hurt her."

"Why not?" I asked, wondering if he still had feelings for his ex-fiancée.

"She's still Gwen, too." He turned to glare at me. "How are you going to get Lily out of Gwen's body?"

Me? Why did this fall back on me?

"You can't," Lily said with a smug smile. "Asmodeus could have, but so sad, he's dead. Now the only way to get rid of me is to kill your sister, too."

Dan looked grim. "Is Gwen even still in there?"

"Oh, yes," Lily said. "The little weakling is still screaming deep down inside."

Nausea roiled within me. Gwen didn't deserve this.

"Maybe you two could share her body," Micah suggested.

"Not a chance," Lily said. "I'd rather kill myself first. And her. See how Dan and Val deal with *that*." Lily struggled a little but Austin's grip held sure.

I winced. She'd rather die permanently than give us what we wanted. Talk about holding a grudge.

Micah spoke up. "David and I can control her now that Asmodeus is no longer able to."

Austin shook his head. "Sorry, pal, but you two didn't do so well controlling your—" He broke off then nodded at the Memory Eater. "Controlling *her*."

"It wouldn't work anyway," I told Micah. "You can't keep Lily under control every minute of every day."

"But I can at least shut her up," David said.

I felt his incubus reach out toward her, and she went limp and quiescent in Austin's arms. But he didn't relax his grip any. Wise bloodsucker.

"What are you going to do?" Dan asked, his gaze intent on me.

I remembered what the Memory Eater had said. "Maybe the demon-exorcising spell?"

"How would that help?" Micah asked. "She's human, not demon."

"Maybe it works on departed spirits, too." Lily was put in Gwen's body by a demon. Did that count?

"You can't be sure of that," Dan said.

"We don't know how it works," Micah protested.

"No, but there's one way to find out," I said. "I'll use it on the Memory Eater first." Damn it, I was going to have to do exactly what the bag of bones wanted and lose even more of Lola.

Holding my side, I took a deep breath and searched for the spell inside me. It was easy to find, stirring up uneasiness in my gut. Once I touched it with intent, the spell filled me, feeling as if it wanted to burst from my skin.

Pointing at the Memory Eater, I focused my attention on her and only her, and recalled the words of the spell. Oh, yeah. *Demon thou art, demon thou shalt not be. Say it times three, I exorcise thee.*

I let the words erupt. "I exorcise thee, I exorcise thee, I exorcise thee!"

The tension left me in a whoosh and the Memory Eater crumpled to the ground in a puddle of black cloth. The spell felt a little stronger, a bit more entrenched in my being. I tested Lola. Yes, I did notice a difference. This time I'd grabbed firm control of her so I wouldn't lose it like I had before, but still sensed a lessening of her strength.

The Memory Eater didn't move in the eerie silence. "Is she alive? Did it work?"

"Something worked," Austin said drily.

Micah knelt down to check her pulse. "She's alive."

I stared down at her. "Can we revive her?" It was the only way to know what the spell did to her.

Tessa came over and pressed a small bottle into Micah's hand.

"What's that?" I asked.

"Sal volatile." At my puzzled expression, she added, "Smelling salts."

Oh. Tessa thought of everything.

Micah opened it and waved it under the creature's nose. She jerked back away from his hand and turned her head away, blinking rapidly.

"How are you feeling?" Micah asked.

She paused for a moment, then something horrible happened. She smiled.

The death's-head image made everyone recoil.

"Memory Eater, how do you feel?" Micah repeated.

"Elspeth," she said. "My name is Elspeth. And I feel good."

There was no more trace of madness in her speech. My hopes rose. "The demon part of you is really gone, then?" I asked eagerly.

She paused for a moment, evidently assessing the composition of her being. "Yes. There is no more demon, no more madness, no more Memory Eater. Only vampire."

Micah helped the skeletal woman to her feet. She swayed slightly, and I couldn't help but marvel at the difference in her. Before, she'd always seemed so tense, so controlled, except when the insanity took over, of course. Now she seemed loose and relaxed. Even her voice sounded normal.

"No problems?" I asked. I wanted to make sure this was safe before I used it on Gwen.

"No. I sense a void where my demon powers used to be, as if part of me is missing. But it has been so long since I was able to use them, I won't miss it."

"But will it work on Gwen?" Dan persisted.

The Memory—no, Elspeth—cocked her head. "It should. The mage you know as Asmodeus brought the spirit in from the demon dimension."

Huh? "What does that mean? Lily was fully human before she turned vampire. Why would her spirit be in a demon dimension?"

"She was evil and had been turned into one who sups on blood," Elspeth said. "The evil vampires who die in this world are reborn as demonic spirits in the next. It's why they try so hard to get back here."

We all stared at her, stunned. So that's what hell was like.

She added gently, "This was well known in my time. You have lost a great deal of knowledge since then."

No kidding.

"You must have a lot to teach us," Micah murmured. He paused, looking guilty. "If you will."

"I will. You always treated me as well as circumstances allowed."

"This is all fine and dandy," Dan said, his voice hard. "But we need to get Lily out of Gwen. Now."

"Are you sure you want me to do this?" I asked. "Gwen's situation is different. I can't guarantee what'll happen." The possibilities ran through my head . . . death, insanity, or no change at all. None of them were good.

Dan made an impatient gesture. "Anything is better than having that monster inside her."

I felt the same, but it was good to have her brother's permission. I nodded at Austin. "Hold on tight. David, if you'd let go of her?" I didn't know what would happen if he was still in control of her when I used the spell.

I felt the incubus leave her and Lily struggled in Austin's hold, yelling horrible things.

Ignoring her, I gathered my will and focused on her. "I exorcise thee, I exorcise thee, I exorcise thee." I felt a little more of Lola leave as the spell whooshed into Lily.

"Nooo," Lily screamed then suddenly sagged in Austin's arms.

The vampire didn't loosen his hold one iota.

Dan rushed over to tip Gwen's face up toward him. "Is she alive?"

"Yes," Austin said.

Well, technically, she was undead. But we both knew that's not what Dan meant.

"Let her go," Dan said. "Let me have her."

Austin shook his head. "No can do. Not until we know for sure that Lily's gone for good."

"Micah and David can control her now if Lily's still there," I reminded him. "Please, Austin?" Dan really needed to believe Gwen had come back to him.

Slowly, Austin released a limp Gwen into Dan's arms. He lowered her gently to the ground and knelt above her. "Can I have those smelling salts, please?"

Micah handed them to Dan and he waved the open bottle under Gwen's nose. She revived with a start and glanced around, then burst into tears, hugging her brother fiercely as she sobbed into his shoulder.

"It's Gwen," Micah said in relief. "I can feel the difference."

Thank goodness. Relief filled me, sweet and pure, but my heart hurt for her. She'd been through so much, and none of it her fault. Thanks to me, she'd been kidnapped, had her body taken over by a sociopath, and turned into a vampire. It must have been hell.

Those of us who knew her gathered around, silently lending our support.

"It's okay," Dan murmured, rocking her and rubbing her back. "Everything's all right now."

Gwen raised her head to look at him and dash her tears away. "No, it's not. I—I'm a vampire now. I didn't ask for this, and I don't want it." She looked at me, pleading in her eyes. "Can you take that out of me, too?"

I really, really wished I could. "I'm sorry, Gwen, it's not possible."

Her eyes widened and tears filled them again. "I can't live like this," she whispered.

"Yes, you can," Dan said, shaking her a little. "You're back. You're still you. Just . . ."

"Just undead," Gwen filled in for him, looking stubborn. "Like the vampires you kill every night."

"No, not like them," Dan insisted and looked up at me, begging me silently for help.

"You know that's not true," I told her gently. "We only kill the bad ones, the ones who murder innocents. That's not you."

She gazed at me with hope in her eyes. "How do you know?"

"Because vampires aren't automatically evil. They become more of what they were in life. Look at Lily. Wasn't she a total skank before she was turned?"

Gwen gave me a tentative smile and nodded.

"See how bad she turned out? Now think about Austin and Alejandro. Totally opposite."

Gwen glanced at Austin who tipped his hat and grinned. "It's true," he confirmed. "I'm sorry you had the choice taken away from you, but I'd be honored to sponsor you into Alejandro's house. And Elspeth, too."

Austin glanced at Elspeth, who nodded, saying, "I appreciate your kindness."

Gwen's eyes widened when she saw Elspeth's face, but she didn't say anything.

Dan started to speak, but Austin cut him off. "There are things she needs to know about herself, things she needs to learn that only other vampires can teach her." He paused, then added, "It's not such a bad life. You'll see." His pocket buzzed and he pulled out his phone.

She gave him a trembling smile, her cheeks wet. "Okay. I'll try it."

Dan helped her to her feet. "Why don't we talk in the parking lot while they finish their business?"

Gwen nodded, and the brother and sister headed for the cars, arms around each others' waists.

I relaxed a bit. Somehow, everything was going to be all right now.

Austin glanced up from his phone. "Uh, Val—"

That's when I heard the scream.

Chapter Twenty-Seven

I whirled to see a whole heck of a lot more people than were there before. Dina . . . and her men.

One of them backhanded a woman and she fell to the ground, her hand to her face. "John, don't," she cried at the man who stood above her.

"That's what I was trying to tell you," Austin said. "Dina wasn't there when Lisette showed up. She'd left already."

Crap. Why couldn't anything go right today? Quickly, I grabbed control of Austin, Dan and the few male demons she didn't already have her hooks into. No sense in giving her more ammunition against us.

Dina had Shade by her side, which pissed me off even more. The other female demons were held in the firm grasp of Dina's puppets, and the male demons under my control were blocked by an undead wall of demons-turned-vampire—four so-called chupacabras who looked barely sane. Dina must be controlling them, too. So why hadn't she controlled the others who had run into the daylight and died? Was she unable to, or was she callous enough to not care?

THE LATTER, Fang told me from the car.

It figured. "What do you want?" I snapped.

She shrugged. "It's my right to join the Naming Ritual."

No, there was more to it than that. This ritual was for Micah's organization, not hers. "You weren't invited," I told her. "Kind of like the other women weren't invited when you named yourself leader."

Smug satisfaction glittered in her eyes. "Prove it."

I couldn't, of course. Not with her holding on to the men who'd been there, and too many innocents in harm's way.

"Then you wouldn't mind undergoing another Naming Ritual?" David asked.

Her smugness turned to anger and she narrowed her eyes at the incubus, probably annoyed because she couldn't make him do what she wanted. "That's not necessary," she said tightly. "But I would like a ritual to determine who should be the next Memory Eater." She waved at the dozen or so men surrounding her. "I have the requisite number of petitioners."

My stomach turned. Why would anyone be willing to do that to someone else? Worse, she was not only willing, but eager.

"Oh, and I'll take the books as well," she added in a sly tone.

Power hungry much?

"We won't do either," Micah said. "We know what you've been doing with those poor men. Experimenting on them, trying to create your own Memory Eater. You're despicable."

"Not to mention what you did to my people," Austin added.

Dina shrugged, looking unconcerned that we'd figured out her evil plot. "Well, if you'd help me find a male Memory Eater, I won't have to do that anymore, will I?"

"You won't if you're dead, either," David spat out.

She laughed. "None of you have the guts to kill me, except maybe the Slayer. But wait, she's injured and I heard she only kills vampires. Too bad."

My blood sizzled, yearning for action, hating this stalemate. "I might make an exception in your case."

Shade moved protectively in front of Dina. "You'll have to go through me, first."

That was Dina talking. I hoped. My gaze focused on the crystal amulet around her neck. I had to get that away from her.

I took a step forward, intending to do just that, but Princess ran from the car toward Shade, crying, MY HUMAN, MY HUMAN, I AM HERE.

Fang was in hot pursuit, but she was fast for such a small dog.

Dina turned toward the spaniel and reared her leg back to kick the dog.

No! I'd had enough, so I attacked her with the only weapon I had left. Swinging my arm to point at her, I yelled, "I exorcise thee, I exorcise thee, I exorcise thee," and ripped the succubus out of her.

Several things happened at once. Dina fell unconscious to the ground, the men she'd controlled staggered with the backlash of their release, and the four chupacabras lurched momentarily before moving toward the demon men, bloodsucking definitely on their agenda.

Crap. I reached out with Lola and snagged the insane ones, yelling, "Stop."

But Lola had lost a lot of strength after using the other spells so close together. I was barely able to hold onto them at all. I fell to my knees, holding my aching side as I desperately clutched the succubus strands with my weakened abilities.

Fang ran over to Dina, his teeth at her neck. I didn't have enough energy to stop him from tearing out her throat, and wasn't sure I wanted to.

But that wasn't what he intended. With a jerk of his head, he ripped off the necklace and brought it to me.

Use it, he exclaimed.

I clutched the crystal, wondering how. But the amulet didn't need anything but my touch, for it immediately strengthened my succubus abilities, enough to let me grab onto them with ease.

Austin helped me to my feet as Shade embraced his dog. *What's wrong with this picture?*

But I didn't have time to explore the pain that gave me. Beth ran over to me, grabbing my arm. "One of those men is my brother, Blaine. Help him, please."

"If I remove his demon, he'll no longer have his demon abilities. He'll be a vampire," I reminded her.

Tears overflowed from her eyes but she nodded fiercely. "Being undead is better than being dead dead."

"These men have killed," Ludwig said, frowning. "How is that different from the other bloodsuckers you've executed?"

"They weren't in control of their faculties at the time," Austin said. "Yet they still managed to attack only animals. There would be no bar to them joining the New Blood Movement."

Micah spoke up. "Would you be willing to sponsor them, too?"

The cowboy vamp hesitated. "In San Antonio, yes. But if they wish to stay here, I'll ask Lisette if she's willing to have them."

"Good enough," Beth said.

Other demons crowded around me, agreeing, urging me to do it.

I dropped my head wearily. Use the spell four more times and give up more and more of Lola each time? A couple of months ago, I'd longed to be normal, wanted desperately to get rid of this demon inside me. But now that it looked like I could approximate the same thing simply by using the spell as often as possible, I hesitated. I was known throughout the vampire community as the Slayer, and many of the rogue bloodsuckers wanted to take me out. If they learned I was weakened, they'd come after me in droves. I'd have to go into hiding until I could build Lola backup and restore the balance, maybe even leave town.

I glanced around at them and took another shot, hoping they'd give up on this idea. "You know I can't guarantee they'll regain sanity?"

Some looked surprised, and Beth pointed at Elspeth. "She did."

I nodded. "I know, but she was a special case. She was chosen as Memory Eater precisely because she could handle the madness."

Beth jerked her head up and down decisively. "It's the only chance they have. If they prefer not to stay a vampire, they can . . ." She paused, then added, "They can do what they need to do. At least this way, they have a choice."

I closed my eyes briefly. Should I do this?

YOU DON'T HAVE TO USE THE SPELL, Fang said soothingly. YOU'VE DONE A LOT FOR THEM ALREADY. THEY SHOULDN'T ASK IT OF YOU.

But they had asked it of me. I sighed. Crap. I couldn't say no, not when I could release these poor men back to their families. I knew what it was like to lose a family. I couldn't do it to any of them. "Okay, but give me some room." I didn't really need it, but all those bodies pressing around me, expecting miracles of me, made me feel claustrophobic.

They backed away and gave me a clear view of the four demonic vamps. One by one, I exorcised their demons, far more gently than I had Dina's, and they collapsed into a loved one's arms.

"Do not rouse them yet," Elspeth said. "It will be better for them if you let them rest, let their minds become accustomed to their new state."

The local demons gathered around the unconscious men, chattering like excited squirrels, except for one older woman who came over, wringing her hands. "What about my son, Adam Bukowski? Where is he? He should be here, too."

GIVE IT TO HER STRAIGHT, Fang said. SHE DESERVES TO KNOW THE TRUTH.

I hated delivering bad news, especially to the boy's mother. "I'm sorry, but I don't think he survived," I said carefully.

Her hand flew to her mouth, and she shook her head wordlessly. Fear, denial, and grief filled her eyes. "How . . . how do you know?" she asked finally.

"I found his wallet where the vampires hid during the day. He probably didn't know to stay out of the sun. And there was a pile of ash nearby."

"No," she said, shaking her head with sharp little jerks. "You're wrong. It can't be him."

Looked like I'd have to show her proof. "Would one of you mind getting the backpack?"

Austin obliged, and brought it to me. I rummaged inside and handed her his wallet, then the belt buckle with the skull wearing a cowboy hat and a snake around its neck. It was pretty distinctive. "Is this his? We found this in the ash."

The woman took the buckle and stared at it. I hoped I was wrong, that she'd say it wasn't her son's. But her face crumpled like the movement of an avalanche, slow at first, then building up steam until total collapse. She broke down, sobbing.

Uncomfortable with tears, I glanced around for help. Thank goodness another woman about her same age pulled her away.

Austin put a hand on my shoulder. "Are you okay?"

Shouldn't Shade be the one asking me this? Dina's hold on him had been broken. Why was he standing off to the side, acting like he cared about no one but Princess?

GIVE HIM TIME, Fang said. HE'S BEEN THROUGH A ROUGH FEW DAYS, TOO.

What is he thinking about me?

Fang gave me a look, the kind that said I knew better than to ask that question. YOU'LL HAVE TO ASK HIM.

Oh, crap. No reassurances from Fang? That couldn't be good. I closed my eyes against the pain that stabbed somewhere in the region of my heart.

"Are you all right, Val?" Austin repeated.

Besides a breaking heart, he meant? Mentally, I took stock of myself. Lola was barely detectable now, maybe strong enough to make one man feel really good, if he got close enough, but nowhere near enough to control any baddies out for my blood. The spell, however, was well ensconced in my being, making me feel like Super Exorcist, able to leap tall demons in a single bound.

Fang snorted.

Okay, maybe able to render anyone alive demonless. "I'm fine," I told Austin. I wasn't about to admit any weakness to him.

"What are we going to do about Dina?" David asked.

DON'T WAKE HER EITHER, Fang said drily.

David rolled his eyes. "What I meant was, what do we do when she wakes up and is no longer a succubus, no longer in control of the local Demon Underground? I can't imagine she'll take it well."

Austin's lips firmed. "Lisette would be more than happy to take care of this problem for you."

Yikes. They might be the good guy vamps, but I doubted they'd be gentle with someone who'd caused their people so much pain.

"We take care of our own," Micah said firmly.

"What does that mean?" Austin challenged. "Give her a slap on the hand? Turn her loose?"

"That won't happen," Ludwig said. "She'll want revenge. We can't trust her not to reveal our existence."

"Well, we can't tell the human authorities," David argued. "And we don't have a Memory Eater any longer to remove all knowledge of us from her."

Ah, geez. Maybe I should have waited a little longer to cure Elspeth. But I didn't regret it. What a hellish existence she must have had.

Micah shook his head. "No, we'll have a Judgment Ritual. And if the determination is that she should die . . . ?"

He turned to look at me. Was this the part where they asked me to kill Dina? Damn, I hoped not. I was tired of killing, tired of being an executioner. How could I fit into the demon community if people only viewed me as a killer? I held up my hands and backed away. "Don't look at me."

Micah opened his mouth to speak, but was interrupted by the sound of a muffled gunshot. Several women screamed and we all whirled around to see Beth standing over Dina, Asmodeus's gun in her hand. She glanced up defiantly. "Problem solved."

Austin rubbed his hand across his chin. "Yep. A bullet through the brain works quite nicely."

Holy crap. I never would have expected that of Beth. Guess I knew who the strong one was in that family.

YOU GO GIRL, Fang said approvingly.

Everyone had frozen for a moment, but now Micah and David ran to her, along with a couple of the local demon men. Micah got there first and gently took the gun from her hand. She didn't resist. He did what we should have done before—he pulled out the ammunition clip.

Tessa ran over, looking stricken. "I'm so sorry, I should have disarmed it, hidden it."

"It's not your fault," Micah said and passed her the empty handgun.

"That's right," David added. "You didn't know she planned to do that."

"Don't hurt her," one man said, standing protectively in front of Beth.

Another agreed. "Leave Beth alone. Dina deserved it."

There was a chorus of agreement from the other local demons present. They might be shocked, but no one was sorry for Dina's death. Even Shade said nothing.

Micah held up his hands to ward off their arguments. "What happens to Beth will be decided in a Judgment Ritual."

"That's fair," David said quickly.

I noticed he didn't argue with Micah this time. Probably because Micah was really acting like the leader I knew he could be. The others looked doubtful, but agreed.

Austin ambled over to look down at Dina, then glanced over at Asmodeus. He tipped his hat back. "What are you planning on doing with the bodies?"

Micah glanced at Beth, who stood with a defiant expression between her friends. "Beth," he said, "if you wouldn't mind . . . ?"

She nodded, and Micah had a couple of men bring the mage demon's body over next to Dina's. Micah advised everyone to back away from the bodies and asked Ludwig to stand by.

YEP, Fang mused. A GOOD FIRE DEMON CAN TAKE CARE OF THE EVIDENCE PRETTY QUICKLY.

Once everyone had backed away, Micah said. "Make it as hot as you can."

Beth nodded and closed her eyes, slowly raised her arms above her head, then snapped them down, pointing at the bodies on the ground. A ball of eerie green fire erupted where they lay, billowing up into the night, shading to white-hot, yellow, and orange and red, with flames rising high into the air.

I turned my face from the heat. Ludwig was already blasting out huge gouts of water, containing the fire, corralling it into that one small area around the bodies.

Dan came running up from the parking lot, Gwen close behind him. "Are you crazy?" he yelled. "This is a neighborhood watch area. Someone probably heard those gunshots. The police may be here at any minute, not to mention the fire department."

Austin nodded. "I was able to take care of the people close by, modify their memories, but with Gwen and Elspeth's assistance, I can ensure no one noticed anything." He held out his hands and Gwen hesitated for a moment. "It's all right. Your presence will act as an amplifier so we can make sure no one here gets into trouble. I'll show you the way."

Elspeth put her hand in his trustingly, and I said, "It's okay, Gwen. You can trust him."

She nodded and while Dan gritted his teeth, she put her hand in Austin's.

"Now you two join hands so the three of us make a circle," he said.

They did, and they all closed their eyes and stood there, looking like they were doing nothing. After a few moments, they opened their eyes and let go of each others' hands.

"You have nothing to worry about now," Austin said. "We took care of it."

Gwen's eyes were wide with surprise. "That . . . that was . . ."

"Interesting," Elspeth said thoughtfully. Gwen nodded.

Huh. I knew the vamps had been able to keep their existence quiet for thousands of years, but didn't realize how easy it was. At least, it seemed that way.

"That's one hell of a talent," Dan said, eying Austin suspiciously.

"Yeah," I said. "Why haven't vampires taken over the world?"

Austin smiled. "Because we don't want it. The New Blood Movement doesn't, anyway. And the method for combining has to be taught. The rogues don't know how."

Thank the powers-that-be for small favors.

AMEN, SISTER, Fang said.

The fire had burned down now, and Ludwig was busy putting it out. Nothing was left but charred earth.

Dan stared blankly at the steaming space. "That was no ordinary fire."

Fang rolled his eyes. WOW, GREAT DETECTIVE WORK.

Beth wrapped her arms around her waist. "It was demon fire—the hottest thing on Earth."

And she, apparently, was an expert in it.

"Did Dina have any next of kin?" I asked.

"Who cares?" a man scoffed.

Micah glared into the crowd. "She might have a family

somewhere, someone who might grieve for her. They deserve to know what happened."

Annie, the delicate soothsayer, shook her head. "She doesn't have any. The only family she ever mentioned was her father, and he passed away."

That's right, someone had mentioned that she'd inherited the amulet from him. I glanced down at the crystal, just now realizing I still clutched it in my hand. Putting it in my pocket to worry about later, I said, "Okay, what do we do now?"

What I wanted to do was go home. Christmas was coming tomorrow and I wanted to get some rest before I had to show up at Mom and Rick's for the combined Yule and Christmas celebration.

Micah straightened, looking stern and very much in charge. "We have some things to discuss. If everyone would join me under the pavilion?"

They all followed him. Everyone except me. And Shade.

He sat off to the side, sitting with his back against a tree, and Princess in his lap. I had to know what was going on in his head. What was he thinking about me, about us?

I wandered over to him, Fang close behind, but Shade didn't look up, not even when I was standing right in front of him. With Princess grounding him, I could see him in his human form. He was still gorgeous as always, but now that I was closer, I saw the tightness in his jaw and the dark circles under his eyes.

Princess looked up. GO AWAY, she said. WE DON'T WANT YOU.

That hurt a bit, as I was sure she intended. "Princess, can you leave us alone, please?" I didn't want to have this conversation with a jealous hellhound listening in.

Princess growled, but Fang went over and poked her in the side. COME ON, SWEET THING. LET'S LEAVE THESE TWO ALONE TO TALK.

Thank you.

DE NADA, Fang said. KISS AND MAKE UP, WILLYA?

That's what I wanted to do, but I wasn't sure how Shade felt right now.

Princess huffed and jumped off Shade's lap. The two hellhounds wandered over to join the others at the pavilion.

I sat down and put my back against the tree next to Shade's. "Hey," I said, feeling foolish. I didn't know what else to say to get him to talk to me. What was wrong with him?

"Hey," Shade echoed gruffly.

"Is that all you have to say to me?" I put my hand on his so I could see his expression.

He pulled away and went back to being swirly and surly. "What do you want me to say, Val?"

I withdrew my hand, feeling a sickening rush of fear. Since I couldn't see his expression, the only thing I had to judge how he felt was the tone of his voice. He sounded weary. "I'm sorry, Shade."

He was silent for a long moment, then said, "Do you even know what you're sorry for?"

"For whatever is making you like this." My heart ached for him, and for me.

Another long pause, then he said, "You left me with her."

"You told me to," I protested.

"Because she promised she wouldn't control me. She lied."

"I didn't know . . ."

"You knew," he said accusingly. "How could you not know? She had control of me, all the time. Every freakin' moment of every freakin' day."

"I didn't know." Tears filled my eyes. "How could I? I didn't know she was a psychopath, didn't know what she'd done to those other men until a few hours ago."

"And you still left me there after you found out?"

"I had to," I protested. "The others were afraid she'd know we were on to her if I rescued you. I wanted to, really I did."

He threw my hand away from him. "Not good enough."

I held the rejected hand against my chest with the other. "You don't understand. We sent vampires to surround Dina's house. They were going to rescue you as soon as the sun went down. Only, Dina wasn't there. And neither were you." When he remained silent, I added, "Ask Austin. He'll confirm it."

"Austin," Shade said, the word practically exploding from his mouth. "Bet he's been having a field day with you. What do you see in that bloodsucker?"

"No—nothing." Tears overflowed, running down my face. "What did she do to you?" I asked in a small voice.

For a long time, I thought he wasn't going to answer, then finally, he said, "I—I can't . . ."

I yearned to hold him, to comfort him, to make all the bad memories go away. But, knowing he'd reject me, I curled my hands into fists to keep myself from reaching out. "What can I do to help?"

"Leave me alone," he said flatly. "Get the hell out of my life."

Chapter Twenty-Eight

Everyone but Val and Shade followed Micah to the pavilion. Seeing Dan talking to Austin, Micah pulled Gwen aside.

"Gwen, I—I—" He broke off. Words couldn't express the anguish he felt at what had happened to her.

Gwen patted him on the shoulder. "None of this was your fault, Micah. Or Val's. The only one at fault is Asmodeus and he's dead now. He can't hurt anyone ever again."

He couldn't believe her composure, and her resiliency. If someone had turned his body into a vampire, he'd probably be drooling in a corner about now. "But your career, your life. They've all been changed drastically." An understatement. How could she work in an ER around all that blood? How could she lead a normal life? "If you need a job, I'll find you one at the club," he promised.

"Thank you. I'll think about it."

"Please, if there's anything you need, call me. Anytime, anywhere." He owed her a debt he doubted he'd ever be able to repay.

Sadness flickered in her eyes. "Don't worry, I'll cope. I have no choice. Dan and Austin have both promised to help." She squeezed his arm, then added, "Your people need you now. Go."

His people? No, not anymore. He glanced around at the demons from both cities, mingling together. Everyone seemed disturbed by the rawness of what had just happened here. Now, while it was still fresh in their minds, while they were still smarting from the knowledge of what could go wrong, they needed to make some decisions.

"We have a quorum," he announced. "What better time than now to hold the Judgment Ritual when we have everything we need, including those who witnessed the event for which Beth is being tried?"

There were murmurs of surprise, but many heads nodded.

"We need a new leader, too," Annie said. "To replace Dina." She glanced at the men who had been under succubus control. "Who did we really choose in the Naming Ritual when Dina emerged as leader?"

The men glanced aside at the four former demons, still unconscious. "Eric," one said.

Annie shook her head sadly. "Such a waste. But since he is no longer demon, he can't lead us. We'll need a Naming Ritual, too." She glanced around. "No secrecy this time."

Even more agreement there. Micah held up his hands and took a deep breath. "The San Antonio Underground needs a Naming Ritual as well. I have resigned from the position."

"What?" Tessa exclaimed. "I thought this was just a formality. You can't resign."

"I can," he said, overriding her objection. "Times have changed, things have changed. What is good for the Underground today isn't necessarily what was good for us when I was named. We no longer have a Memory Eater, so we no longer need an incubus to control her. It's time to find a better leader."

Ludwig protested, "You're a good leader."

He had to say that—he was a friend. "Thank you," Micah said. "But am I the best for San Antonio at this point in time? I don't know. And you don't either. The ritual will tell us the truth." He glanced at David and Pia. "And I promised David I'd hold one." But this was no longer a simple vote of confidence. It was for selection of his replacement.

David shook his head with a wry expression on the half of his face that wasn't burned. "How can I condemn you? I made a stupid mistake myself, tonight. I release you from your promise."

That was gratifying, but it didn't change the fact that Micah saw his past mistakes more clearly now, just as he saw the future more clearly. He had screwed up. "It doesn't matter," Micah said. "My resignation is effective immediately." And he'd never heard of a resigned leader who had been appointed again.

"Okay, let's do this," Annie said, breaking the tension.

Ludwig gestured at Austin, Dan, Gwen, and Elspeth where they were standing off to one side. "What about them? We've never had outsiders at our rituals before."

Micah thought for a moment. "The Book of Rituals doesn't say they can't attend."

Elspeth stepped forward. "If I may?" At Micah's nod, she said, "It is unusual, but not forbidden, to have outsiders attend. Not inside the circle, but outside, as observers."

Tessa glanced around the pavilion with a challenging stare. "I think these people have earned the right to be here."

No one argued with the soothsayer.

"Since there are no objections, they can stay if they wish," Micah said. And, for the benefit of the Underground's two new leaders, whoever they might be, he added, "As Elspeth just demonstrated, her centuries of experience in the Underground will be of great use to us in the future, to remind us of how things used to be done and help us regain knowledge of what we have lost." The fact that she was now a vampire shouldn't weigh in the equation—one of these rituals had put her in that position.

He didn't give them time to think about it or protest, but said, "Tessa, Annie, I believe you have the necessary robes?"

The soothsayers nodded and gave everyone a midnight midnight-blue robe to wear. Tessa had even made small capelets for the two hellhounds, which they wore with pride. Besides providing a sense of solemnity and the tradition David insisted they needed, the robes imparted a lot of warmth on a night like this. And, as the night deepened, everyone would appreciate that.

Val came up to Micah, wiping something off her face. Tears? "What's going on?" she asked.

Micah glanced in the direction she'd come from and saw Shade sitting under a tree. Had they had a fight? Was there trouble there? "We're going to have a ritual and need everyone present."

"Okay," she said with a forced smile. "I guess it's time I actually participated in one."

He hesitated for a moment, not certain whether he should pry, then asked, "Are you okay?"

"As well as anyone could be who's been shot." She rubbed her side. "The vest may stop bullets from penetrating, but it sure as heck doesn't stop the force of them. I don't think I cracked a rib, but I'll have some heavy bruising tomorrow."

That wasn't what he meant. She knew it, too, because she wouldn't look him in the eyes.

SHE'S HURTING, BUT SHE'LL LIVE, Fang told him.

Micah nodded at the hellhound. "Could you tell Shade we need him, Fang?"

SURE.

Tessa and Annie had everyone but the non-demons sit in a large circle on the grass outside the pavilion, nothing between them and the sky. The men who had recently had their demons exorcised were still unconscious, but Elspeth watched after them.

Tessa and Annie fussed with the seating arrangements, and Micah wondered why they were being so picky, then realized they were ensuring the succubus and incubi didn't sit next to anyone who might be influenced by their nearness. Smart move. It wouldn't be a good idea to have lust interfere with the ritual.

Shade pointedly sat far away from Val. Micah sighed inwardly. He hated to see that relationship fail. It was good for both of them.

Micah took his place in the circle as Tessa and Annie lit the round metal brazier they'd set in the center. That was the signal to start.

Everyone quieted and hushed those who hadn't attended before. Gwen, Dan, Austin, and Elspeth sat outside the circle across from him, watching. Micah had half-expected Dan to leave, but evidently Gwen wanted to stay, and Dan wasn't about to leave his sister's side.

Micah caught Gwen's gaze and she gave him a thumbs-up. "Good luck," she mouthed.

She still thought of others, even though her whole world had just fallen apart. Her support and her strength touched him. He smiled back at her.

The two soothsayers, the only ones garbed in hooded white robes, picked up the Book of Rituals together. Ancient and fragile, the coffee table–sized book had a carved leather cover with the remnants of gold leaf clinging to the decorative scrolls and title on the cover. Inside, it was hand painted and hand lettered, a work of art in itself. Other cities had to make do with copies, but Micah was proud that this one had been brought from England long ago. It was probably as old as Elspeth. Though they'd copied the book onto disk for everyday use, they still used the real thing for rituals.

When it was totally silent, Annie and Tessa presented the book together to Micah. "We would like you to officiate," Annie said.

Micah thought about protesting, but the stern gleam in Tessa's eyes beneath her hood warned him against it. Rituals were the soothsayers' domain. What he wanted was irrelevant. He supposed it made sense from their point of view. After all, he had officiated at a few other ceremonies over the years and was probably more comfortable doing so than anyone else here. Truthfully, he was happy to do it one last time.

Micah nodded and rose, accepting the book. "I would be honored."

The soothsayers withdrew to stand opposite each other across the brazier, the flickering light making their faces look mysterious and solemn. He stood at a third point next to the brazier, so they made a triangle, and stared into the fire.

This was the last time he'd officiate at a ritual. Seeing their expectant looks, he realized what David had been trying to tell him. It didn't matter that the ceremonies were outdated and a bit corny. It made them feel special, a part of something important. And if that's all the rituals did, it was worth it.

Micah took a deep breath and began with opening remarks. "This organization was founded by our ancestors to provide a refuge for those with demon blood who cannot pass in normal society, a place to find assistance in dealing with the rest of the world . . . a family. Safety of our fellow members is paramount." He glanced at David, who nodded. "To that end, we agree to abide by the strictures and guidelines set down by our ancestors."

He turned to Beth and said gently, "Beth Williamson, will you accept the judgment of your peers and abide by any decision they make?"

She looked scared to death, but nodded. "I will."

"Then, please, join me in the center."

She rose from the circle and came to stand across the brazier from him, forming a square. She trembled visibly as he read the solemn ritual words from the book, concluding with, "Soothsayers, Beth Williamson is accused of murdering Dina Bellama. What is the circle's verdict?"

They brought their hands down, palms together beneath their chins and gazed into each other's eyes as they tested the will of the circle. "Guilty," they said in unison.

Goosebumps prickled over his skin. He'd never been in a ritual before with more than one soothsayer. Two made the decision seem twice as real, twice as weighty, twice as final.

A few gasps sounded around the circle and Beth bit her lip but didn't say anything. She hung her head.

Micah was reluctant to ask for sentencing. Unfortunately, he had to. "And the circle's judgment?"

They paused, and from experience, Micah knew they were judging the weightiness of her crime and weighing the opinions of the circle.

They turned toward Beth, their unfocused stares implacable. Again, they spoke eerily in unison. "The deceased was guilty of far more heinous crimes. Her sentence, death. For Beth Williamson, there was no crime, but the execution of justice. She is free."

Thank heavens. Beth's hand flew to her mouth and she choked back a sob as the approval of a popular verdict filled the space.

Micah smiled at her. "Beth, please rejoin the circle."

Two hands parted without letting any of the energy escape, and the circle welcomed Beth smoothly and warmly into their midst as tears of joy streamed down her cheeks.

"Justice is done," the soothsayers said together. "So as it has been, so it shall always be."

The circle repeated the words after her. "So as it has been, so it shall always be."

Now it was time for the Naming Ritual. He turned to the other bookmarked page and frowned. This wasn't the version they'd used when he was named leader. Why had they selected this one? Well, he'd find out when everyone else did. Soothsayers didn't make mistakes when it came to rituals.

"First, we shall have a Naming Ritual for the Austin Underground," Micah said. He read from the text, the circle repeating the words after him.

"Part demon, part human, we are secretly born.

"Persecuted, violated, forsaken, forlorn.

"For freedom, for privacy, we have all made a pact.

"Three to serve: one to lead, one to protect, one to act."

Micah glanced up. "Soothsayers, what is the circle's will? Who shall lead?"

Again, they judged the circle's intent, the knowledge of the demons present representing all of the Underground's opinions whether they agreed with them personally or not.

Simultaneously, Tessa and Annie brought their palms together and bowed their heads. Micah didn't know all of the demons in this city, and had no idea who they might choose. It could even be someone who wasn't present.

They deliberated for a few moments, then Annie stepped away from the fire and spoke. "One amongst you embodies everything a leader should be . . . strong, compassionate, decisive, and just. It is what this community needs in its time of grief and rebirth." She turned to the right to face one segment of the circle. "The people name David O'Hara." She bowed toward him. "You are called to lead. Will you serve?"

David looked stunned but stammered out, "I—I will."

Micah hadn't expected that, since David wasn't really a part of either organization. But he would be a good leader. The energy in the circle rose in approval. Micah read the next line from the book. "Soothsayer, what is the circle's will? Who shall protect?"

Annie stayed facing David. "Another amongst you has all the qualities of a Paladin. Brave, chivalrous, champion of the underdog. The people name Pia Fontaine." She bowed toward Pia, seated next to David. "You are called to protect. Will you serve?"

Pia looked bewildered, as did everyone else. The Underground hadn't named a Paladin in decades, so people didn't know what the position entailed. Micah explained, "The Paladin is an ancient position that hasn't been used in modern times. The leader's Paladin functions as his right hand, defending demonkind, protecting the weak, and meting out justice as the circle wills."

And it was certainly better than turning someone into a Memory Eater. Everyone stared at Pia. Those who didn't know her seemed stunned that such a slip of a girl could merit the title of Paladin, but Micah knew it was a good choice.

Annie bowed to Pia again. "Will you serve?"

Pia glanced uncertainly at David and must have seen something in his eyes, because she nodded fiercely.

Micah glanced down at the next line in the book. "Soothsayers, what is the circle's will? Who shall act?"

Annie turned to face the outsiders. "A Lethe is not necessary. None shall act."

"The Lethe is the proper term for how Elspeth served us," Micah explained. "But we called her Memory Eater."

There were gasps around the circle, and expressions of relief when they realized no one here would have to fill that role.

"The Naming is complete," Annie said. "So as it has been, so it shall always be."

The circle murmured the words back at her and Annie returned to the center, facing Tessa once again.

"Now we shall have a Naming Ritual for the San Antonio Underground," Micah said. This was it. The last moment he would have this position. Regret filled him as he wished he'd made different choices, wished he'd been a better leader for them. He planned to offer the new leader all the support he could, give him or her the benefit of his experience, both the successes and the failures.

Taking a deep breath, he repeated the opening words of the ritual and asked, "Soothsayers, what is the circle's will? Who shall lead?"

Tessa and Annie bowed their heads and paused, the longest pause of his life. Then Tessa stepped away from the fire and spoke. "In these troubled times, the people seek strength and protection, but also compassion, humility, and a willingness to serve. One amongst you has learned these lessons well."

She turned to face Micah and his hopes rose. Was she looking at him or someone behind him? He couldn't tell.

"The people name Micah Blackburn." She bowed to him. "You are called to lead. Will you serve?"

TOLD YA, Fang said in his mind.

Micah froze, stunned. At this moment, he felt unworthy, undeserving of this honor. Surely someone else would be a better leader.

NO, Fang said. THEY WANT YOU.

Micah bowed his head. Leading the Underground was a privilege, but a great responsibility, too. Could he do it? *Should* he do it?

It was rare that people were given a second chance in life, a chance to correct their mistakes. And if they thought he was the best, who was he to argue with the collective mind?

Feeling humbled by their faith in him, Micah let his voice ring out strong and true. "I would be honored."

Chapter Twenty-Nine

I was so happy for Micah, I suddenly found myself grinning like a fool. He would be a great leader, more so now that he'd had a chance to learn from his mistakes. Relief filled the circle. It seemed no one had been confident that he would accept.

Micah glanced down at the book again and continued the ritual. "Soothsayers, what is the circle's will? Who shall protect?"

Tessa turned in my direction. Oh, crap. I closed my eyes, praying, *Not me, please let it not be me.*

The soothsayer continued whether I wanted her to or not. "One serves as Paladin already without the title. The people name Valentine Shapiro." My eyes flew open and she bowed to me. "You are called to protect. Will you serve?"

"No!" exploded from my mouth without thought. The circle's energy reeled with shock. Crap, they probably never had anyone yell in a ritual before. "Uh, I mean, thank you very much for the honor, but I decline."

NICE SAVE, Fang said. BUT A TAD TOO LATE.

The energy didn't seem to calm down at all. Dang it, I shouldn't have yelled. But I was ostracized enough from everyone. They already saw me as the Slayer, the girl who killed people, no matter that the people I executed were monsters. How could I ever have a normal life, make more friends, if they all saw me as some larger-than-life heroic damned Paladin? Besides, it was just a fancy word for an executioner. I didn't want the job. Someone else could do it for a change.

WHAT WILL YOU DO IF NOT THIS? Fang asked.

I don't know. Anything else.

The ritual continued, but to my surprise, Tessa didn't ask anyone else to be Paladin. Instead, she turned to face Micah.

He looked confused for a moment, then must have realized she wanted him to read the next line. He glanced down at the book. "Soothsayer, what is the circle's will? Who shall act?"

Tension and dread filled the circle. No one wanted to become what Elspeth had been.

Tessa turned toward another part of the circle, away from me. "It is rare that anyone has the strength, balance, and fortitude to become a Lethe, but there is one such here tonight. The people name—"

"No," I shouted again. "You can't do that." No one should ever have to endure what Elspeth had. How could they contemplate dooming a fellow demon to eternal insanity? It wasn't right.

People looked horrified, and the energy wobbled again. I wasn't sure if it was because I'd messed up their stupid ritual again, or because they realized any one of them could be a Memory Eater. Whatever the reason, I didn't care.

Tessa turned toward me. "Do you agree to serve as Paladin?" she asked, sounding implacable, not at all like the Tessa I knew.

"No." Hadn't I already answered that question?

"Then we must choose a Lethe."

She turned away, and I noticed she was staring right at Shade. Holy crap. I couldn't let her turn him into a Memory Eater like Elspeth. "No," I said again. "We don't need either one of them. Ask Micah."

He wouldn't answer, but looked to Tessa. He was leader now. Why didn't he answer himself?

HE CAN LEAD EVERYWHERE BUT THE CIRCLE, Fang told me. THERE, THE SOOTHSAYER HOLDS SWAY.

Tessa answered instead. "The circle has spoken. It must be one or the other."

"Can't you choose another Paladin?" I pleaded.

"There is no other," Tessa said with no emotion in her voice. "You must choose."

Crap, crap, crap. Why me? I didn't want to be Paladin, didn't want to be executioner, but I didn't want to doom Shade to the hell of being a Lethe, either.

Wait, maybe there was an out, a way to force her to choose another Paladin. "How can I be Paladin, when I'm already keeper of the *Encyclopedia Magicka*?"

"One does not preclude the other," Tessa intoned. "It makes you more eligible, not less."

I glanced wildly around and saw Austin. "I can't. I have a contract with the vampires. It would be a . . . a . . ." What was the term? "A conflict of interest," I finished triumphantly.

Austin rose, and at a nod from Tessa giving him permission to speak, he said, "There is no conflict of interest. The contract ended when you stopped the chupacabra menace, per our agreement."

Damn it, why didn't he back me on this?

HE WOULDN'T WANT A LETHE EITHER, Fang said. IT MEANS A VAMPIRE WILL GO INSANE, TOO.

I'd forgotten about that part.

Then Austin had to add insult to injury. "The New Blood Movement approves of Val Shapiro's level head in this important position."

I shook my head. "If the contract is void, that means I go back to working for the Special Crimes Unit."

This time Dan rose and asked for permission to speak. Good—he'd confirm it.

Tessa nodded at him and Dan said, "I'm sorry, Val, we thought there was an unspoken understanding. With your efforts in cleaning up San Antonio, the rogue vampire threat is much less. And the other scuzzies feel uncomfortable working beside you. Once you accepted the contract with the vampires, Lt Ramirez had to make a hard decision. You have been terminated, without prejudice."

Damn it, I didn't even have a job now? Grasping at straws, I said, "But . . . but without a job, how can I pay for my half of the townhouse? Gwen will have to go it alone. I can't leave her in the lurch."

Tessa nodded at Gwen this time. Gwen had to come through for me.

"I'm sorry, Val," my roomie said. "I'll have to give up the townhouse now that I'm . . . now that I've changed. Austin has promised me a place in the mansion."

I couldn't believe this. Would no one back me? I looked at Fang.

SORRY, BABE, BUT I AGREE WITH THEM. YOU ARE THE BEST PERSON FOR THE JOB.

"So I'll be homeless and jobless," I snapped. Back to where I started. "What kind of Paladin would that make?"

Micah shook his head. "Club Purgatory belongs to the organization, not to me. The leader's salary comes from it as well as the Underground's investments, as does the Mem—the Lethe's. The Paladin's would, too. You will always have a home with the Underground."

I wanted to cry, rail and scream at the world, but all my protests had been refuted, shown for the lame excuses they really were. I didn't want to make this decision, didn't want to turn myself into an executioner. But I didn't want to turn Shade into a Memory Eater, either. What would happen if I didn't make a decision?

THAT'S THE SAME AS SAYING NO, Fang informed me. AND SHADE IS CHOSEN AS MEMORY EATER.

"You must choose," Tessa repeated.

I closed my eyes. I couldn't believe I was actually going to say this. Reluctantly, slowly, I said, "I accept the position of Paladin."

Tessa nodded gravely. "A Lethe is not necessary. None shall act. So as it has been, so it shall always be."

The circle, all but me, repeated the words, and, at the soothsayer's bidding, everyone released their hands, the energy streaming into the night sky.

The others gathered around Micah and David to congratulate them, and Tessa and Annie emerged from their trances, asking what had happened. I wandered away from the crowd, apart, alone like always.

OH, STOP WITH THE PITY PARTY, Fang said in an annoyed tone. YOU'RE NOT ALONE. YOU HAVE ME AND MICAH. LOTS OF FRIENDS. BUCK UP, BABE. YOU'VE BEEN DOING THIS JOB ALL ALONG ANYWAY. NOW YOU'LL GET PAID FOR IT. WHAT'S SO BAD ABOUT THAT?

You know.

YEAH, BUT YOU DID THE RIGHT THING. YOU SAVED SHADE.

Yeah, once again the Slayer rode to her boyfriend's rescue, emasculating him. I searched the crowd for him and found him off to one side. He was holding Princess, so I could see his face. It was stolid, uncompromising, promising he'd never forgive me for saving him, for not letting him make the decision for himself.

But if I'd done that, I'd never have been able to forgive myself.

He looked away, and pain stabbed through my chest. I didn't regret the sacrifice, but was it even needed? *Would he have accepted the position?* I asked Fang.

HE WOULD HAVE, Fang informed me. HE'S THAT LOYAL TO THE UNDERGROUND.

Shade turned and walked away, and Princess looked over her shoulder at me. THANK YOU FOR SAVING MY HUMAN, she said simply, without a trace of her usual arrogance.

Whoa, Princess was polite? The world must be coming to an end.

Fang poked me in the leg. CUT IT OUT.

Okay, slight exaggeration. It was just my own personal world that was coming to an end.

From the pavilion, someone called out, "Hey, everyone, it's past midnight. Merry Christmas!"

Hardly. I had a job I hated, had lost my boyfriend, Gwen had been turned into a vampire, my succubus powers had been overwhelmed by the power of the exorcism spell, and I'd just had a big fat target painted on my back, inviting every rogue vampire in the area to try for the unprotected Slayer.

Merry Christmas? Yeah, right. Ho, ho, holy crap.

CPSIA information can be obtained at www.ICGtesting.com
Printed in the USA
LVOW081201270412

279413LV00002B/4/P